VIGILANTE SPIRIT

BY JACK ROBERTSON

TRILOGY OF ANGELS

This is a work of fiction. All characters and events portrayed in this book are products of the authors imagination and are used fictitiously. Vigilante Spirit is the first of the Trilogy of Angels series.

To order additional copies of *Vigilante Spirit* contact
Amazon KDP

Robertson, John Chester

Third Edition
2021

ISBN 978-1-7322684-0-1

Contents

Water over the dam..3

Out of the swamp 13

Rescued 27

Grace..42

Gin 60

Rebirth 72

Polecat puppy 86

Buzzardville..111

Shame..132

Charm City..151

Devils to angels..164

Twin troubles 190

Chaos 214

Discovery..233

Turmoil..252

Christie and Clyde..269

Gee's dilemma..285

Bilgewater pirates..296

Liberation 317

Passage 329

Regeneration..351

Seduction..361

Destiny..377

These characters

are completely fictitious

and are not related to anyone

in any dimension

of this world or any other...

I think.

- Jack Robertson

Especially important to this series-

Christopher Dorsey

Connor Dorsey

Courtney Dorsey

Lisa Dorsey

Bianca Hoch

Carly Gaver

Carol Robertson

Delanie Robertson

Eugenia Robertson

Lauren Robertson

J Chas Robertson

Vigilante Spirit

1

Water over the dam

It's another nice quiet afternoon to do nothing. What day in William, A. Gold, the 3rd's life isn't? Will has way more wealth than he or anyone else needs. Except for a tiny painful spike of guilt, his world would be perfect. *"Why think negatively?"* *"That's all in the past."* He grabs his fishing pole and heads over to the lake.

Once in his boat, it effortlessly drifts away from the tiny pier. A constant counterclockwise current slowly carries it to the top of the dam. Then, it moves gently along a dull grey twisted wire cable. The vibration rock him to sleep. Will should reach the opposite bank soon. Before hitting the far bank, the swirling current always returns him to the pier. The boat faithfully repeats this until Will grabs the rope dangling from the pier. It won't if he's still napping.

This journey just takes just long enough for Will to snooze, pretend to fish, and wake up completely refreshed. Cooling him, the bright sun passes from directly overhead to the west. Asleep, Will in his little boat floats quietly across the top of the dam. The current tugs so slowly to the other side. It's eerily silent; only the sound of softly falling water. His body nestled in the bow is limp. Will is oblivious to everything.

The fishing line follows uselessly; it trails behind in the water without a nibble. It leads to a trailing, red and white bobber. No chance of catching anything for the bait fell off as soon as it touched cold water. Today it won't matter. Any fish that may have bitten, if bait were still on the line, lurk sheltered down deep near bottom. The fish sense something happening, a low rumble Will couldn't hear even if he were awake. They are still.

Lazy fishing allows Will to justify these *"siestas"* to anyone who might pass by. The line in the water is just an excuse. In fact, he doesn't need to justify midday naps to anyone for he is a man of means and the sole heir of his fathers' estate. Yet, because Will is otherwise so self-important, he won't permit himself the luxury of unexcused laziness.

Following the mindset of Will Junior, his late father, Will the third despises inefficiency in others almost as much as he hates spending money. His dedication to thrift and keen investment

4

acumen means Will has never worked outside of his home. Not even for one moment.

While Will has never married, this bachelor dimly acknowledges having fathered a child. It was through a brief affair with a barmaid. He rarely allows this minor indiscretion to reach the front of his thinking. He's too self-centered to even care how his offspring fares. Occasionally his conscience nags. Ignoring his instinct to do the noble thing, still it comes to mind. Trying, to soothe it, he made certain provisions in the event of his death. For the child he doesn't know with a lawyer who he's never met…and never will.

His genetic issue is just something he keeps in limbo. To Will it's almost the fault of the child to have been conceived. Its' existence is barely real.

This mistake is barely worse than the day he accidently knocked his can of bait overboard. Will hopes he will never actually meet his offspring. To do so would be a real downer, proof of his imperfect being and no doubt boring.

Usually when his boat returns to the pier, he steps out and return to his big home on the hill. Occasionally he might catch a fish or two. No one ever says, *"Nice catch Will!"* And no one comes here to bother him or his boat because Will owns this part of the shore. His father secured it with a locking fence.

Without worry, he is confident the twisted wire cable above the dam will never fail. When he was growing up Will and his dad fished here. The gentle slide along the twisted wire cable was always steady and firm. Old dependable, there's nothing to worry about. *"Best of all, it doesn't cost anything!"*

A willow branch near where Will left the pier, conceals a jet black raven. Will can't see her, so he doesn't see her watching him. She sits silently among the leaves without moving each time he comes here day after day. She doesn't respond as a raucous male begs her to fly off with him. Her attitude has that defensive air of a lady waiting for someone… someone who never seems to arrive.

His shining feathers flash sunlight into her eyes momentarily blinding her as he dances and flutters. This draws her gaze momentarily from Will and his boat. Abruptly, her body stiffens in alarm. In this mans' last mortal moment, the raven realizes his peril and cries out to warn Will. Still no sound comes from her throat. Finally, her tortured being screams out, much too late…unmercifully too late! Now no audible warning can halt this ride to doom.

She shrieks in terror at the male raven, abruptly aware this avian imposter is no more a living creature than is she. Scornfully he sneers at her in ridicule. The demon vanishes. Until this very instant the day was a nice day just like every other. For poor Will, it's a day as never before… his last in human being.

Moments before this distraction, an overdue calamity struck way upriver. Miles upstream a neglected earthen dam finally collapses. Its' pent up energy triggers a huge wave. It projects an enormous surge of destructive force. Instantly this swell of water rolls downstream. The dependable grey cable submerges slipping beneath the hull… just enough to clear. Disaster is upon him. Never again will his body rest with this raven to watch over him. Her feathers wilt in disgrace.

Uncounted decades of careless upkeep are avenged in this moment. Surging waters from faraway mountain storms easily overcome the insignificant manmade obstacle in its' ancient sunken path. The demon distracted the ill-fated raven from knowing the danger.

Enormous hydraulic pressure silently elevates the small lake. The swell lifts Will's little boat nearly as high as the ravens' willow.

Their eyes meet. In this critical moment nothing can save them from crashing over and into the abyss. Will and his boat slip over as gently as before. They fall into eternity.

In a micro moment, as he nears the crushing rocks, the man stiffens and is alert. Too late was the raven; he will not survive this fatal plunge. With a spasmatic jerk, defying his doom, he reaches for his shirt pocket. A button is pressed. Up in his study in the house on the hill his computer activates a doomsday application. It executes orders for his massive securities portfolio. Next it issues his standing order to execute his will. In his final gesture he forever alters the fortune of another ...his only child. The raven observes without emotion, Will dies poor!

An angel sighs, *"If only you pushed the button sooner." "A gift given when no longer needed by the giver is still a gift." "But it doesn't score so well with the Almighty as generosity from one who is alive." "If the button was only pushed before you went over the dam, you would have been spared the journey on which you now embark!"*

In this mystical moment of Will's eternal existence his mind bursts in a loud flash... a new spirit is born as his living human being passes. Will begins a mightier voyage than he could have imagined when he left the pier. Those, here in this valley of an older dimension witness his rebirth as an echo spirit.

This innocent new mind moves in its' strange cloudy infancy. It is without memory of where it has been, where it is now or when it left where it was. It is a being of fresh intelligence making a first lucid analysis of self.

It wonders- *"Why am I in such a black miserable swamp?"* *"I may be on a mountain top or at the bottom of an ocean."* Then almost maniacally, *"Am I invincible? ... I think I must exist."* But *there is nothing of me that seems destructible."* Looking down to where his feet should be... *"I have nothing destructible!"* It is very little comfort for him to realize that he cannot be harmed because he has and is nothing. His only being is intellect and without stain. Suddenly he yearns for adventure. *"Bring it on!"*

Anywhere on this planet may be a fine starting point for someone with intelligent substance even if without physical being. He wonders, *"I am free and flowing; what does this all mean?"* He continues to ponder, *"Where am I going; why do I exist?"*

Something nearby is alive. Not only is it alive, but it also nuzzles him. Contact with anything alive is an invigorating experience. Now everything in this new world is a curiosity. He asks the thing, *"What are you?"* It doesn't answer but is with him.

Being with something alive now isn't quite enough to suit him as it was a moment ago. It now bothers him that it doesn't care whether he is warm or cold. Whimsically, he decides it shouldn't matter to him either. His mind is adapting.

Whether this thing is vertebrate or invertebrate, or even if it is friendly or not. It only matters it's a moving living creature. Anything living is what he intuitively feels he needs to be with. He craves the awareness of anything alive nearby. He reasons at it nervously, *"Whatever we are going, we ride together!"* He is high with excitement and leaps onto the creature, *"Let's go!"*

He is transported through masses of green algae seemingly very fast. But this steed obviously is merely a wobbly snail. They bob up and down to the surface and into the mud as one. His first experience with this murky world is a delicious learning experience. And so, a new sense of wonder floods his mind.

He reverts to asking, *"What am I?"* Questions come to his mind: *"Is it possible this is just a fleeting thought, or even a nightmare that exists for a while; then I will wake up?"* *"Will it disappear like a wisp of mist on water?"*

Skimming just beneath the surface, he can see through the eyes of his primitive host. Even so, it perceives only shades of light, dark and grey. This monotone quickly becomes boring. Awareness comes to him that riding in a snail is not and cannot be the reason for his existence.

Deciding with a new sense of self-worth, *"Something out there requires my talents."* *"I must learn what."* Now his wonders, *"What is my destiny?"* His time to ponder passes. Violently, without warning, they are snatched up violently by a stronger creature, something bigger and more powerful. His snail has been swallowed with him inside.

Spirit, snail and whatever swallowed them fly high over the swamp ascending into the clouds far above the shining surface. He suddenly knows he must jump out of his recent host into his new host. His snail buddy was swallowed. He makes his move and is pleased. Peering out through the sharp eyes of this new creature he sees that the world above and below is in bright sunlight and is much more beautiful.

Now in flight they are one with everything below and above. They glide effortlessly honking toward shore and a green forest. Still remembering nothing, he doesn't worry about the answer to the big questions. Even stranger, since rising above the swamp in this creature he can't even remember the questions.

Buckshot hits them hard drilling through both bird and the invisible stowaway. The blast is so powerful the shot passes completely through. The hunters' ability to hit the bird has some benefit at least to himself. No tiny pellets to pick from the meat still on the carcass. This hunter uses buckshot for everything. Shock and death occur in the duck more quickly than pain can be felt. It's body becomes rigid then limp; muscle shuts down as it drops like a stone. The spirit finds the whole experience interesting.

He feels a sense of déjà vu. Falling creates a weird sense of nothingness but it is something he felt recently but cannot exactly recall. Uncertainty grips him. Mercifully, the spirit is consumed by a need to survive. Feeling neither pain of pleasure, at least he knows he isn't hurt.

His thoughts are completely distracted by something new and bad. The gigantic explosive force killed his only transportation dead. They plummet down through a cloud like a hailstone.   In awe he realizes, *"My duck is dead!"* *"Damn, this ride is over!!"*

Vigilante Spirit

2

Out of the swamp

Abruptly, things he thought were important a moment ago aren't now..

Mighty jaws have just clamped down on his ride and are a lot bigger than the dead bird.

His trepidation fades as he tries to size up these new surroundings. Bright bird eyes he peered through moments ago are now terminal. This creature shows no remnant of its' former spirit. It is as dead as any creature can be. The spirit consoles himself with the thought that whatever he is, he still exists…even though he's being carried out of a swamp in a duck that's in the jaws of a dog. His mood lightens, *"Things are improving!"*

A faint remnant of his lost humanity inspires him to offer a simple eulogy. *"On a gentle wind, we floated upon clouds buoyed by the warmth of the sun." "Thank you for showing me this joy... Thanks forever."* Chuckling to himself. *"I hope you taste good!"*

Maybe the spirit and the fowl would have traveled endlessly to wherever migration had carried them. *"If only that buckshot had missed its' mark."* Spirit muses, *"So that's the end of living; possibly I'm lucky not to be alive." "Was I ever?"* This useless mood passes, and his self-confidence returns. *"Whatever else I may be, I 'm unique...even if I'm a weird creature in a really weird place."*

Deciding he hates sitting on this dead duck. it's time to move on. He wants to catch a ride with any living creature that happens to show up. Looking around he hopes to find something suitably mobile. Snails and ducks are excluded from now on.

Almost on cue, the big dog vocalizes seemingly woofing, *"Ralph!"* Its' large toothy jaws tenderly grip the newly dead duck. Sprit pauses for a moment. Then, he assesses the dog as his new transportation resource. He jumps on. At once he can look out through the retrievers' eyes. Everything seems much closer. *"That duck was farsighted."*

Immediately he sees a broken-down young man holding a shotgun. The duck shooter stands upon his rickety pier waiting for his dinner. Dog swims towards his master. The dripping retriever responds obediently to the shooters' sharp command to drop the duck. Dogs' huge jaws open and obediently the corpse falls at the hunters' feet. Without the courtesy of even a *"Good dog"*, the man casually reaches down and scoops up his trophy.

Spirit wonders. *"Who gets shot next?"" I'm glad he can't see me."* His vision blurs rudely. It is because the dog he's in is shaking from head to tail dispersing water in all directions. *"A-hah... We are alive, but uh-oh... we do have fleas!"* A big fly buzzes just overhead. He thinks to himself, *"Maybe I can jump onboard and get away from this   flea   trap!"*

Spirit doesn't jump. Ignoring his own fleas even as they take turns bouncing from his nose and before I can react, dog jaws snap the bug from the air. I watch it shoot past me on the way down his throat. *"This cur is a menace to everything that flies." "I'm glad I haven't got wings."*

But nothing I had experienced so far prepared me for the complex personality of this dog. Although very gentle with the master, it is also big, very strong and dangerous. I can hear the bug thinking as it descends into the dogs' gut. *"Damn, who would have thought that stinking mutt could move so fast?" "Wow, wow, ow!"*

Spirit continues to think, *"I may be stuck here now, but I'm getting far away from these filthy fleas as soon as I can figure out how."* Thinking about the hunter ... *"If he gets mad and shoots the dog like he did the duck, something that can happen any time, I am going to learn to walk...fleas are disgusting."* He vows never to travel by flea.

Some time passes. Fortunately, he is beginning to understand the sounds dog hears. He learns that the dog can be *"Good dog"*, as when we bring back things to *"the Man."* Or he can be a *"Bad dog!"* as when we chase and bring home skunks. The spirit decides, *"Maybe the man is irritable because the dog eats the skunks just outside of the cabin, instead of letting the man eat them?"*

He considers the process of duck hunting. Anything would seem to make more sense than the man sitting on the pier, or in the brush, half-frozen waiting to shoot something. He decides, *"It would be better for the man to shoot skunks and have "Dumb ass", retrieve them all at one time the way he does ducks."* Listening unseen *"Dumb ass"* is the name the angels call this animal. *"Hmm, I wonder how long that would last if the dog became smarter than the man?"*

Up until now, the dog hasn't understood his masters' chagrin over the skunks he retrieves. As far as dog is concerned, *"Ducks stink; skunks taste and smell great!" "Maybe master is missing the very best food." "Dumb ass" dog catches and eats another skunk."* Then without hesitation he spies a pile of deer droppings. *"Ahah, we are rolling in some kind of fine perfume!" "Maybe if I smell good the man with give me some of his dinner?"* The dog lays down with a thud and takes a nap with his eyes wide open.

Inside of his cabin, the man cooks his duck dinner over a rusty old round wood burner. He lets the dog in. Forgetting the dog fetched his duck dinner, the man ruminates- *"Maybe this stinking dog is as worthless as he smells!"* But, if the truth were told, the dog knows the man stinks worse than him. The spirit is undecided. *"I don't know who is right because I don't have a nose." Both are watering at the eyes."* He decides to figure out a way to improve them. The spirit can hear the humans thinking although neither the dog nor the man realize they are thinking. Spirit concludes neither has much worth hearing.

The dog thinks- *"The man is weird.... especially with his walking on two legs nonsense. I run faster on all four"*. The spirit incites rebellion within the canine suggesting. *"Maybe he's too lazy to walk on four legs"*. The dog just snorts but doubt registers in his doggy brain for the first time.

Something also is registering with Spirit that this dog understands what he just thought. *"Hmm!"* The spirit wonders- *"Something seems very familiar. Did I ever walk?"* However, no memory of walking comes to mind. Certainly, his memories begin with that first splash.

The dogs' wits are kindled and kick in for the first time. He thinks of their relationship and becomes frustrated. Whoever told the hunter he is boss? Everything seems to happen according to anything he wants. He wants an easy meal, so he shoots a wretched duck. Then, he wants me, his "Dumbass" to fetch the duck and "Dumbass" me, with my jaws that could tear him apart, just jumps in the water and brings the poor dead duck back...and then he doesn't share. Finally, despite his own agitated state, he comes to a grand conclusion, *"Dog does not need the man at all!"* Observing the rebellion, he has inspired, *the* spirit resolves to become an advocate to this poor dog. Mischievous angels have tagged the Dumbass name on him. It sticks in both dimensions.

The spirit reasons in a voice only another spirit might hear, *"This dog catches skunks and eats them."* *"So- if dog eats skunk then it only makes sense to think that dog would like duck as well."* *"This scrounge doesn't intend to share much with the dog."* *"And., why does dog cry when man yells "Bad dog?"* *"Dumbass is really a lot nicer than his master."* *"It isn't fair!"*

The thinking process has pushed the spirit nearly to the brink of exhaustion. Angrily he demands an answer from someone or anyone. Spirit asks in every direction, *"What's my job?"* *"Why am I stuck in this miserable flea trap anyway?"* *"Why am I even here in this weird world?"* *"Since I wasn't hurt, why did falling bother me?"* *"Why did I take a ride on that stupid duck in the first place?"*

From somewhere unknown a voice answers, *"You are an echo spirit."* *"Please try to figure out the rest more quietly?"* *"Most of us have better things to do than listen to your meltdown."*

The spirit is both astonished and grateful to realize someone else is around. At least he isn't totally alone. But no matter how repeatedly he tries to communicate with the voice, there is no answer. Now to make the best of things.

Rather than just be helpless, it seems his best course is to manipulate this dog to do his bidding. Very quietly he wonders, *"But what do I want it to do?"* Thinking of how easy it was to get into the dogs' head he speculates that for now it is easier to manipulate the beast than the man. After all they both have fleas.

He focuses on the dogs' mental process. It immediately stops scratching. Its' dull eyes slowly brighten. They start to see things in a completely new way. Quickly the retriever recognizes that the man has been using him to do all the really nasty work. The dog thinks critically about the world around him for the first time ever. Suddenly, he's not a happy pooch.

"When I shook the pond water from my fur it was obviously full of germs!"

Dog worries *"Who knows what microorganisms are in that swamp water?"* He scratches at his fleas again. *"Why didn't the lazy man fetch the damned duck himself?"* It doesn't occur to him; he doesn't know what microorganisms are or why they might be bad.

Dog is fed more powerful reasoning mentality. From somewhere in the canine cosmos well beyond the dogs' tail encouragement comes to the echo from the earlier voice, *"Now you are both learning!"* Dog hears as well and is startled. Spirit doesn't try to communicate with the voice for fear it will go away entirely.

The sun sets over the cabin. As darkness sets in, the man and his rebellious retriever settle down as usual. Morning comes and the newly self-possessed dog and man, who mistakenly still thinks he is the master, trot slowly towards the pier. The chilly morning sun has not yet erased all the dark clouds. The man is at peace with his world. But the dog is extremely dissatisfied with his lot in life.

The dog is highly irritated. Mumbling repeatedly in his canine mind, *"This is all wrong..." "The man is too lazy to fetch his own dinner!"* Oblivious, to his revolting retriever, the man simply thinks of the next duck dinner he hopes to have. But his dog can only think about germs. Their relationship has hit bottom. The dog doesn't notice that his fleas are now gone. Spirit gave them marching orders. They left at dawn.

Spirits' influence has shattered their bond. Dogs' revenge comes on the pier just as the man stoops to tie his boot string. The hapless hunter doesn't realize who shoves him or how it happens as his dog gently tips him off-balance. Momentarily he teeters on the edge of the pier and suddenly he is face down in the swamp mouth wide open. Spontaneously he gulps in green water struggling in panic to get out.

In this moment, Spirit understands his inspirational influence is complete. Then the newly enlightened dog whimpers and true to its' basic instinct leaps from the pier. He clamps his teeth down very hard on one leg and then pulls the man safely to shore. A retriever is still a retriever even if he is no longer his masters' best friend. The spirit is delighted at what he has done. *"Avenger is my true nature!"*

That same voice that he heard last night answers, *"You are who you should be..."* Spirit asks hopefully, *"And who is that?"* The voice responds- *"You are an echo spirit".* Spirit responds- *"I am a spirit?"* He queries, *"What's my name?"* The voice sarcastically replies, *"Your name is whatever you want to be called."* Equally sarcastic, the echo replies, *"Ok, suppose that I just call myself Spirit. Ok?"* As no answer comes back, he decides his name is Spirit.

There's no negotiating with a voice from nowhere that won't answer.

Spirit now has some assurance there are others in his troublesome dimension, even if he doesn't see anyone. As for this dog, he feels way too much sympathy to leave him with the man. Now he worries about the new intelligence he has stirred in the animal. It has created an ability in the animal to feel angst. Moreover, now it can act on its' feelings.

Without his dinner, even though safely on shore, now the hunter is in pain. His severely bruised left leg throbs. Moreover, his sudden gulp of dirty pond water will give him cramps. These maladies will have him shuffling on his unhurt leg back and forth to the outhouse for a week.

Pains in his stomach, backside and leg worsen his disposition. Any initial appreciation he felt when his dog dragged him to shore is forgotten. He remembers now that the hurting began when he felt Dog pull him to shore by this sore leg. He sees the deep teeth marks in his skin. It hurts there the most because surrounded by filth it's infected.

Medical treatment would be a long way from this cabin, and he has no way to get there except on one leg. The pain keeps his mind occupied throughout the following day. He finally reaches the conclusion that things just do not add up. What is adding up is that the dog pushed him in and bit his leg on purpose. *"Where's that dumb ass dog anyhow?"*

When his father was alive he knows, his father would shoot this worthless animal. He remembers his father yelling, *"Any damn dog turning on me gets no second chance."* Thinking very dark thoughts, Hunter glances up at the shelf where his shotgun should rest. It dawns on him the shotgun is still in the water next to the pier. *"I 'll fetch it tomorrow when some of my pain is gone ... I hope!"*

Dog very clearly realizes his imminent danger and runs unseen away from the cabin and out of his masters' view. Over fields and gullies he trots. Soon he is miles away from the only home he knows. Uncharacteristic of his species he pants a happy grin and has no intention of ever going back. He has completely escaped from the man. *"I'm free!"*

Back at the cabin, the man continues painful stumbles in and out of the brush in search of berries and wild mushrooms... anything he can find. Each time he enters the cabin he looks longingly at the shelf where his shotgun should hang. Perhaps it will magically reappear there. He worries, whether it ever work again. Just now, under the pier, a tadpole peers down the guns' barrel and decides to make it home.

Looking for something to worry over, Spirit thinks to himself he has gone too far by emancipating the dog. He muses- *"If Dumbass is smart enough to laugh, pretty soon it's going to be time for me to find a new way to get around."*

An old, weathered farmhouse appears ahead. Worried of becoming captured, the retriever and its' unseen stowaway follow the winding deer path up into the forest. They need to be as far away from the curious eyes of those who live on the farm as they can.

Stealthily, they circumnavigate the field. Soon it is well behind them. Moving into the trees again they are engulfed in the cool dark green of brush and timber. They haven't been seen and the echo thinks they are alone. Then their trance like state is broken.

In the small clearing ahead, something appalling is going on. Three men are methodically punching and kicking a hapless fourth. The poor victim is outnumbered and doesn't stand a chance against three. Spirit urges the dog to charge at them. Leaping forward, the canine growls and becomes a raging monster. It is now a snarling beast charging at the group roaring with fangs bared. It looks and sounds like something wild coming out of the jungle.

Spirit amazed mutters to himself, *"I didn't know I could do that!"* A voice next to him replies, *"You didn't!"* Somehow the echo has relinquished control of this suddenly vicious retriever to the victims' guardian angel. This anything but angelic protector urgently prods the dog at the three robbers. Dog has become a mighty beast as well as an incredibly smart one. An echo spirit, an irate angel and a possessed pooch have just made this battle a whole lot more even.

Vigilante Spirit

3

Rescued

Spirit realizes that which causes coincidence to change the way things turn out is beyond comprehension... Perhaps the answer lies only within the realm of The Almighty. Whether coincidence or sheer chance have anything to do with the events unfolding at this moment is involved won't matter. Because it will all become settled in short order.

This collision of the problem and solution is perfect.

Flaming hate burns from the bloody red eyes of a normally timid dog. Powerful jaws snap cutting and tearing evil flesh. Whatever fierce ancestors' gory instincts were infused in the creation of this beast are amplified. He now is well beyond vicious. Clearly his forbears vanquished dragons and lions. Nothing of his recent civilized ancestry remains. An avenging angel is in control.

Unprepared for his mind-boggling strength the cowardly trio is horribly confused. Instinctively, it tries improvising weapons using rocks and sticks. Knives are useless because they can't reach the animal. Their arms and legs are slashed. Their fingers shred like dry twigs. Their red blood stains the green meadow. More pain and suffering follow defensive moves. Looking on in astonishment Spirit senses a wolf-devil. He's wrong; the canine is bestowed the mighty wrath of a righteous guardian angel.

Canine fangs repeatedly bite down without mercy. The dirty three attempt to surround their bizarre enemy to attack him from all sides. This tactic backfires. Separate attacks position each one to be vulnerable to counterattack. They can't fend off his quick omnidirectional pivot. Each is now alone in battle with this demon. It anticipates each move. Everything they attempt makes it much worse. Leniently, the beast stops short of completely killing them. Their intended victim is frozen with fear.

Prone in the dirt, the hiker watches in fearful awe. While not under attack, he's worried he too will be the focus this rabid beast. Why else would a domestic animal act like this? Still down, but trying to run, the hikers' feet swing back and forth. His attackers ignore him entirely. Mere minutes ago, they tried to rob him, now they just need to escape alive. The terrible trio is reduced to blubbering cowards trying to escape. The demonic dog holds them at bay while biting anything that moves.

Hikers' intense pain subsides to a surreal twilight blur. He obviously is no longer in danger. Boot kick marks bruise him from head to toe. The robbers did not want him alive to point them out in some future courtroom. So, they were kicking him to death.

They didn't plan to attack him; he was just a target of opportunity. Their target was the farm the dog avoided on the way here. When these robbers saw the hiker alone and helpless, they simply attacked. The money they steal fuels their addictions. When that is gone, a new victim was targeted.

Punishment for this and past atrocities was apparent to the attackers but ignored. Cravings triggered their savagery whenever it got underway. If this chance encounter with this youth and his protector hadn't happened the farm down the trail was next. The good farm family will sleep peacefully tonight and never imagine the horrors this hikers' coincidental encounter with terror has spared them.

Although hazy, the hikers' vision is clearing. He is shaky as he comprehends what just happened. Tortured screams from his attackers have cleared away his shield of shock. Although now just an observer, he glares with hatred at them as they scramble away as fast as ripped leg muscles can move.

His loathing lingers inside. Still, because he was raised as a Christian, the hiker believes he must forgive them… but not right now! Belatedly, his attention is drawn to his benefactor. Despite all he has just endured he still thinks a simple dog has saved him. He doesn't understand why a simple dog has beaten them.

Fully alert he analyses the dog. Amazingly it's just a mostly Chesapeake Bay retriever. Yet it has torn three assailants up horribly. It sinks in, *"This is a hunting dog, not an overly vicious breed."* He takes a deep breath and decides not to think. Again, he is relieved. No one is hurting him now. *"It's amazing…the dog is so calm now and obviously not rabid."* Hiker is very grateful to this animal for saving his life.

Belatedly Spirit contributes to the youth by telepathically forwarding the pain from the battered youth down the trail. The three, now nearly a mile away, hurt more from the Spirits' burst than even the injuries from the beast. When this pain reaches one he foolishly throws down his revolver. The Lord and man may forgive, but those in the middle settle scores.

This robber would have tried to shoot the dog back there but couldn't stop to grab it. It was useless to even try. Throwing his weapon away is a fatal mistake. Now, in addition to being stupid, he's completely defenseless. This is an untenable state to be in because of the treacherous nature of his companions. Their fear to escape the dog gave this dirty trio a brief surge of energy. It fades as their distance from the meadow increases.

When this new wave of exhaustion takes over, their meager water dissipates quickly. Thirst has them gulp down the water from a plastic bottle only one thought to bring along. The one called Buck is sizing up his options more critically than the other two. Buck's selfishness doesn't bode well for his two companions.

Things are much better at the place they ran away from. Back in the meadow it's peaceful again. Sounds of distress are gone from the ears of those who remain. The echo who now calls himself *Spirit* waits silently. The retriever is back in his gentle dopey dog persona. Time seems motionless.

A small cut just above his left eye and the bloody splatters on his nose are the only hints of his recent battle. Here no one calls him *Dumbass*. He has their respect.

This happy dog even licks Hikers' wounds. The lads' blood no longer streams; it hardens and clots. Still, the youth shivers at the thought of the retriever reverting to the monster he was a short while ago. He notices, although so badly hurt, he has little pain left. Hiker thinks naively, "*My body has really toughened up on this trail.*" Roman, his guardian angel, feigning sleep, just moans at this foolishness.

In the waning afternoon sunlight, the forest meadow shines with color and beauty. Its' deep green is punctuated by an abundance of wildflowers. Dog and youth, seemingly alone, stop walking and suck in the sweetly scented air into their lungs. Dandelion fuzzy seeds float gently in air from the forest as though erasing the dents in the turf from the struggles. Soon the meadow floor will be without blemish.

Vitality returns to him. Hiker is refreshed by this fresh energy and puffs out his chest thinking somehow it was he who defeated the robbers. Strength surges back into his arms and legs. The echo floats nearby and enables rapid healing by some means even he can't comprehend.

Spirit tries to ask the guardian angel, *"Did I do that?"* No answer returns. Still, Spirit comes to believe he's here for some very noble reason albeit mysterious. He ponders, *"The hikers' guardian angel possessed this simple animal and caused it to attack evil. Now he's gone,"* *"Maybe I too can get around more on my own?"* He experiments; it seems workable, but clumsy. *"If I keep up my confidence, I can be more than just a passenger."*

"Perhaps my mission is to reduce the pain of creatures in trouble?" He enjoys the idea of being a force for good. He decides he really does have powers. But, he hasn't a clue how to use them. Spirit reasons that such power would come with great responsibility. *"However, slight my contribution was in bringing this man back from the edge, it was real and a successful victory over evil."* *"It's great to be real!"*

Hiker, still feeling some stiffness, pushes his body up on wobbly legs. He places each weary foot in front of the other until the cadence of his pace returns. The canine looks up at him. Back to being just a submissive retriever. It walks with him just as dogs have always since the first chose to befriend a worthy human. It doesn't walk at his heel, leading the way instead. But for certain, dried blood on its' chin is evidence this very peculiar beast is no friend to the lowest of humans. And the most confused of all is poor Dumbass.

Every good dog goes where its' chosen human goes for a very sound reason. For both species understand an ancient essential truce between them. It comprises the pledge made eons ago: humans always will share their food…and then some. The retriever rejected his former master who took much and gave little. Food is to be shared with this human. The dog puts his paw down decisively hard on one resolve, *"No skunk eating for this dog anymore!"* *"People want to think we're their best friend, but it really has a lot to do with food."*

There is no honor in the man-dog bond without food. And he's hungry. The dogs' tongue touches his lips. *"My mouth is dry, and I am thirsty."* His mouth dried up when the wetness of the healing canine tongue had clotted the hikers' blood. Dog licks his lips thoughtfully. It is obviously not a great leap of imagination to understand that each is ultimately good for something besides friendship. They are mutually edible.

Hiker searches the clearing where the robbers ambushed and beat him a short time ago. Amazingly his large backpack remains where it fell. Spontaneously, or so he thinks, he digs into a tight pocket of the pack pulling out a chunk of jerky and a water bottle. Dogs' pleading gaze compels him to share this meal. Hiker yanks a chunk off with his front teeth and offers it. The same mouth that had destroyed evil fingers a short time ago reaches ever so softly to retrieve the outstretched tidbit. Dog takes it with the familiar gentleness he used in fetching the hunters' game birds. He laps a drink from the canteen.

Intuitively Dogs' eyes open wider as his sensitive nose signals *"Self! There is more food where the jerky came from!"* Seductively he extorts the grateful human to reach into the pack for more. These two new buddies, oblivious of their unseen spirit companion, descend together with casual determination down a steep trail beneath the trees. The human tosses another hunk of jerky. Dog muses, *"This boy has promise!"*

Far distant, those fleeing the meadow continue limping painfully up the mountain and experience a worse desperate reality. In this graceless escape, they constantly trip and stumble over sharp loose trail rocks hurting all the way. Ankles sprained; they are relieved to be coming to where they left their ride. Mal, who had a decent upbringing, starts to thank God, then realizes he needs to keep a low profile in that area.

Coming to the dented van, Buck screams kicking at the side as he realizes it won't carry him out of this mess. All four wheels are gone. Some mystical scale has balanced both justice and revenge. Mal says, *"This is the trouble we've made for ourselves."*

They have been outmaneuvered, injured and have no hint of from where their foe came. They fear the beast is still after them. Now they imagine him up ahead and back from where they have fled. It's their turn to feel the panic they inflicted on the innocent youth. A chapel bell way down in the valley slowly tolls morbidly calling them   to   their   graves.

A mother will soon bow her head in prayer within the chapel. She will give thanks for that which she has received and ask to be forgiven for her failures. Particularly one such failure is Mal.

Mal and his bad companions are really only sorry to have been beaten. He is sorry his achilleas tendon is bitten nearly through. He struggles gullibly up and down the mountain trail with the two he still thinks are his buddies. Finally, just enough of his blood drips along the way. He loses consciousness.

As Mal's eyes are closing he can see Buck, his pal, steals the water he needs if there is any chance for his own survival. Lips burned with thirst, eyes close bitterly, he now understands more than he ever wanted to know.

The forest is deadly still. Black vultures circle patiently waiting to pluck out his eyes. Though unconscious, Mal tries to remember how his mother taught him to pray; failing he despairs into near oblivion. Natures' dutiful vultures land close by waiting. Others trail those who left Mal to die.

A mile or so further down the trail the remaining two thugs crawl over logs and trail washouts hindering their way. Resting for time, one pleads for just a sip of water. As the water bottle is extended, his partner swiftly slips a blade just below the reaching limb. Mortally wounded he frantically reaches for the gun he threw away. *It's gone!*

Buck sticks him a second time. He casually wipes spurting blood from the knife on his buckskin jacket. Retrieving the water he limps on alone. Buck sneers jeering at his former pal, *"We didn't have enough; now I do!"* But someone in a more just dimension sees an intolerable imbalance and completely disagrees. Buck just sealed his doom.

The widows' worthless son Mal abandoned her some time ago. Grace is returning up the twisting mountain road with all the caution a nearsighted lady can muster. She left the chapel in the valley an hour ago without staying to chat. This was highly unusual for her. Outside of friends in the congregation, there's no longer anyone still alive for her to have a conversation. She lives for those moments after each service. Grace once cared for her two boys and a worthless husband. There is no one now, except the Lord. She loves the Lord, but she misses her son almost as much, nearly more.

This is the dangerous season to drive wherever there are deer. For, this is their rutting season. Males range all over these mountains seeking challenges. Grace's old Chevy climbs higher. The thin old road to her cabin cuts back and forth as it makes its' way up a steep slope. Momentarily her tired mind drifts away from the road. She thinks of her prodigal son... of Mal.

She loses focus of the road only momentarily. Her tired eyes glaze over. In this fleeting instant, Graces' car strikes what she sees as a deer. She barely glimpses its' brown hide with a streak of red. It bounces over her windshield then over the side of the embankment falling out of sight far below. Grace is sorrowful for a moment and makes a promise to her Lord to drive so carefully as to never again waste one of His beautiful creatures.

Crossing the road, Buck is struck with such explosive force he becomes airborne. His body is propelled over the guardrail before being hit dawns on him. He plunges very slowly for a long distance.

If Grace been inclined to stop, she would have been amazed at just how long Buck hangs up in the air. It's long enough for the murderer to recall his every sin and everyone he hurt, including her very own Mal and the buddy whose life he has just taken.

At first, he thinks he will land as lightly as a feather in the wind. Then just at impact, his descent accelerates; he hits very hard. Next, he hopes he will quickly die. He won't. It will take almost a week. Bucks death is so slow. He can't move; his back is broken. True to his evil being each day he snarls his defiance back at the world. His sneering death mask will mark this soul for eternity. He will never have buddies again. Even in hell he will suffer in a solitary eternity. The vultures gather closer.

In a week, Buck's soul will be conveyed by The Grim Reaper. Gee, as his friends call him, is an angel whose vocation is to collect all, both elegant and awful. He avoids his formal title The Grim Reaper. When collecting souls, he performs their initial evaluation. The reaper will make his way here when the sneering one completely dies after vultures have feasted upon his rotting carcass. One glance at this unrepentant sneer will give them clear bearing to his face.

Gee will then explain to the soul of Buck: *"If Grace had missed you Buck, justice still would have still prevailed." "The trail you followed has washed out and now is a cliff." "You would have died just the same." "Evil was your foundation." "With certainty, you turned your soul in the direction of perpetual agony."* Two of the evil three now know their destiny. They are worse off than the dust from which they came and will return. Mal's former friends are beyond saving but his bleeding has slowed. And then too, there is the matter of what to do about those prayers Grace uttered for him.

Almost home now, with a mothers' intuition, Grace prays quietly once more for her lost sons. Her faith is pure and mighty. Prayers are rarely answered promptly, yet there are exceptions. Grace prays with her entire being. In the great beyond. One who listens says nothing but is touched by the innocence of this lonely mothers' soul.

Vigilante Spirit

4

Grace

Her nerves are badly shaken from her collision with what she perceived as a deer. Fortunately, she is near her cabin home. Her personal danger and damage to her car from hitting a large animal isn't lost to her either. Getting the car fixed if the windshield had cracked or any serious body damage would have really been tough on her limited income. Still feeling guilty, she rationalizes wild four-legged jaywalkers are a normal hazard of these backwoods roads.

This isn't the first close call she's had with rutting deer. Because this section of the road is so far out, very cars use it. Grace worries if ever she has an accident, whether she would be found before it would be too late. The word "cellphone" isn't in her dictionary.

Far from the grocery stores, out here Gods' wild creatures are an essential source of food. Grace isn't one who hunts for sport. She even butchers her own meat. Food is vital. Therefore, harvesting game for the table must be right in the eyes of the Almighty. Even so, wasting any living creature is wrong. *"Running over and leaving roadkill is a sin especially if it happens because I'm careless."* She smiles at herself because she realizes she has been thinking out loud with nobody else in the car.

Since leaving the father of her sons, the only man she counts on is The Lord. Without Him, Grace would have given up long ago. Straining to see the narrowing gravel road, she squints as daylight fades. Her eyes are alert to detect anything else crossing her path. Grace humbly begs her Lord for forgiveness. Mercifully, God doesn't reveal to Grace the only buck she hit was a human one.

Arriving at her cabin, she's relieved; nothing has bothered her home. It's just as rustic and orderly as when she left for chapel this morning. Grace goes in and starts to go to lie down. Then for no apparent reason, other than a weird apprehension, she changes her mind. She puts on her boots. Grabbing her rifle, she will walk off the jitters.

Except for trips like todays', she has been alone here ever since her Mal took off with his weird friends. After sitting behind the wheel of her Chevy for several hours, it feels good to walk.

Grace is very conscious of being a woman alone on the mountain. She is especially aware of her vulnerability from critters of all kinds. For comfort, her fingers caress the cartridge clip in her jacket. The

N.R.A. is the only organization Grace belongs to, except for the little chapel in the valley. She reflects, *"The good Lord gets my soul for eternity, but the NRA will keep me alive long enough to get there."*

This rifle is something she can't do without. Not only does it let her have fresh meat, but there's also nothing else to protect her since she left her man and older son. Before leaving them with Mal, she worried her life and that of her youngest were in constant danger from his bipolar mood swings. Her fear of that man was far worse than being isolated here on the mountain.

Night isn't the best time to be out here alone even though she knows these woods. As a human, Grace is nearly blind at night, while nocturnal predators see or smell nearly everything. Moving away from the light of her cabin allows her natural night vision to kick in. Fortunately for her, no clouds block the moonlight. Grasping an unlit maglight in her fist, her rifle is cradled in the crook of her arm. Just to be on the safe side she slides the clip in. She's ready for anything.

At last Grace, the mountain woman, is in control. She's at one with the wilderness. Her feet sense firm places in the trail she can barely see. The air on her face is cool and refreshing; her fears lessen. Still, drawn by some primitive instinct she needs to keep going. She is a good distance from her cabin and her pace is steady.

Gone is her church lady persona. Her legs propel her up and down ridges effortlessly. From time to time, she pauses to listen to something she senses but can't quite hear. Something in the breeze conveys an ominous message. It points to something important, but what? Grace lets it guide her to wherever it takes her.

This moonlit night isn't entirely quiet except when Grace or wild creatures become still to listen. Multitudes of forest creatures of all sizes and shapes move stealthily within their own space. Predators crave the darkness to stalk their prey and hide from others further up the food chain. Grace is merely human. She moves relatively noisily, as if out in the sunlight of the day.

Predator noses sense two humans of related scent. Grace moves closer to the other of her kind with each step. With nothing apparent to guide her, she is drawn as to a magnet. Perhaps it's a remnant of primitive maternal instinct like a mother bear drawn to her cub. For unlike the wilderness mothers, Grace cannot consciously sense her cub and has no inkling he's even near. And yet she knows she must go on.

The path meanders down into a valley then up over ridges and again descends. Even for a younger woman this is no easy trek in daylight and much less at night. Then, mercifully and abruptly her instinct and even divine providence mesh... into harsh reality.

Her foot brushes something soft. She nearly stumbles over her bloody son. The figure on the ground would seem a mere obstacle in her way. Curled up at her feet in these rocks Mal is like a dying animal one in misery and pain. His corpse would have been breakfast awaiting the first vultures of dawn. Rocks would be his coffin, his pallbearers these trees. The monster he was is extinguished. Fortunately for everyone, so are his former associates.

Grace gasps at the horror before her eyes as she clicks on her light. She nearly drops the rifle. Mal doesn't recognize his mother for several moments. He raises a feeble fist to strike at whoever wants to finish him off. Recognizing his mother, Mal sighs deeply. Just as when she soothed his childhood injuries he wails, "*Mom... mom it hurts ... help me... Oh God help me!*" And for the first time in years the Lords' name passes his parched lips. He who hears Mal, hears all, but says little to most. Yet, Grace has heard and knows His Word. She gives silent thanks. Finding Mal before it's too late is her sign He heard her. Grace and Mal cry out to all of the forest to hear, "*Praise   be   to   the   Lord!*"

Now to get him to the cabin. She squats on a rock cradling her exhausted sons' head. She kisses his forehead as she did so often when he was a child. A ripped off a piece of her blouse bandages a wound and stops the bleeding. Mal senses he might survive. But now the moon is behind a cloud and the way home is up the long hard trail..

They can't stay here long for hungry creatures smell his blood. Some would prey upon him even now if she were not here. Bracing against her, Mal rises to stand. But he is weak, and his legs are stiff. Once up, he falls against her heavily almost knocking her over. Though well past the strength of youth, Grace is determined to save Mal. She pushes his dead weight to a standing position and steadies him for their trek up the mountain. His feeble attempt to regain balance throws them both on the ground.

Grace tilts her rifle downward returning its' clip to her pocket. She slips the stock under his hand. Mal uses its' stock as a cane. This rifle may never fire another round because its' barrel is pressed repeatedly into the rocks and dirt. Painfully and very noisily they limp up towards the cabin.

Agonizingly they gradually work their way. Just out of sight, predators wait hopefully. No other sound is heard. Grace's teeth are bared at every pairs of eyes luminescing around as they pass daring them to threaten. Her teeth aren't smiling; she snarls at anything close. She bluffs everything with her teeth as the apex human predator she is not at this moment.

Agile Mountain dwellers know how to get up and down ridges. But, neither has ever tried to find their way against such odds in the dark. Loose rocks and his weight throw their balance from side to side. As he stumbles, she twists against his weight. It causes Grace to sprain both ankles. She brushes off her pain with the yowl of a bobcat.

Mal struggles on mostly in shock. His deep bite wounds bleed through the makeshift bandage Grace had used. Both worry they might not make it as her tiring body supports his struggling steps. Neither wastes a single breath by talking. Something growls deeply back at her a short distance behind them. Grace, fearing her first growl may have been a bobcat mating call, growls back trying to sound more like a puma than a bobcat. Nothing more is heard in reply. The moon slips behind a cloud. Surprisingly, nothing attacks; they hear the sound of an infants' cry in the distance as the unseen male bobcat looks for love farther into the forest.

Once more, the clouds part just enough to release the moonlight. The outline of her cabin looms up the slope as a shadow against the sky. Grace's determination to reach its' safety is greater than her pain. Mal feels such agony his movements are spasmatic. The push of wind against their backs rises from the valley propelling them almost to the cabin door.

Without the wind, bringing her wretched son up this last stretch of steep trail would have been improbable. Shelter is just within the cabin door. As they arrive, the wind subsides. Grace propels him into its' dark interior where she quickly revives the flame in her woodstove. Her tea kettle is soon bubbling.

Prodigal son Mal is again within her loving care. Home means he may survive. Feeling his mothers' pain and anguish adds to his misery. At her urging, he begs for forgiveness from the Lord he once knew. Mal promises his mother he will never associate with either of those two loser friends again. Only the Lord knows how easy it will be to honor this promise. Both of those ugly souls are bound for an even fouler destination. And each will take his turn at the pleading his case and lose. They will argue its' merits based on the unfair leniency given to Mal. But, to no avail. For the case of the prodigal son is an established precedent.

Vigilante Spirit

5

Moving on

On the other side of the mountain, Spirit somehow is aware of everything that befell the robbers. He senses the unrepentant Buck slowly dying in the dirt of his own doing but feels no sympathy. Buck's only sorry he didn't hijack the car before it hit him.

Hiker's tranquil campsite seems a world away from Grace and her sorry son. Soothed by the warmth of this campfire all here are considerably happier. The Dog and Hiker have bonded and are enjoying their camaraderie. This is far better for this human tonight than their first meeting in the meadow. Spirit is satisfied this day was a success as well.

If Grace were to look out of her cabin window, she could see their distant campfire glow in the blackness of the valley below. She won't look though. She's focused entirely on nursing her son. Mal confesses everything to his mother in a delirious babble. Neither Grace nor her son will look or venture outside of their cabin until those by the campfire have long gone. And should they ever meet face-to-face, though Grace is guiltless, her shame would be unendurable.

Thinking about how to get food along the trail, Hiker knows enough of survival to gather wild mushrooms, avoiding poisonous toadstools. Mushrooms are about the only wild forest things he knows people can eat, or not. He counts on using his credit card when he reaches some store along the way. This needs to happen soon because he's feeding the dog now. Or so he thinks. When they step back onto the trail tomorrow, Dog will pretend to be very impressed with Hiker's mushrooms. But he really prefers food with more zest.

The echo has no use for food but is fully enjoying the campfire. Although he's been indifferent about where he's going, he still wants to know the *why* of everything. He instinctively knew it was his job was to help someone in trouble. Today all here in both dimensions have grown in one way or another. Each is content. Something is about to change everything for the echo. Out of nowhere someone new materializes…

Without warning, a woman in buckskin slinks into their campfire circle of light. Unlike the hiker who sees nothing, this dog can see spirits. He gives her a welcoming glance. For his keen nose senses nothing dangerous about her. Grinning down his nose, he thinks,

"Hello lady, hopefully you have jerky too!" Smiling, she stops to pat him. She offers no jerky. *"Hmm, it would be rude to chew on her buckskin while she's wearing it."* Drooling slightly at the thought of chewing her buckskin, he hopes, *"Maybe she'll take it off later!"*

The hiker can't see her at all but smells the sweet scent of honeysuckle. He's still sore from events of the day and he slumps. With eyes half closed, his hunger abated, he just sees the campfire and his canine benefactor. Social obstacles out of the way, the lady in buckskin senses the hunger of man and dog. She bribes the dog with a bit of food from a deerskin pouch the dog was sure wasn't there a minute ago. *"The man can get his own food."*

Spirit is confused but doesn't object to her bold move in feeding his companion. This is better than watching the dog hunt for another skunk. And she is very lovely…

Attempting to ingratiate himself with this new food source, the dog offers to go catch her a skunk. She declines and instead hands him a chunk from the same pouch as before. *"You eat!"* she commands. *"This is for strength. Wild mushrooms make you cramp."* Dog swallows the strange musty tasting mouthful without chewing. Surprisingly... it suits him. He becomes very sleepy. His guardian angel sighs, "Dumbass fell for it."

Some future day, when Dog has moved on, he will think about the tidbit she gave him and will try to smile about this meal... But, without the Spirit's infusions of intelligence, eventually he might just slobber. Someday he may become just a dog again. Now he's a happy pup with a full belly...and very tired.

Spirit is beside himself, *"There's something extremely exciting about this woman!"* He welcomes her. She pretends to ignore him. Her raven hair and smooth barely tan complexion project her sensuously in the dancing flames. Now both the human and dog are sleeping; the echo is only interested in her. *"Nothing about her seems soft or vulnerable... yet she's beautiful."* She's more mysterious to Spirit than the nighttime forest.

Her hand gently caresses the bruises and cuts on the sleeping hikers face. If her liberty with the dog was self-confident, it's even more so with the man. From an even smaller pouch, she places something on his wounds. Speaking only with her eyes, she communicates with Spirit her only wish is to help the youth. The echo spirit is satisfied she will do the boy no harm. And his guardian angel Roman is also pleased.

The moon gradually subsides. The visitor in deerskin curls up alongside of the dog by the fire and soon seems asleep. Hiker lay snoring by the fire. Spirit peers through the flames at the woman and the animal. The echo is impressed at how naturally she sleeps on the ground without a cover next to the dog.

He wonders whether she would have even needed the dogs' help to defeat the attackers in the meadow. She appears to have considerably more muscle definition than either the dog or the hiker. Then he realizes her body is merely an illusion. Although she's like him a spirit she can move about easily without riding on other moving things.

Hikers' dream state drifts to the events of the day. He is both the victim and the beneficiary of chance in random attack and his rescue. Coincidence and chance has carried him to these final moments of light sleep. Then touching another spot that was painful earlier, he drifts into a deeper sleep than he has ever known. Even in his dream, he wonders why his own mind became so much more alert after the robbers jumped him. His last happy thought," *Where has my pain gone?"*

Shivering slightly in his sleep without waking. Hiker presses his body deeper into the soft earth." He mumbles in his sleep. *"Tomorrow I will get as far from here as my feet will carry me."* *"This mountain has given me way too much adventure..."* His thoughts dissolve into oblivion. The hiker drifts in deeper sleep that nothing that will happen will disturb.

As for the dog, its' intelligence will return eventually to a more normal state for a canine of his breed. But the craftiness that led him to tip his old master into the pond will always stay with him. His craziness on this weird day is forgotten. It would not bode well for him to repeat his savagery. However, something learned so well is not soon forgotten.

His heroic day is over. All he can do now is dream of catching rabbits and partridges and maybe even a stray chicken. No more ducks though. His legs jerk as he sleeps in the light of smoldering campfire embers. Still, the dried blood flecks from the evil ones remain on his muzzle. He licks his nose. *"Never forgotten at all."*

In the morning Dog will be hungry again with renewed urgency in his belly. He starts to chase a skunk but changes his mind remembering the disgusted faces his old master made. Instead, Dog accepts and swallows another hunk of jerky from the hikers' pack. To reciprocate he pounces on a curious partridge. Rather than tearing it apart, he gently brings it to the human. Hiker cleans and roasts the small bird. They share this barely significant snack.

This is a new experience for the retriever because this man shares the best parts after the food is cooked. Usually the dog got those visceral parts the hunter wouldn't touch. Dog likes meat any way he can get it. He's a big animal and that partridge just wasn't enough…he's still hungry. *"Hmm…maybe I can sneak in a skunk later!"* He won't though; rabbits are also abundant on the trail. Dog affirms to hunt for a partridge instead of a skunk. But he could backslide if one comes his way. The canine may smile again. But he will never again become a demon…unless absolutely necessary.

The Spirit and the beautiful woman will be gone when the sun rises above the treetops. He is now just a big dog temporarily endowed with abnormal intelligence. At least more than anyone might expect from him. The dog feels joy but only the youth smiles in his sleep. Spirit didn't create these thoughts in either of their minds. He suddenly had something more interesting to think about... the girl in deerskin.

Back in her own world, Grace offers a morning prayer thanking Him for this miracle. Today and forever after her prayers of appreciation will continue. She starts to wake Mal to bathe his wounds. She leans over him then decides to let him sleep awhile longer. Judging from the slow healing of the bite wound, he won't be able to move too well for several days.

Nearly a week later, Mal finally stands without help. Grace drives him down the mountain to a tiny health center. It passes as the town hospital. There's not enough business here for a medical doctor. Fortunately, the town veterinarian knows just enough general medicine to save the injured leg from the infection. Mal stabilizes slowly with a blood transfusion and antibiotics. He's not the first human to be treated here. They all thank The Lord again when the vet confirms Mal doesn't have rabies or parvo. The vet laughs, *"If he had them, I'd put him down in a minute."*

This son will never resume his low status as a thug. His walking will always be impeded by a painful limp. Besides a wobbly bearing, this leg will always serve as a reminder to walk a straight moral path.

Punishment for past misdeeds will hamper every step he will take throughout his lifetime. The vet can hardly imagine the extent of his damage to his Achilles Tendon from the teeth of a single pooch. Mal doesn't try to explain.

As Grace prays once more in chapel pondering over Mal her body trembles. Sadly, she realizes, *"If Mal got into this much trouble, how much more did the one I left back with his thieving father?"* In repentance, again this faithful servant of The Lord bows her head to pray for His mercy for her other son.

But that other son is one whose sad fate has already been written. Some cubs never return to the mama bear. For many there is no second chance. Only He knows why. Still Grace knows she must pray for both of their sad souls.

There are longings as well on the other side of the mountain. But, by far more exotic beings, for the echo spirit is in love. And he will follow her …if he can.

6

Gin

Hiker stares into the burning coals reflecting on the strange way the day turned out. The orange flames create wild mysterious images seeming to mean something then become nothing but dust. A lone yellow flame dances in the center. Something about it reminds him of the dream he just had about a beautiful girl in buckskin. Eventually it dies out as does her image. Her dance wasn't for him.

He thinks back to his decision to leave college. The idea was to gain a sense of his true path in life. The ambush was a major detour. Yesterday, he learned how dangerous the world can be out here. *"Maybe by hiking further, I'll learn more than I did during my first 20 years"* Youthful optimism overcomes fear of the unknown.

"What should I do about this dog?" After his terrifying beating by those maniacs back on the trail it seems like a great idea to have the dog with him in case they're up ahead. The confusing question, *"How can anyone trust an animal with such a Jekyll-Hyde*

personality?" Then acknowledging, what would he have done without the dog? Realistically he admits, *"I could be laying in the bushes dead!"*

The dog feigns indifference by sniffing around the spot where the girl had fed him last, hoping she'll take the hint. No buckskin scent, no scraps and no more food. He doesn't care whether the hiker likes him so long as he shares his food.

The possibility the ambushers may be following and attack him again is large in the humans' mind. His need for protection seals his decision to accept the animal… providing the dog follows. Anyway, how would he get rid of the animal? Or force him if he chooses not to have him follow? He doesn't know its' name. Not a word has passed between them sitting here in the firelight. Yet they are completely at ease with one another. The dog reads every thought but covers his amusement with a deep friendly *"Woof!"*

Spirit is oblivious of his mortal companions. His attention is riveted on one of his own kind. He is totally smitten. When she arrived, he tried to keep his focus somewhat averted to be polite. Her aura is darkly brilliant. He muses, *"I'm hallucinating." "This person doesn't seem real." "But then again, maybe I'm not real either."*

"She seems to be like me only much better... It isn't her physical beauty". Very soon he will clearly understand the wisdom of this thought. But, by then he won't question his attraction.

Almost embracing the fire, she had rested close to the flames, but not quite touching them. Gin has been away from this kind of warmth for way too long. Distant memories of campfires with her dog put her in a nostalgic mood. Dog was more company to her than anyone else. She thinks blissfully, *"It's been ages since I patted a dog." "Too bad I can't even now." "But I didn't come here for a dog."*

Her mind focuses purposefully on Spirit. She seems to see through him. He looked to the flickering fire to redirect her mind. Acknowledging one another at last, he whispers, *"Are you ok?"* Without a word, she nods affirmatively. *"May I ask who you are?"* She responds with something unintelligible to him. He repeats his question. Indulgently she repeats only a word that sounds like *"Gin."*

Gin hasn't time for small talk. She has her mind made up. He understands this is all she will say. Naively he wonders if she will tell him more in the morning when she has rested. He's wrong. Tonight, they will be very busy.

Spirit continues peering at her through the dogs' eyes and even peeks at her through those of the hiker. She knows he finds her desirable. This is her moment.

He is way behind and only now realizes, *"Somehow she knew where I was."* Gin senses he finally understands her purpose in coming to him. Her eyes pull at him with beautiful magnetism. *"She hears me thinking .... this is exciting!"* Gin almost loses her composure in joyful amusement.

Spirit's heart would have flipped now if he had one. He's completely intrigued with this creature he senses is like him ... an echo spirit! Even though she calls herself *"Gin"* and appears in a human form, she's not a real person. *"What's with the body?"* *"You are hiding in a body!"* It is obvious to him this lovely body is just her host. He thinks, *"I'm in a dog but I'm not pretending to be one." How can this be?"* She demurs, *"I'm worthy of being myself and you are not."* He shuts up not wanting to show ignorance of his past.

Spirit looks at Gin and his mind is passionately delirious. Fortunately, his excitement does not radiate into his own host. With physical limitations, the dog could die on the spot from Spirits' explosive emotion. This mortal dog might feel better now. Even so his body went through a lot. Few living creatures can shift shapes to the degree this dog changed and survive.

It gets late. Hiker drifts into an even deeper sleep. As his breathing becomes regular, Gin silently rises and glides out of the camp. As silently, Dog follows her out of the fire circle and back down the pathway. Then he remembers the hiker is alone and vulnerable. Choosing to follow his new friend for now, Dog returns to the campsite. They pass on the trail without a word going opposite directions. Dog doesn't turn to follow or offer him a ride. Spirit follows Gin, moving for the first time without help from a host body.

Since his first splashdown, Spirit has attached himself to every living host of opportunity. Thrusting through the woods by himself is great. This one who calls herself Gin is a compelling relief from his pathetic existence.

Love is its' own motivation to those of every dimension, and especially here where Spirit finds himself. In a surge of ardent energy, he pushes the campfire far behind. Like an infant taking its' first wobbly steps he falls down the trail trying to capture love.

It's easy for an experienced spirit to hover and even to fly. Unfortunately, it's exceedingly hard to learn how to steer in any one direction. This echo state didn't come with flying lessons. Worse Spirit lacks the fundamental rudder of an aircraft. His acrobatics, as he bounces off the trees on both sides of the trail draw the amusement of every ghost, soul and echo who ever were here. His arduous pursuit hits the forest like a tornado.

As the rising sun announces morning, Hiker awakens to the sound of troubled birds in toppled trees. His canine companion, having gotten little rest snoozes nearby. But something else is different. Sitting up he finds his map lying on the ground. He thought it was lost. Unfolding it carefully he learns he is just under four miles from a small town with the odd name of *Buzzardville*. *"If I don't get to someplace soon the buzzards will get me here!"* *"Buzzardville. look out here I come!"* He hasn't a clue what awaits him.

He's had enough. It's about time to get off the trail and to make a police report in town about his attackers. *"It's a damn good thing this dog came along when he did!"* His guardian angel having returned once more receives no credit from anyone. But Angel Roman doesn't care. After dealing with the ambushers, he found something in an amber bottle stashed in an old hollow stump. That bottles' contents had him completely engrossed. It's the only reward this un-angelic immortal cared about last night.

The young man doesn't get to decide the dogs' future this morning. Whimsically, the dog gives the hiker a final lick and takes off running through the brush. They enjoyed the campsite for a night. Now, in the daylight, for now that time has passed. These two are going separate ways. This isn't due to a lack of friendship. Each just has his own agenda today. And Dog isn't ready to be any mans' dumb anything at least now that the boys' guardian angel has returned. They will meet again.

Gradually mastering the art of steering himself, Spirit follows Gin's trail. He weaves from side-to-side towards her on the trail zigzagging pathetically. Still he perseveres and learns. Catching up with her has become compulsive. Gradually her path leads them back towards the cabin of Hunter, Dogs' former master. Spirit passes the farm whose family barely missed harm yesterday. Driving mules pulling his wagon the farmer is fertilizing his field. He will never imagine how close to disaster he and his family were yesterday.

With time to spare as Spirit labors far back on the trail, Gin pauses respectfully at the hollows on the forest floor where her mortal family lived long ago. She honors the spirits of those who came before her and even those who came after her to this place of rest. In this rarest of moments, they respond wishing her good fortune. As the sounds of her suitor grow closer, very quickly the place becomes still again. Her mortal family spirits return to their sleep.

Nimble Gin has her own designs. For she has set her cap to marry. And having read his simple mind now the girl knows she didn't need a living body to attract him. As for why she wants him: Gin was first drawn to him by a mystical attraction to his innate kindness.

First, when he rescued the dog and yesterday when he stowed away within the battered hiker until she soothed the boy. She finds Spirit extremely appealing because he is her opposite. Together, they will make one better than the sum of both.

When she bolted from the campfire and took this trail. This pathway back to where the dog had come from she was confident Spirit would follow. At first, seeing only the dog was behind her was disappointing. She sped on intent on ditching the pooch. Dog may be bright but he's not her type. Although confident, Gin couldn't determine that the Spirit trailed her until she heard all those trees he was knocking over. *"Who knew this would be his first attempt at self-propulsion?"* Like anyone just learning to walk, Spirit needed something to hold himself up. It wasn't until his unbridled force dropped a dozen trees did he manage to learn to drive himself.

She has just enough time to return her body to its' resting place. Gin bids farewell to her family and waits patiently. Soon the whole forest, and even Spirit, senses they are coming together. That he was been conceived from the mind of old Will Gold as his boat went over a dam only a short time ago simply doesn't matter to Gin. This is trivia in the realm of the echoes. Only who he is now matters.

Her own death came from the fangs of a copperhead long ago. She became so angry when the snake bit her ankle she grabbed it up and bit off its' head for spite. She may have survived had she not looked it in the eye as her teeth sunk in. It had teeth too. She died from her bite of spite.

Although she wants him as meek as he is now if she had known him when she was alive maybe not. While Will was quiet, she was anything but and she was as strong as any man around.

Then there is the matter of the several thousand years' difference in their ages. Neither of their parents would have approved of this marriage if anyone asked them. Existence in this dimension is less complicated. No one here ever asks or objects to such differences in time for it would be pointless.

Some famous old ghost once said, *"After a century, or so, children just do whatever they want."* Gin came up with the idea of a possible future with Spirit while the poor echo was still ruminating in the pond snail. She even spoke to him once or twice. But she wouldn't answer when he tried to carry on the conversation. It would have been pointless to her. It was not until he made his way out of the swamp that he was able to succeed for himself or anyone else.

Like so many of her human female counterparts Gin fully realizes an attraction to a potential suitor that is based more on the future than where he has been. She decided, *"He is clueless about nearly everything important."* Such has been the mechanism of mutual attraction between men and women in most dimensions for as long as anyone can remember.

Spirit is totally frustrated by his slow pace of pursuit and tries without luck to hitch a ride on an eagle and then a silver fox. Before long he sights and chases the distant glow of her wake. *"It's a good thing she left one I can follow."* Humbly he recalls the dog didn't have this much trouble staying on the trail. His thoughts return to Gin. Although Spirit doesn't recall much of how he started, he knows he is and always has been a male in nature. And that means he can merge with the spirit of Gin. Then he experiences a moment of self-doubt. *"Back at camp she seemed almost oblivious of me."* *"Does she really want me?"*

A nearby ghost awakening by his noises answers him by saying. *"This too is the way of courtship."* *"In some basic misconception created by nature, male suitors never stop chasing women."* *"In truth, we men are the ones captured."*

And Gin seems to be about the same age as Spirit but obviously isn't. He neither knows nor cares. For their moment of flirtation by the campfire created a vital connection. His self-confidence like the campfire burned low and after rekindling flares high again.

The waiting Gin feels compassion. However, regardless of his state of mind, she has no intention of letting him know he is the only reason she returned to her seductive mortal state. This is her beauty secret. Last night she was slightly more beautiful than she was even in the bloom of her youth. Spirit sees his love as beautiful and mysterious even though he feels pain. The old ghost yawns and says to no one, *"They will do well as one."*

In her campaign to attract Spirit, she borrowed several physical attributes from her sisters. As with the living, lady echoes anticipate romantic relationships infinitely more quickly than their opposite gender. And once they make up their minds little deters them.

Now she has returned those splendid maidenly attributes back to their earthly resting places. And Spirit will never notice.

Vigilante Spirit

7

Rebirth

Gin's sad to relinquish her heightened physical beauty. She flashes a last sensual smile in the direction of Spirit before shedding it in favor of her spiritual being. Further back he abandoned his attempt to catch a ride on another creature and is hot on her trail. And with that fading smile her human body slowly vanishes. The earthly composition is gone. A hazy blue luminescence remains drawing Spirit into her true being.

Spirit senses the warmth of her welcome and rises confidently and smoothly for his first and final smooth ascent. *"Are you following me, she intones coyly?"* He whispers, *"Of course, Look at all of that dammed forest I've just trashed trying to get to you."* He confesses *"I have been attracted to you from the moment you touched my mind".* Gin purrs, *"Are you a serious suitor?"*

He confesses his love, *"You are where I know I am meant to be,"* *"You are the answer to my eternity and why I exist."* *"If you will have me, I would you."* *"I want you to be as one with me and I with you... Will you be mine?"* In the way of all in every dimension, Gin pauses for agonizing moments… then accepts Spirits' proposal. And for endless ages they will never part, as it is the way of the echo.

Spirit and Gin pause enthralled upon the very pier where not long-ago Spirit and his poor duck were retrieved. This mismatched pair although abruptly betrothed are destined be a success. The moment they unite their child will replace them. As for the idea of *for better or worse*, neither feels anything could be worse than where they've been before now.

Undeniably Spirit's arrival was embarrassingly graceless. This couples' definitive reward is their creation of the more dynamic spirit they are about to become. Both are extremely happy to become a single new superior spirit. As they wed they will sacrifice their beings. Gin and Spirit will disappear; it is a wholly perfect unification. For echo spirits become their own child. Waiting here, their anticipation is building. They have been very lonely echoes as Gin and Spirit. Instinctively, they understand there is no possible annulment or divorce from this or any other echo union. They can never return to who they are now.

This is no legal decree nor one of will. It's a straightforward component of metaphysics within their dimension. Wedded spirits become another who is neither and yet both. They quietly enjoy these quiet moments as individuals.

They dare not touch. Their mystical moment will occur at the instant of touch. As to what they are to become, it's a person they will not know. In time their offspring can also marry. Or this child may simply fade indefinitely as did Gin before Spirit arrived. It took encouragement from an angelic raven to convey Gin to this moment.

Humans might find this total sacrifice considerably too generous. From those spirits arriving to witness this event, many compliments will be bestowed and follow the refrain- *"Congratulations upon your achievement!"*, mostly to Gin. Not much will be said to Spirit owing to his recent arrival. No one knows him; Spirit's a newcomer to this dimension.

A wispy angelic figure says nothing and silently starts to exit just before the great moment. She is deeply affected because it was through her ravens' eyes poor Will went over the dam. Then, something sinister catches her eye. On the roof of the cabin a familiar sight hides behind the chimney. With a powerful thrust she tips that demonic creature up, over and down the pipe into the coals of the fireplace below. It is the crow that tempted the Raven leading to the death of Will Gold. A demon does not burn but its' wretched host the crow is free.

Without observing anything of the exorcism, both Gin then Spirit vow before all in attendance to be one for so long as their new being may exist. Their auras connect; they are one. An entirely different force is tasked with the destruction of demons.

When vows of this dimension are made, they cannot be heard by any living human. Not even if one knew to listen. So, we cannot repeat to you exactly those uttered.

Yet, eloquence is inherent within this moment. Mutual acceptance and loyalty are bonded to this couple. Without further hesitation, they reach out to one another and become one. Total separate and then combined sensual awareness of each overwhelms them and they are awash with euphoria and ecstasy.

Their energy produces an explosion of sparkling luminescence over all attending. A human's eye, were one here to see, might physically experience this moment projected against the white smoke above the cabin chimney. Inside of the cabin, the sleeping hunter stirs only briefly. Echoes never allow a breach of secrecy. For few humans could deal with the idea of even one much less many alternate dimensions besides heaven and hell.

An image reflects momentarily upon that fluttering smoky canvas. First, images remarkably like the features of the late William Gold then the face of a stunning Native American woman unfold magically. The images shift, blend and fade slowly. Slowly a new face appears. It begins as a child, then a teen. Gradually, their progeny achieves maturity... all within timeless moments.

Inconspicuously, the dog has lain in a low spot within the reeds near this old cabin. Just inside his former master sleeps. It watches the wedding take place; but the dog doesn't care or seemingly comprehend. If his nemesis, the hunter, were to wake up he would only think his runaway retriever has returned. Seeing spirits is as normal for some creatures as not for others. But the hunter doesn't awaken as the dog retrieves a dead crow from the ashes of his fireplace and carries it away from the cabin where it is set free without being possessed.

Dog is essentially an invited guest. Oddly, his invitation came from the Gin when they were curled up by the campfire. The witless groom was too busy chasing Gin to even realize the animal known around this cabin as *Dumbass* was on the way to the wedding. Whether Spirit realized he was getting married before he got here will be debated by others for centuries.

Although Gin said goodbye to them as she passed their resting places, the brides' mother and sisters are proudly wearing the matching gowns they fantasized way back on that day Hunter thought he fell, but really was shoved, off the pier.

Normally dogs aren't interested in weddings. For them life is simpler: see a pooch smooch a pooch. This cabin is the last place Dog wants to be. For him, this is a dud of an event because there's no food except for smoked crow, which wouldn't taste that good. Women seem to understand weddings. Dogs and men just don't.

Moments ago, in the human dimension, the body of a man identified as that of Will Gold was discovered by The Maryland State Police. It was spinning in a swirling pool just downstream from a dam nears his residence. Some other nicer day a tiny boat will be found not too far downstream. If Will returned to life at this moment, he might insanely tell the police he just got married. Though Will is now in a better place, no one will ever guess where. Only the raven knows the truth. But poor Will is never waking up again in his world.

Echoes are guided only by the logic of the mind or minds from whence they sprang. Two of these unique creatures are now just one. This joining is solemn in the world of echo spirits. It is the event of echo reproduction. marriage and rebirth. It's why everyone of this dimension are invited as witnesses. Even though angels may attend, most consider echoes to be weird. But the angel who is leaving now is a believer in echoes and she is very sad.

With the betrothed joined, the atmosphere by the edge of the pond is alive with spirits and even a few local ghosts. All the ghosts graciously show approval with happy groans and moans loud enough to be even heard by the living. Their sighs pleasantly resonate over the water. Nature pauses to listen; there is no one living who hears them because the hunter sleeps dreaming of things he has never seen.

For the finale, a wondrous melody beyond the range of human appreciation bathes all who hover beneath this silvery blue sky. Far too quickly for those here, a solo herald trumpet proclaims this celebration over. A soft rhythm only heard in the minds of earthly composers such as of poor deaf old Beethoven sweeps over the pond. It's a sound never really heard by mortals for its' true purpose. It signals a renewal of essence.

Wedding, conception, and birth are complete. Momentary silence...as the music fades. Spirit and Gin are no more. Their offspring dances and floats upon a bright new cloud. An echo is born. He is *Vigilante* and is greater than the sum of his parents. An angel states, *"This echo will prove to be far mightier than either."* Vigilante has inherited Spirit's determination and the inner strength of Gin. He carries the power of Gin's ancestors back before the era when Will Golds' arrived on this continent.

With little memory of his parents, hopefully Vigilante can escape most limitations of both. Instinctively, his mind contains what he needs to know to survive in the world he will find beyond this humble birthplace. The celebration ends: all invited and uninvited vanish. This newborn, although unschooled, is up and ready. Vigilante will seldom revisit the uncertainties that plagued Spirit when he came from this swamp.

Very few in the human realm remember Will Gold. But some will come to mourn him. Especially a raven and an angel miss poor Will. Others who really don't care he's gone were mostly involved in his business. They will miss their fees and commissions more than the person who wrote the checks. Even those like Will who leave so few footprints on the earth manage to commit both fair and foul acts.

There were a few weighty misadventures such as the affair Will had with a barmaid. Most people he knew worked for him in some capacity. He left no family behind except for one he did not wish to know. Living a self-centered lonely existence is why so few care he's passed. Even his online existence was cold and critical.

Even so, his echo's son, young Vigilantes' first perception of a mission is truly great. He wants to bring justice to those in need and to fight evil. Still, even the noblest spirit is limited by his lack of a physical body. Not understanding the experience of his father, he may make the same mistakes.

Vigilante decides, "*A human would be nice to practice with until I have more confidence in my ability to know what's going on.*" Vigilante sizes up the first body in sight. It is the former master of Dog. It's the hunter just waking up in the cabin next to where Vigilante has just been born.

Depressing to see, and Vigilante can, is Hunter's smelly unwashed body. It lazes in its' almost perpetually flatulent stupor.

He continuously stares into the fireplace of his rundown hovel. It is not the nice clean cabin his mother left behind.

This lost soul barely survives in a semi vegetative state. He sleeps and eats without a plan or purpose in life. Only when hunger pains send spikes to his belly does he go anywhere. His body would actually have a putrid odor if anyone living were here to experience its 'effluvium other than the dog. Little wonder the dog preferred skunks.

The scent of the hunter hits the breeze as he opens the cabin door. The dog makes a fast exit from the reeds now that the wedding is over running as fast as his legs can move. He remembers how fast the hunter could draw a bead and shoot.

Even old Will Gold was more social; no one knows this man. This wretched hermit is a perfect inaugural client for Vigilante. Even the last skunk hiding in a hole under the cabin bugged out when the dog wasn't around. The dogs' body scent diluted the hunters'. The skunk now bunks next to the outhouse. It smells better and the dog can't smell him.

Dull half-open pale blue eyes gaze with disappointment into the fireplace. Hunter senses something was there. It's becoming dark in the cabin. Eventually he must gather more wood. Shrugging he decides, *"Later!"*. Dirty fingers reach up to rub droopy eyelids. He scratches, stretches and releases wind from both ends. Smiling, he's very proud of his accomplishment.

Vigilante decides the hunter is way too filthy to be his host. He will follow the man instead. Echoes have a basic perception of smell. Instinctively this sense tells him this mans' body is filthy. The first step of his undertaking will be to get this person up to a reasonable standard of sanitation... at least as clean as the critter by the outhouse.

An ingot of his intellect passes into the mind of the hunter. From this moment on, his life will change. Vigilante hopes it changes for better. Nothing sudden stirs within his head. But Hunter gets up briskly and uncharacteristically decides that he needs a bath. Stripping, he steps to the corner and reaches into a rudimentary kitchen sink. He grabs the rusty handle. Icy cold well water spills down the wide lip.

Each pull on the handle pumps a generous stream into a pot he empties into an old grey galvanized tub. He perches buck naked in the water holding one end of the pot over his head. He pours clean frigid well water over his dirty body for the first time since he was a child. Goosebumps on his arms and legs feel their first water since the day he was pushed into the dirty pond. He spies a yellow sliver of soap in the corner. It was lost long ago by his mother.

Shivering cold and wet, he retrieves it from where it fell in the dust. He always knew it was there but wasn't inclined to bend over that far. Because his nearly forgotten brother Mal had an evil sense of humor. Mal would boot him in the rear whenever he caught him bending over. Ever since, Hunter has avoided exposing that area of his body, even though he lives alone.

Such is the hunters' reentry to sanitary civilization. Clean is a sensation he hasn't experienced since his mother Grace left him and his father to *'fend for themselves"* as his father always expressed her departure. *"Your worthless mother took Mal and ran off with him leaving us to rot!"* Not bathing is rebellion against the few habits of hygiene she had insisted upon. His cleanliness vanished until now.

Hunter was only half-grown when his father died accidentally. The old man taught this son, who he favored over the younger, just the barest ways to exist. He wasn't shown much more because his father feared he too would leave. They fished, hunted and ate anything large enough to cook, bite and swallow.

Feeling sorry for himself he reasons, *"Is it any wonder I'm angry?" "When that rotten dog pushed me and the gun off the pier into the pond my innards got shaken."* To the hunter, the gun means eating something other than fish. The hunter used it with his dog. He moans, *"Back when I had a damned dog."*

At last almost clean, he hates the idea of wading into the swamp. But realizes he must if he's going to eat meat again. Reaching the pier, he gently lowers himself over the side and carefully fishes the gun out using his big toe hooked into the trigger hole. Although the gun was old the safety worked; he hopes the safety was on when it fell. He shivers even more thinking of what it might be like if it goes off now. But the safety wasn't on.

Vigilante intervenes and stops a ticked-off minnow from bumping the trigger. Because fate will always be its' own master, the simplicity of that shot may be less painful than his own. As for the tadpole, it reluctantly exits the gun barrel and is snatched up by a waiting bass. The hunter watches and waxes philosophically for the first time- *"Life goes on...or it don't." "I just got lucky."*

Vigilante wants this isolated human recluse to realize his full potential. He thinks improvement is possible because he believes in the innate power of the living mind. Relative to other living creatures, a persons' is enormous. But Vigilante doesn't even stop to wonder why; he knows this to be true. His tactic: awakening the young mans' self-respect is just his first step.

The echo will yank this man he's named *Hunter* out of his lethargy. While he can stimulate Hunters' mind, it can't be totally controlled. However well-intentioned his efforts are, everyone has a free will. Unfortunately, this won't happen the way Spirit and that crazy angel transformed the dog. Dogs are easy and Roman, the hikers' guardian angel, had enormous power. It became a monster and back to nice pooch again in one afternoon. From somewhere comes a *"Who-yahh!"* It's Roman.

Vigilante hopes this guy Hunter will learn to experience more of life than his muddled past would suggest. *"The slow and easy way obviously isn't working fast enough to suit me."* To move progress along, he bombards the hunters mind telepathically pushing him to think about doing something other than sitting and sleeping. So, he enlists help from a strange source…the polecat by the outhouse.

8

Polecat puppy

Neither Mr. Skunk nor Hunter are sensitive to their own foul scent. So, Vigilante disguises the white streak on the polecat and convinces Hunter it's a lost puppy dog. Moreover, one needing to be petted, fed and kept inside of the cabin because it's so little. Hunter has something other than himself to care for. Mr. Skunk can't believe   his   good   fortune.

Gradually there is some progress. The delusional hunter feels compelled to keep the cabin warm for his young puppy. *"When it gets bigger I'll teach it to fetch ducks."* Instinctive habits die hard. Despite Vigilante's best efforts, Hunter still isn't very motivated to be clean. Lazy doesn't go away easily.

Vigilante has way too much to accomplish to wait until the man wakes up on his own. That could take forever. Even his former dogs' new ability to understand laziness in his master was another reason to run away. Hunter takes after his late father. When Vigilante implants a suggestion, if it's anything that takes physical effort, Hunter tries to forget the thought. He flops and naps wherever he happens to land... even in the wretched old outhouse or on the pier.

Then an unfortunate accident happens. Polecat and the hunters' big foot happen to collide in the cabin. The polecat has his own rotten instincts. Even though the hunter is lazy, the cabin instantly becomes unfit for human habitation. The housebroken Mr. Skunk turned puppy reverts to his true nature. The revolting skunk stench wafts its' way all the way to where the real dog roams. Dog hungrily stops to sniff the wind but moves on.

Achieving considerable distance from the cabin the dog reflects on his old master. *"Lazy-ass is a great name for that slouch who called me Dumb-ass."* The dog arrives at the edge of the farm whose family he recently saved from robbers. One of the farm boys shoots him with a bee-bee gun. It stings but rather than run away yelping Dog just sneers and flips him off with his right paw. The unnerved brat runs home screaming- *"Mommy-mommy!"*

Back at his cabin, skunked Hunter pinches his nostrils and closes his eyes craving another nap. Vigilante keeps him awake by forcing his eyes open. Hunter tries to sleep with eyes wide open, with thumb and forefinger holding his nose. To keep him alert, Vigilante implants an idea- *Hunter is thirsty*. It works. That starts a frantic cycle that moves him to get up, go to the sink and then outside. Drink ...walk... pee... hold nose. Vigilante celebrates *"It's working!"*

Eventually he can't drink, pee or walk another step. For what seems to be an eternity, he lays on the floor gagging from skunk scent gritting his teeth. To get him up and moving, Vigilante induces him to violently hiccup and experience severe flatulence. The resulting spasm from front to rear propels him in circles. It's so effective he spins like a slow-motion pinwheel. Vigilante ups his game to a higher level.

Hunter becomes hungry… very hungry. Not to be outfoxed, soon he fishes, eats and naps on the pier. It's obvious to Vigilante; this man is just plain lazy. But there's something oddly familiar about this lazy cycle. For some reason he can't remember Vigilante recalls the joy of napping while fishing. And he wonders, *"Why?"*

Dog lopes along the trail now very far from his old master' cabin. Although he and Spirit had gotten along well, he has little intention to become close with anything even vaguely human. Now emancipated, Dog knows he doesn't like being possessed by spirits and angels even worse than he hated fetching dead ducks*." It's bewildering."*

"Thinking like a man and biting like a lion, for no apparent reason, is way too crazy!" Dog remembers everything that happened. He understands becoming very smart for a while. It's clear to him that his burst of intelligence is slowly fading. He doesn't

care; it's lonely to have so much to say stored in his head. *"There isn't anyone to talk to... even if I could..."*

Enough intelligence remains that he realizes he wants some human companionship. He wants his human to feed and love him. He thinks enthusiastically, *"Maybe I can even play with kids!"* Then reflectively, *"But I am going to be the boss!"*

"But not kids with bee-bee guns." He licks the spot on his backside where the tiny copper projectile hit and stings. The sheer fun of his giving the farm brat the *doggy-finger* strikes him as wonderful. So hilarious that for his first and only time he laughs out loud.

Dog is trying to decide his future... *"what I want and don't want."* He's resolute he won't fetch ducks for anyone but himself. On the other hand, retrieving a ball tossed by a nice child seems like it would be great fun.

Whimsically he muses, *"Maybe someday I can shoot ducks and people will fetch for me instead?"* Reality sets in. He discards that notion altogether as he realizes that he doesn't have a finger needed to pull the trigger. *"Even flipping-off that farm brat strained my paw."* He licks it. That reminds him he's hungry; time to eat has arrived with its' familiar hunger pangs. The immediate problem: catching a critter worth eating. He must hunt just to survive. No leftovers will be tossed to him from anyone soon. He has the problem of everyone who has ever gone it alone. It's the realization freedom and independence are a lot of work.

He lifts his wet nose eagerly sniffing the wind for any food source scent. His nose points to a clump of honeysuckle. He leaps in without seeing his prey using only his nostrils to guide him. Instinctively he savagely snatches at a fluttering shadow. One sharp snap of his fangs and he's chewing on a partridge. *"I can make it on my own!" "But I really would love to know how to cook this bird."* He chews snobbishly. *"Raw fowl... entirely too primitive."*

Hiker, the beneficiary of the dog's lapse into an unevolved state is unhappy too. While near death from the beating he was completely helpless. His mind was very foggy and unstable then. Now the whole miserable experience has had time to sink in. *"It blows my mind to fully comprehend how I was rescued." "Now that dog is gone too."'*

Roman and Spirit, who came to his aid, lost interest in him once he was safe. From that point, Spirit focused only on Gin. And Dog has taken off on his own quests for the time being. Something is missing from Hikers' life another hike just won't solve.

Now that Spirit has dissolved into Vigilant, they have loftier goals. Even Roman, the boys' guardian angel is seeking solace elsewhere. Poor Hiker misses the dog.

Back at the cabin, Vigilante continues working to restore the hunters' vitality and the ethics that Grace had tried to teach him as a child. Sadly, nothing can completely overcome his fathers' bad influence.

As far as his memories of his father go, Hunter doesn't even remember his fathers' face. Sitting with his back against a pier post he's still loafing. A catfish takes the bait and is hauled onto the pier squirming. Having just caught a fish for supper, Hunter only cares about eating and nothing more. Nothing bothers him when there's food in sight. Even less after he fries and finishes it off. His belly is full and soon he's fast asleep.

After he first lost his father, Hunter wallowed in self-pity. Remembering his mother, now he has vivid memories of her soft sad eyes. After all these years he still misses her. Grace's wisdom and pride once guided him. Remembering mom, he walks back to the cabin, he cleans and airs it out. He mumbles, *"Skunk smell may never go away."* Its clinging stench is strong enough to drive the man out and away.

Vigilante senses a slight surge of ambition in this persons' mind. *"This man is starting to learn who he is."* Somewhere inside Hunter is recalling better ways learned at his mothers' knee. He vaguely remembers her few simple prayers. He misses mother and even his brother Mal. Looking up at the stars from a tattered blanket on the ground he tries to mouth the words. *"Our father who art in..."* But then he falls asleep. Tomorrow morning he won't remember even trying.

Awakened by the rising sun, Hunter scrutinizes his face in a cracked old trash pile mirror. His newly washed finger traces his jaw beneath his shaggy beard. After rinsing his face, he reaches for his only razor. It's the same old blade he uses to gut and skin critters. *"Ouch!"* It's too dull to cut hair.

The jagged metal blade brightens as he strokes it on a rock. Flecks of rust give way to a sharper edge. Wincing, his eyes squint in pain as the blade snags a matted whisker in the tangle. Still he's making good progress towards looking civilized. A surprisingly mature face emerges replacing the hairy mask that mostly concealed his head just moments ago. He's shocked to see how closely he resembles his dead father. Seeing himself brings to mind his fathers' face.

Freshly shaven, he gathers up his meager belongings into a bundle. Then he looks at the uninhabitable cabin. Mr. Skunk peeks around the outhouse. He's the only critter who will live here for a long time. It arches its' back smugly and it won't pretend to be a puppy anymore… *"I'm a proud polecat!"*

The sun warms his clean face for the first time he can recall. His eyes lead him to a faint path through the brush. Walking onto the thinnest hidden trail, he follows a barely visible line. Where it leads is rarely seen by anyone.

This path is so overgrown with thorny blackberry bushes it seems unreal. But Hunter remembers it well. A disturbed copperhead glares up at him. Retreating from anything so big as this man, the viper deliberately uncoils and slithers off. The hunter continues following the faint line; it leads him into an ancient clearing.

Eroded old gravestones mark the earthly resting places of his neighbors' ancestors. Like grey sentries each protrudes from the dirt in erect objection to any intrusion. Rarely does anyone come bringing flowers anymore. So, residents aren't disappointed he has none. Even so, they know in their own time more will come to stay. Even some will have even been loved. It becomes obvious a lost loved one isn't why this visitor came.

A chapel is centered in the clearing just ahead of Hunter. Like the cemetery it's abandoned. This place of the Lord presided over this field of stones for a very long time. It hasn't heard prayers and songs of worship for decades. Nearly forgotten, its' sagging roof is slowly falling. It barely remains, having suffered countless nibbles from termite armies. Stained floor planks survive in scarlet clusters. A white altar, visible from outside, is remarkably preserved. The skeletal remains of its' builders lie nearby beneath engraved slabs. Their *honorable souls* were quickly welcomed by The Lord upon their arrival. Outside are many *forgotten souls* whose scant attention to the Word leaves them decaying in perpetual mediocrity. Finally, there are those *nowhere souls*. These simply bore those who matter.

Long gone are those whose mighty hands who once scribed beloved names into these churchyard stones. Many have stood here a century or more. Most words are barely visible on these weathered rocks. Very few loved ones could carry marble this far and limestone was nearby. Some sad stones record an infant life of only a day. Still, the sweet essence of their innocence remains etched here and in heaven.

Though this is a chapel of The Lord. no one visits to worship now. Even so, some new bodies have been interred out in this forgotten place. As Vigilante looks around in awe, he sees that not all souls buried have moved on. And they see him as well. Here and there overgrown shrubs testify someone once cared to give the place a nice appearance.

Some of those who linger now hover near the pathway to the chapel. They plead with Vigilante to stop and chat. Others sit hopelessly waiting for whatever is to become their fate. While this is where their worldly remains rest, it isn't their destination. Still, no one is in a hurry. In life these were lonely country folk; this is their last church social. Most have nothing to fear. For these worked so hard just to survive there wasn't much time to get into mischief.

Vigilante watches in surprise as Hunter walks up to the altar and slides a small alter stone to one side uncovering a hiding place. He pulls a rusting metal box from where its' stashed. It contains his fathers' stolen loot. His dad was a robber and a thief. Greedy, but freshly washed, fingers touch musty banknotes and jewelry along with coins of silver and gold. From a grave outside, the ghastly corpse of the robber, ever selfish, sneers at his son from his hole in the weeds. Even now, he covets his box. All here know it to be what it is... a legacy of evil. Naively his son dares to inherit his curse...and the curse awaits.

When his mother abandoned this son and her husband, out of desperate need she could have taken this loot to support her younger son Mal. Poor Grace was saved from having to confront this curse because she didn't know it existed. Had she run away with this, who knows what grief would have come to her? In that small town where so few have cash or jewelry, her husbands' victims may have exacted much more in revenge than was stolen.

Even this favored son wasn't aware of this box until his fathers' dying moment. This confession was made while he lay mortally wounded from a black bears' claws and teeth. His father wanted this treasure to buy him care to heal. There was no nearby emergency healer and no ambulance to find one.

The irony of this is, some of the money he had stolen was money old Buzzardville had raised to buy an ambulance. He provided no details to his son except the place in the chapel he hid this box. Yet Hunter has the sense to know this money was ill-gotten. The curse was enacted by the vengeful souls of those others whose lives were lost for lack of that conveyance of mercy.

A lingering ghost exclaims, *"Pity, is- no guardian angel is here to stand guard over this boy!"* This son is on his own, without spiritual support. His father desecrated this chapel; Hunter takes up this curse. The abuse of this place of worship as a cache for stolen goods leaves the entire righteous spiritual community aghast. *"The sins of the father leave his sons without friends"* groans one from within a grave. His fathers' corpse chills in terror yet offers nothing.

As the boy and echo pass the weed ridden graves one sage proclaims, *"That lad has just one living soul to offer a prayer for him."* Grace, his mother has no idea of the destiny of this son she left behind. She is of no use to him now. Grace is so focused on the son she saved. She gives scant thought or prayer for this backwoods boy.

Another ghost picks up the lament as the echo and human pass ... *"Why, no guardian angel? How can he survive now?"* *"He has followed a pathway to the abyss?"* *"Who's to protect him now he too is a thief?"* Vigilante winces realizing that helping even a second-hand thief may be against his mission. Yet, having started this boy moving he can't just abandon him. He realizes this boy needs guidance.

A sarcastic soul chuckles at their concerns. *"Hey man, you and I never had a guardian angel either!"* *"Look where we are today."* *"Who says he needs one?"* Interred nearby, his one-day old sister pipes up giggling. *"Brother, just look around!"* *"Are you really anywhere?"*

Decades gave way to centuries after the earth embraced these mortal bodies. It's as though none ever walked among the living. No one alive now even remembers most to mourn. Those here are all mourn for one another. They release a pitiful wail like one from souls in prayer. Yet, few here are as worthless as Hunter's father… whose soul is truly damned. Most simply are in limbo.

A ghost sits upon his cold white stone and cries to heaven, *"If prayer is only for the living, or so we are led to think, who can truly say when life begins and ends?"* Heaven says nothing although it knows.

Although he's become the sole heir to his fathers' curse, the son feels no guilt. Hunter sees no sin in his deed. Vigilante tries to stir his conscious. He feels something momentarily, yet in seeing, he dismisses it from his mind. Conveniently he wants to believe it's only his imagination and ignores his only warning. Plodding on his way, the son doesn't glance in the direction of his fathers' place of burial. *"It's mine...it is mine!"* his father screams. No one cares.

Glad to be alive; life is for the living. And heaven and earth know Hunter feels neither guilt nor righteousness. Vigilante follows trying to change his mind but realizes this boy has never known wrong or right before. His mind was simple. No one now can make him understand either. He has only the instincts of the beasts he hunted.

Oblivious to all except themselves, two resident souls have been arguing ever since they arrived here. Vigilante is intrigued over the things they are saying. They distract him from worrying about those stolen items in the box. So, he quietly keeps score.

Pastor Paul is the ghost of a minister who when alive brought the Word of the Lord to this once populated area. His perpetual debate is with Mr. Isaac, a teacher of science and mathematics. Neither was involved with any public discourse when living. Both were respected by all who heard them…at least back then.

Each constantly argues an opposite origin of man. Only egos, as hard as granite, perpetuate a debate no one ever told them to have. Their spirits exist just to argue. Unflinching, each rejects compromise by ranting on. Like mules they chomp on each morsel of faith or logic from between clenched teeth. Looking for a weakness where there is none they spit each syllable with righteous indignation at their opponents' lack of wisdom. It will go on eternally at this rate. They unceasingly repeat stale arguments.

Pastor Paul cites Genesis, creation and biblical truth passed down through scripture. Mr. Isaac, with academic condescension, continues his arguments for evolution. For Mr. Isaac, natures' mutations evolved into ever higher creatures. Each evolves through trial and error. Survival of the fittest and sheer chance lead gradually to the earthly creatures of each age.

Neither ever acknowledges any slight value in the others' argument. There is no retreat from this contest. It propels them endlessly. Obviously for these well-meaning wretches, there is no difference from one decade to the next. They are grounded on a sandbar in a stream of stubbornness. Every ghost stuck in this churchyard hates listening to their noise. No one has a choice. Hearing is their purgatory.

Wading into the battle uninvited, Vigilante scolds. *"Preacher and teacher... you each are failing to understand!"* They stop outraged at this nincompoop. *"I'm not a party to your fight, but it's obvious neither of you has enough information to win."* Both just groan sarcastically.

He challenges the teacher. *"Mr. Isaac, you are deceased; we are here."* *"Doesn't this prove there is a reality beyond mortal existence?"* The teacher fumes, *"NO!"* *"This is obviously a nightmare, and I will wake up!"*

The preacher feels victorious until he hears; *"Pastor Paul, it's obvious you have not studied science."* *"Believing God made everything, are you not also required to believe that God created science as well?"* The preacher first nods affirmatively, thinks it over, then shakes his head shouting *"NO!"* In some confusion and being above all else honest, he partly relents, *"The Lord also created science as well as everything and everyone in the universe."*

"Doesn't it only make sense to both of you that you continue your discussion only after each has read the books of your opponent...?"

"Ok?" The preacher believes the end of the world is near and prays before answering. He promises to read everything ever published and quickly return.

The teacher agrees enthusiastically. He mistakenly thinks the *Holy Book* must be an easy read for such a scholar as himself. Borrowing the testament of the ghostly minister he will soon spend considerable time in confused enlightenment. In sheer folly, he attempts to apply scientific methods to each idea expressed. He cannot. Then hanging over him is this nagging suspicion. *"This is reality; it is not just a dream."*

It took only moments for the Vigilante to disrupt their debate. Although he is new to their dimension, he can't imagine why some would believe this all could have occurred without the Master's plan. Vigilante wonders whether any human is truly intelligent. Especially worrisome to him- his vitalized hunter lad is a strong indication people aren't very smart.

Returning to the area of the wretched cabin, Vigilante watches as Hunter dumps the contents of the box onto the pier. In addition to loot, several official looking papers fall out. One has the name of his brother ...*Malcolm*. The hunters' name is on one. He is shocked to learn his own full name. His middle name is very strange. Until this moment he didn't known he has a middle name.

Vigilante thinks. *"This mans' name doesn't matter."* Vigilante ignores the papers. *"Character matters more than name."* Frustrated, he still doesn't know how to make this mans' mind change about keeping this cursed loot, by improving his character.

The hunters' father isolated his family from the outside world. He almost succeeded. Hunter knows of the world outside because of something his father once discarded and forgot... a broken radio. The boy found it in a heap of old rubble behind a shed. First the boy plugged it in; then he shook it when nothing happened. Inside of the radio, an old glass tube containing the thinnest wire filament made contact; it slowly lit, and sound came out of a very tinny weathered speaker.

While no electric was ever installed in the cabin, a long-hidden wire snakes beneath the leaves over to an isolated pole. His father hadn't bothered to unplug it when he tossed the broken radio onto the pile. The electric wire and the shed were put together and forgotten by long gone moonshiners. It's still hidden beneath the underbrush. Boys find everything forgotten.

On one side the sole outlet dangles. The broken radio was a novelty that wore off when the tube first went dark and no longer worked. He never shared anything electric with his Grace. She never had electric. Even now she has it, but always goes to bed when darkness falls over her mountain. It's the way of many who live in the country. They don't miss what they didn't have.

When the boy accidentally made the radio work, he learned a lot. The radio station transmitted old news because little happened new in this area. He knows about a town he visited with his mother as a child. Now, having found his papers, he imagines a much larger world out there. Perhaps once in town he can locate mother and brother Mal.

Returning to realty from thinking deeper than ever, Hunter mouths his middle name for the first time. He repeats it over and over savoring its' sound. Casually he tucks the birth certificates back into the box. Reluctantly entering the cabin. He shoves the box and everything else he may need in town into his dead fathers' ragged pack.

He walks outside again. The cabin door has no lock, so it doesn't cross his mind to try to secure it even though he doesn't plan to come back. No sun shines upon his face this time. A dark cloud makes the day gloomy.

Forgetfully he whistles for his dog and heads for the big trail. It leads to town by sheer chance in the opposite direction from where his dog has gone. Far off in the distance dogs' sensitive ears lift in recognition of a faint familiar sound. Hesitating momentarily dog lowers his head. With an agitated whimper dog runs fast ... once again further from his former master, *"No man owns me!"*

Hunter rarely sets foot on this road. And no one else does either for it is overgrown and only barely passable. But to this young hermit the trail feels like four-lane highway. Legs fall into a steady long comfortable stride. One needn't stop to worry why he's going or what he will do when he gets there. He has money and he thinks it will be all he needs. *"Something big is finally happening in my life!"*

He feels the greatest rush of anticipation and excitement of his twenty something year lifetime. *"I'm really on my way." "For the first time I'm leaving the woods to see the big world out there!"* Cramps of excitement knot up in his stomach. Feeling rich and mighty the hunter jogs down the road with even more determination in his stride.

The nearest town is many miles from the cabin. But he went there once with his mother, back on one his early birthdays. He remembers it because that was the last birthday he has known. He has no hard feelings about his mother because he knows his brother Mal was sort of crazy mean. Their father regularly tried to beat Mal into obedience without success. He believes his mother ran away with Mal to save his brothers' life.

They all knew his father well enough to know that if he could have caught them, they both would be dead. His father seemed to tolerate Hunter more than anyone else in the family, so he was safe. *"I will find my mother!"*

Hunter decides, *"It's wiser to arrive in town tomorrow morning when I'm rested and clean."* Hearing this, Vigilante feels proud. So, when the towns' faint glow breaks through the darkness of the woods before him, Hunter leaves the trail to find a place to sleep. He's tired and will rest but not because of laziness. He took a long walk today and has reason to be tired. When morning arrives, he will find his way into Buzzardville. Descending from the trail on a faint deer path he follows it to a stream. He's thirsty again, but not like he was back at the cabin *"I wonder what was wrong with me?"*

Carefully stepping so as not to surprise any snakes his feet slosh in cold water along a shallow stream bed. He comes to a place where spring water gradually has cut a cleft into the hillside. He follows the feeble trickle of water to its' source and soon reaches a brushy hillside. It leads him into a hidden overgrown hollow.

Cleaning out the debris he slides down onto what he sees as a good spot and instantly falls asleep. Vigilante settles nearby into a smaller hollow and feels as though he is guarding the snoring figure from predators. Mornings' dawn seeps down gradually through the greenness overhead. He wonders if this is the way of a guardian angel but is corrected when from somewhere a voice whispers, *"NO."*

Birds awaken at dawn. Vigilante stirs the man by attracting a noisy one nearby that pecks and flutters without the proper caution needed by such vulnerable creatures. With a lightning like movement, a hawk, oblivious of either Hunter or Vigilante, snatches up the defenseless little bird. It hasn't time to do more than utter a single fatal cry. Hunter feels little sorrow for the stricken creature but is concerned about his own breakfast.

This noise and commotion might awaken the dead had there not once been a wake for all who fell dead before in this wood during a long-forgotten skirmish. Hunter slashes the air with a stick and robs the hawk: it flees like the coward it is. The smaller bird is not wasted; Hunter eats almost anything when he's hungry. With something in his belly, the man stares at the green canopy above shivering in the morning chill.

Vigilante hasn't given up on him; he's not even bothered by the hunters' theft of the bird. *The problem is- there's this damned box.* As the human leans forward to scoop water from the cold stream something causes him to trip losing his balance. Nothing living pushed him this time, least of all his long-lost dog. The shock does nothing to improve his mood. Suspiciously he looks around half expecting to see someone.

Hunter falls into a small deep spot in the creek. Over time a pocket of water has been trapped behind a log. His clothes are under water just long enough to wash off the odor of yesterday followed by a night of sleep on critter droppings. He washes clean but feels that his clothes are too cold and wet for this big trip to town. And, luckily, he has money to buy new ones when he gets there.

He pulls dry old jeans from his pack bundle. Then he carefully takes out the shirt with a hole his mother had patched for his father. She had barely gotten to the task before bugging out. He is a bit embarrassed the patch is of different color. *"I'll buy a new shirt too."* He puts the shirt on buttoning it as he climbs back up onto the trail to town. Hunter thinks, *"This is going to be a really special day!"*

Vigilante doesn't share his optimism because there are dark forces from another dimension gathering over the town. Hunter is moving into shadows he cannot perceive. The unlikely pair slog mindlessly into danger. No angel or possessed demonic dog will appear to alter this curse etched in granite.

Vigilante Spirit

9

Buzzardville

They are coming to Main Street. Hunter doesn't remember
much about this strange town. Not even the big sign he passed

proclaiming -*Buzzardville*.   His eyes are wide with wonder. *"I haven't seen this many people in my entire life!"* It's frightening. When he and his mother were here the town seemed so much slower. He remembers holding his mothers' hand wishing she were with him. He hardly knows what to think. His mind is blown. It's nerve wracking. He has only a shadowy memory of the streets.

Thinking back to that day, he remembers going into a barber shop and getting his first and only real haircut. He wants to relive that great feeling. Not to be deterred by little recollection of which direction to go, he reinforces his reasoning, *"This is the only way mother and Mal could have come."* He hopes someone here might be able to tell him where to find the barber. In his mind he tries to rehearse what to say assuming he gets up the nerve to ask anyone.

Then thinking, *"Maybe I can talk to someone old enough to remember us?"* *"Someone old enough to have been an adult back then..."* He can't think of words to say. So, he just keeps walking. Hunter reasons, *"There can't be many dressed like me coming here."* And then looking around self-consciously, *"Why's everyone staring at me?"*

Asking someone isn't a bad idea. Old Buzzardville's porch sitters see very few people arriving on foot. Someone might remember seeing a lone woman with small boys even so long ago. Or, one may even have heard another mention such an unusual sight. People in small towns remember strangers. If only he can find the courage to ask.

As people pass him on the sidewalk he tries to speak; not a word comes from his lips. He can't even form simple words much less ask questions. Nothing happens no matter how hard he strains. No words come out.

Those closest in blood within his own family mostly ignored him. His brother, mother and father have been gone for a long time. Craving the sound of other humans last year, he tried to make the junked radio tubes light up again. A tube cracked when tried the same tapping that worked before. Living in seclusion with only family members, as they disappeared so did conversation. His father rarely said anything to him. His brother Mal got nearly all of their attention because he was always acting up. *I was the good brother; look where that got me.*

Vigilante follows him in gloomy anxiety. Although he wanted this man to grow as a person he simply unleashed his instinctive weakness. Worse, Vigilante can't justify helping Hunter because he came to town to sell stolen possessions and spend cash from robbery. For an echo, who sees his mission as one to do good, abetting dishonesty would destroy the ethical fabric of his being.

As they pass a yard where a boy is trying out a new slingshot the pebble bounces harmlessly off the Hunter's bundle. He sees the boy and just walks on. An opportunity to speak and somehow dodge fate is lost. It won't return.

Ominous forces are on a collision course with this carelessness. It's obvious to Vigilante something evil is going to happen. But what? The echo is helpless to change whatever is in store for his protégé. Still, he follows along hoping things will get better and whispering things like, *"Turn it over to the law" "Tell them you found the box and want it returned to its' owners."* His advice does not register as Hunter spots a red and white striped barbershop pole ahead.

Hunter doesn't understand that when his father robbed these people he changed people here for the worse. It's made them bitter.

More has been lost in Buzzardville than was taken. They lost their innocent trust of outsiders entirely. Doors once never locked are doubly secured with deadbolts. Every stranger has suffered suspicion since the day Hunter's father knocked over these townspeople.

Worst of all, Hunter has the loot with him. Naively he lugs the cursed bundle containing the box slung over his shoulder. Besides currency and coins, it holds the gold locket his father ripped from a terrified woman. Inside of the locket is the only picture ever taken of her grandmother. The robber snatched it from her right in front of her husband as she held her baby. Hunter's carrying things that mean a lot to these people and their kin.

Her normally proud husband had to withstand this insult in helpless humiliation, because the robber said, *"I will shoot everyone if you don't hand them over right now."* Taking what she gave him, he reached over and yanked a gold chain and watch from the shamed mans' pocket. These had been passed down to the man from many generations. They were his only keepsakes. For this victim, it's irreplaceable. Such humiliation remains a symbol of his lost manhood.

The youth doesn't know or care who owned the locket or the pocket watch. Nevertheless, he knows they were stolen. With every footstep taken towards the Main Street barbershop he comes nearer to the epicenter of deep hatred from an enemy awaiting long fantasized revenge. Hunter's adversary happens to be the very long memory of the sheriff. Even at this critical moment, He doesn't sense danger. But it surrounds him like a beast waiting to pounce. For the moment, his enemy still hasn't discovered him. The cloud darkens. It's eerily quiet.

Adding to their torment, as good Christians, these folks would like to follow the love thy neighbor rule and to forgive transgression. They refuse to forget. *"Forget hell!"* they yell at one another after a few beers at the town bar. No one here forgets or forgives anything. Still walking and clueless, Hunter won't think about the origins of the box no matter how hard Vigilante presses his conscience. *"I'll sell what's in it for any money I can use to help me find my mother and brother." "This is my inheritance from my father."* Because he didn't take it from anyone, he feels his conscience is clear. But that isn't the way these people think.

As with some other small remote towns, some of the folks who live here are way too closely related... *Buzzardvillains,* they proudly label themselves. With one mind, everyone recalls all too well one terrible day. When anyone is hurt; all are. Even children not even conceived then feel it happened just yesterday, rather than two decades ago.

Right after the big holdup they hired their first lawman-. *Sheriff Lott McPherson* He's been on the job ever since. Before the robbery no one felt the need for a peacekeeper or even a jail due to their liberal interpretation of what in other places may be called- assault and battery. Sheriff McPherson is the husband of the same woman threatened and robbed on this very day twenty years ago. And *Sheriff "Mac"* is now and will remain that disgraced man. His office is right behind the very spot of the robbery.

Buzzardvillains take great pride in being law abiding. Few of these good folks have ever been in any trouble other than a payday brawl. As Sheriff McPherson says, *"That don't count."* A fistfight is a rite of passage for normal young men and even for some women in this town. Just bare knuckles though, none of that big city stuff like guns and knives. Other than minor scuffles, none of their cousins, or any other relatives argue. Old families own and run everything that matters in Buzzardville. Recently he was provided a deputy. Because as one elder pointed out, *"Our good Sheriff Mac is my kin but he's getting a bit long in the tooth for his job!"*

This observation severely shocked everyone. Even those who heard about this disloyal remark second hand. No one has even made eye contact with that loudmouth since the day of the nasty remark. Still, a deputy was put on just to be on the safe side. The reason, their wives told them they should. It all went down at the town meeting. One makes the motion; others mumble, *"Second."* Looking down at the floor, everyone says, *"Aye."* Seeing no discussion. The chairman announces matter-of-factly, *"Motion passes."* No one ever brings the subject in public again including the sheriff. Mac's deputy is either his nephew, or second cousin; nobody knows; nobody cares. The wives are happy.

A close-knit community, Buzzardville is just bold enough to glare at most outsiders who passthrough while pretending to ignore them. Strangers are considered nonexistent except when doing business, such as selling apples or apple pie. Then outsider money is welcome. But even these customers are treated with exaggerated politeness. Although unappreciated on the average day a stranger is safe. Buzzardville may well be the only small town in America where no one ever says, *"Y'all come back!"*

The Bird, a tabloid of town trivia is published only once weekly. Sheriff Mac is reading it by the light of the window facing the street. Holding it folded in one hand while watching the street he complains, *"So many strangers coming; nobody knows any- body!"* Old Mac breathes out an exaggerated hiss to his deputy dragging out the *"a-n-y-b-o-d-y."* intentionally making it sound like one long sentence.

The lawman has just read a police item in *The Bird* about some newcomers'   dog:

As reported to the sheriffs' office, a black Labrador retriever was seen running

down Main Street at midnight with either a duck or a skunk in   its'   mouth.

He chomps down on his tobacco chaw sneering- *"Lord only knows what kind of new trash it is that doesn't feed their animals. Our folks wouldn't let them run around unfed all night."* "New trash" includes anyone living here under than six generations.

The sheriff spits a tobacco chaw wad in the general direction of the red can in the corner. He used to hit the side of the can back before his cataracts got so bad. He refuses to go away for an operation fearing someone will steal his job while he's gone. His teeth clamp down on a fresh chaw and he rolls it around in his cheek. It gets chewed a few dozen times. Then it's ejected in the same manner with similar inaccuracy.

Frowning at the *Newcomers* column in the paper he mumbles to his deputy, *"You deal with their crap... I'm fed up!"* The deputy grunts agreeably and spits his own wad at the can in a slam-dunk splash leaving both the wall and floor wet. The sheriff mutters, *"God dam showoff!"* Wet brown streaks run down both of their chins. The piece caught in his mustache is reprieved from joining the mound on the wooden floor. He huffs, *"I look out for the good folks... them what belongs here!"*

The words are barely out of his mouth. His attention focuses through the office window directly across Main Street. Two bleary eyes lock onto what he sees as the despised robber image burned in his memory. *"The rotten holdup man from all those years ago, is* coming directly at me." "That piece of human garbage shouldn't have come back; I got the drop on him this time!"

His eyes stop on the strangers' shirt and his blood runs cold. "The last time I saw that shirt I shot a hole in it and he's still wearing it. He's back to finish me off!"

The sheriffs' tired old brain fills in images his blurry eyes can't fully see. This piece of crap robber had on this shirt the day his beloved was harmed. His hand reacts. Instinctively it grabs his pistol. This louse has topped this lawman's' *Most Wanted* list for as long as he has had this job.

Vigilante tries to scream "DON'T SHOOT!" No human ear hears him. Even the young deputy doesn't comprehend what is happening. The old lawman steps through the door; calmly raises his arm, takes aim and fires. A short blast erupts as the bullet crosses the street. It's as though a canon is fired. Deaths' messenger is on its' way. Just an instant before his mind said, "Shoot him first, before he gets you. He's come back to finish you!" Vigilante's warning could not penetrate that fear.

The decades in between the two intrusions will register tomorrow, a day too late to save this target. Blood spurts out of the hunters' forehead. He drops dying a mere yard in front of Hiker, who by the sheerest coincidence is walking towards him. Hiker instinctively turns in horror towards the source of the gunshot as the youth falls dead at his feet.

To compound the Sherriff's confusion, at this moment another young man with a modern backpack and something the size of a rifle moves into his dim field of vision from directly in front of the hunter. As Hiker strides down the street he feels a touch by an unseen presence. His neck hair stands erect, and he is alerted by fear that stops him in his tracks. Instantly, the hiker turns away stepping back.

His horror becomes understood as the barrel of the same pistol pivots towards him. Another shot is fired. The second loud *boom* is followed by a cracking glass vibration from just behind him. Hiker defensively shifts his body again. The shot missed him. Instead it hits the plate glass window just behind where he is standing.

Hiker is mesmerized with fear. The shooter barely missed hitting him. The deputy reacts and grabs the sheriffs' pistol. Although this round misses Hiker, it crashes through the fine gold lettered glass front window of the barbershop behind him. Gus, the father barber can only watch his cherished window proclaiming □□□ & □□□ □□□□□□□ *shatter* into a dozen pieces.

Old Gus perceives the hiker to be an insane vandal breaking his window with the hiking stick in his hand. His body reacts to his false assumption with a huge rush of adrenaline. Forgetting his only weapon is a hot towel in his hand and not his razor, the old man rushes out after Hiker. A dead man lies on the left side of his door and his vandal is on the right side. He charges past the bloody corpse without stopping or even glancing down.

Frozen fear has melted into a wet trickle running down his leg. Hiker runs for his life. His feet take on a survival speed they have never known. Neither old Gus nor Hiker focus on the fact that they are running from a freshly slain corpse. Hiker is so afraid of crazed old Gus, the dead guy on the pavement and the shooter are far from his mind. He's running for his life.

Because the sheriff and Gus grew up together, he doesn't try to get his gun back from the deputy in fear of hitting his barber and friend. The son half of *GUS AND SON* was in the back room when all this commotion started. He comes to the front of the shop only to see his raging old father chasing someone. Presumably, this is the guy who just broke the shop window. He sees his father ridiculously snapping at the culprit with a wet towel. Old Gus's son knows better than to run out and join the chase unarmed.

He grabs what he knows is a real weapon. It is the straight razor his father was too excited to take. He also snatches up a big seven-ounce bottle of Aqua Velva after shave. This is just in case the situation warrants a hand grenade. Thinking *"This is my backup weapon!"* he charges in pursuit his mind screaming, *"Pop let me get him!"* No one on the street sees the Hunter's bloody corpse.

Although his youth and head start gave him a good lead and he's halfway down the street, Hiker twists his ankle. Vigilante pumps up Hikers' adrenaline as high as he can. He feels frustrated to the point of defeat. *"Where in hell is your guardian angel?"* He continues to push the limping backpacker along. But the bad ankle is slowing him down. Vigilante is pushing so hard, poor Hiker seems to be hopping down the street on just one foot. The gap between pursued and pursuers is closing fast.

Today there's no help from Hikers' guardian angel. Roman is sidetracked. Although he started to follow, now he's back with son of Gus sniffing the Aqua Velva becoming snockered. Even when Hiker was attacked by Mal and his buddies in the meadow, the reason he was so vulnerable in the first is his guardian angel was dallying at a clump of hemp growing just off the trail. Roman, although an angel, has serious substance problems.

No one could have anticipated the demented actions of this half-blind lawman. In his mind the sheriff saw Hunter as the boys' father. He imagined the shirt wearer as the assailant from that humiliating day... He took up the badge seeking justice. Today was his best day if only in his poor tired mind.

Vigilante doesn't try to avenge the hikers' death. Instead, the moment Sheriff Lott McPherson suspects he killed the wrong man he hears- *"Blind revenge is the absolute demise of all noble deeds in both humans and immortals."* For a good man, guilt is a terrible punishment.

Even though he doesn't publicly acknowledge his shooting error, the sheriff makes an appointment to see about his cataracts.... in a faraway city. The trip and the glasses are being financed from part of the proceeds of a rusty old box found in the possession of a deceased vagrant. In *the Bird* the article will include the sentence…

Owners of some items could not be reached and were deemed to be public property. However, the sheriffs' office was able to restore certain items to their rightful owners.

He finally understands who the robber father of the deceased was. His trip resulted in the restoration of his vision. But he rationalizes, with the death of the felons' son now the score is even. With the reason for his career no longer important, he will not run for reelection. A dead felon father and the loot on him makes the matter is settled as well. Still, the hunter's ghost feels only a huge injustice though the shine shines and the curse is gone from old Buzzardville.

With the race down the hill practically lost, finally the spirit sees a way to help the fleeing hiker. He reacts by blocking the pain from his injured ankle just as Spirit did once before in the meadow. Running now on his injured ankle, the hiker races towards the river like an animal from a fire. This burst of strength doesn't happen a second too soon for the barbers Gus's son, a former high school track star, barely misses Hiker with his razor.

Poor old wheezing Gus stops halfway down the hill. For no apparent reason, his towel becomes tangled in a window flowerbox. Breaking his pace drains his anger. Exhausted old Gus stumbles and falls to the pavement. Seeing his fathers' predicament, his son heaves the Agua Velva bomb at the hiker as hard as he can.

The sweet contents of the open spiraling Aqua Velva bottle permeates the air only for a moment before something foul drowns out its' scent. Old Mr. Gus's big son is bent double with stomach cramps. His pains make him turn around and run as fast as he can back up the hill. He rushes into the restroom of his fathers' barbershop a moment too late. His dignity was far too great to use the one in *Hilda's Beauty Salon,* although it was only halfway back up the hill. Thus, the chase is lost to the barbers.

Hiker reaches the river at the bottom of the street and plunges in. His pursuers gave up. But if they stayed a bit longer they would have watched him land in mere inches of water. It makes a miserable hiding place. Now his arms hurt worse than his ankle did. Vigilante doesn't numb Hiker's pain the way Spirit did after the meadow incident. Roman, the boys' wayward guardian angel, has his attention. The angel is floating down the street in their direction and definitely isn't sober.

Everyone in town knows the water is polluted with *Giardia* bacterium well enough that every local child learns to steer clear of the river in elementary school. Up at the top of the hill the dead one is being collected onto a pickup bed and everyone is breathing easier. The collective conclusion is the two were both out to get the sheriff.

Nothing of the sheriff's error will be reported in *The Bird*. Little Gus mumbles his way around the shop for weeks with simmering anger, *"That son 'um of a beach ran like somethin' else!"* *"Who'n the hell was he anyway?"*

The hikers' invisible guardian angel is almost passed out on the payment. He was in deep focus on the Agua Velva when all hell let loose, and the bottle top came off. Woozily, Roman belatedly ruminates about Hiker, *"I think I better see what that boy is up to..."*

Those witnessing their sheriffs' actions won't discuss it even among themselves. However, another warning concerning the danger of *Giardia* will appear on the second page of *The Bird*. On the front page, the headline will read *Chicken Thief Dog Shot at and Missed*. The article will mention that a vagrant has been humanely buried by Mr. Harry, at the usual place for those without means. It will be followed by several lines encouraging all residents to have their pets immunized to prevent rabies.

The river becomes a lot deeper as Hiker proceeds downstream still thinking he's being chased. His empty water bottles help buoy his backpack in the water. He will alternately float, swim and wade until well out of reach of all out to get him before leaving the safety of this river. He trusts any of its' rapids far more than he does those maniacs back in Buzzardville.

Now accompanying the hiker, Vigilante helps by telepathically repeating to keep his mouth closed. Hiker heads for a sandy spot along one side. His feet touch bottom where the stream becomes shallow. Some pain returns to his ankle. But the cold river reduced the swelling. Unfortunately, being very thirsty along the way he allowed a little of the deceptively clear water to enter his mouth. This foolish luxury will result in misery tomorrow.

In the back of the pickup, dead as those ducks he once consumed, rides this poor son of a robber. The hunter can never tell anyone his name, and no one will know. For one bullet went directly through his bloody birth certificate. He rides on the truck bed, eye open awaiting disposal. His ghost thinks, *"Dam getting shot hurts!"*

Hunter isn't mourned; he was just another troublesome stranger. While the chase was on back in town, people gradually trickled by to see his corpse and trade meaningful glances. When his lifeless body was carried away in the bed of Mr. Harry's old truck, some Buzzardvillains who arrived too late for his sidewalk viewing were disappointed.

Harry, his undertaker, likes to say, "*I'm the designated driver for everything dead.* "And he's the first to also admit he's the town drunk. But, drunk or sober, Harry is an indispensable element of Buzzardville. Some even whisper he's the richest man in town.

Arriving at the storage facility, intelligent-inebriate Harry pushes the corpse onto the tailgate. Then Harry half carries, and knee bumps the body through the rear door of the veterinarians' office. Gradually he slides it down the steps into an old restaurant cooler serving as Buzzardville's morgue. This is where any animal found dead on the pavement or on the road is taken.

Most of the towns' unfortunates, mostly those who fail to pay parking tickets, eat roadkill stew while in this jail. Of course, dead critters are stored in a more modern building. All in town proudly recite, "*The new freezer meets health department requirements...*" Then in a confidential tone, "*If anyone ever bothers to inspect us.*"

It is true this dead hunters' temporary mortuary has a low

standard of sanitization. But Hunter doesn't care. It seems almost as though he's back home in the cabin. He feels like he's sleeping. Padlocking the cold dark locker door, Harry reasons, "*It don't matter if this old locker is dirty cause this boys gonna be buried in dirt anyhow" "Whew!" "Don't I need a drink?"*

The sheriffs' office proclaims the old case closed and issues a formal order for burial. Harry is given it verbally by the sheriffs' assistant. He notices the man is sweating and won't look him in the eye. Now even Harry knows the truth.

Arriving at the burial site, Harry thinks he's alone and fishes a partly full whiskey bottle from beneath the cover of the unfinished dig. He always starts a new grave as one is occupied. The=empty bottle is pitched into the new grave. Harry is primed for reverence and meditation. He closes his eyes and goes to sleep.

Noting neither the digger or deceased are completely dead or alive. A wandering angel intones-

> *Soul in shock, body broken,*
> *Never again to hunt or fish,*
> *No word of sorrow spoken,*
> *Why Lord why?*

The hunters' corpse lays soothed, *"It's the kindest prayer anyone has ever said for me."* Harry wakes up hearing voices…for neither for his first nor last time…he murmurs *"Amen!"*

Vigilante Spirit

10

Shame

Vigilante returns to Hunter's corpse and stays as though he can be of some use… The dead boys' bewildered ghost asks, *"Why was I shot; who are you?"* Vigilante is too ashamed to admit it was his horrible mistake to awaken this mans' mind. It's all too complicated to explain to a new corpse. If it was allowed to exist in its' normally lethargic state, Hunter may still be alive.

Both learned dear lessons. But for this young man the final grade was a "D" for death. Hunter was someone who needed to remain low-key to survive. Simplicity was all he could handle. Vigilante belatedly realizes even a pathetic life beats being dead.

The millstone of doom rolled upon Hunter's lifeline the instant he chose to ignore the seriousness of his fathers' crimes. Its' curse shrouded him as the damned box was moved from beneath the cold altar stone. Carrying it here... to Buzzardville, of all places, danger became deed. Inspired by its' curse, the lawman pulled the trigger of the gun that killed him. Vigilante doesn't bother to answer Hunter's imploring spirit. His ghost really knows why he's dead. Vigilante is boiling with frustration.

No evil demon placed curses over either father or son. For certain, crimes create hatred so intense it spawned a curse. His fathers' crime created the curse; Hunter claimed it. It attached to their souls as though glued to graveyard granite. A dirty deed was their   doom.

Vigilante tries to explain, *"Death would come to anyone who came wearing the shirt worn on the day of the robber. Suppose your mother had taken your with her instead and left Mal behind."*

If Mal had worn it to town, he'd lay here dead." Vigilante spares Hunter the misadventures of Mal.

Mal was far meaner than Hunter yet is safe through Grace's motherly love. Hunter's ghost replies, *"So, Buzzardville was a baited trap set and waiting for that cursed old rag. The sheriff's trigger finger was just its' enactor."* Vigilante doesn't reply.

On the day Hunters' father fled after robbing him, young McPherson was frozen stiff with fear. His mind changed the way things went down to create his response as less passive. He rationalized his reaction was in manly defense. In fantasy, he imagines first securing both wife and child. Then remembers shooting at the robber from a small pistol hidden is his jeans. His fantasy is just an element of the curse.

Fortunately for their relationship, the sheriff and Mrs. McPherson never talk about the incident. She knows her man well and never considers he could have done more to protect her. Delusion cauterized his wounded mind. Whenever she overhears him talking to others, she simply puts it out of her mind. If she must comment she demurs, *"It was all so dreadful. "The Sherriff did all he could." I don't want to talk about it."*

As Sheriff Mac remembers the way it happened: he had a tiny gambler' pistol, one not designed to hit anything more than a few feet away. Thus, the round barely grazed the robbers' shoulder. McPherson deludes himself it marked that shirt well enough for him to remember. It's the same one with a patched hole still on the dead boys' body.

Though hazy old eyes, the sheriff imagined a patch on the spot from his bullet. Unassisted by the curse, McPherson would have missed from across the street. When asked he will say, *"The debt's paid; justice is done."* Even, if Hunter came intending to return the loot to rightful owners, he would still be a goner. At least he would have died an honest man instead of a dead thief. As for the curse, when Hunter fell mortally wounded, its' dark cloud was gone.

Buzzardville's amassed hatred was unmerciful. Vigilante reasons, *"This wasn't justice." "No warning shot was fired; no order to halt given."* A rattlesnake gives warning. Natures' designs, colors and even deadly creatures give notice. Vigilante groans, *"Nothing... no warning, your life was just blown away."*

Miserable guilt-ridden, Vigilante knows the truth. The sheriff is nearly blind and very delusional. Even worse, this so-called bullet hole in the shirt was actually caused by an ember from the cabin stove. True, it was worn on the day of the robbery, but Grace had sewn that hole. Why this fantasy? The sheriff remained frustrated and helpless over being robbed. Trying to reconcile his shame, over time he created that bullet hole burned its' hole in his imagination.

Worse, the robber was bluffing during the holdup. For his pistol was one he carved out of wood. Hunters' father was a robber and a thief, but not a murderer. That day he left his shotgun home. It was fortunate for him. For if he had a real gun and even accidentally shot one of his victims his eternal damnation would be sealed rather than highly probable.

But Vigilante sees things differently. He doesn't believe a curse can triumph over Hunter's life of laziness. He believes, *"The alternate outcome for a mindless one should not be equal to that of one whose mind is clever."* He argues with the universe: *"If Hunter came to town with the contrite heart of one trying to restore the goods to rightful owners, why would he still be cursed by his fathers'*   *ill-gotten*   *legacy?"*

The answer comes- *"but he didn't."*

In Vigilante's ideal world, rational fate would surely sway all that is right to respect Hunter's weak mind. For the echo, an alternate outcome based on good intentions should have favored the boy... *"Virtue must trump evil,"* he screams. Therefor this whole outcome is wrong. He cries in anguish to the heavens, *"The curse was wrong!" "Justice must win!"* A voice from somewhere replies, *"He knew he did wrong!"*

Once Hunter's soul leaves his body, he will be gone forever. No one will grieve. No chapel bells will toll... no kind words spoken. Not a tear will fall except by this echo spirit who knows the boy's mind wasn't strong enough to make an informed decision. Vigilante doesn't even blame the sheriff. Seeing the object of his worst fears, Sheriff McPherson need not have waited to be killed.

For Vigilante, this is his blunder. *"It is my fault!"* Making mistakes may be essential for maturity. But this is an error not to repeat. He confesses to the universe he wasn't a good mentor. Good counsel would have deterred this boy from tragedy.

Consumed by his guilt, he reluctantly turns away. He cannot

bear to look at the youthful corpse. But, in doing so, he misses something vital…a surviving soul.

He turns his attention back to the hiker. That one survived the horror of Buzzardville. But was nearly caught up in Hunter's tragedy. *"My destiny isn't to protect him for he has a guardian angel." "Assuming he's sobered, Roman should be with him by now."*

Finding the exhausted hiker downstream from the town, Vigilante watches him come to a bridge. It crosses over the river. Above an embankment, there stands a familiar fast food sign. Hiker's hunger pangs are now worse than his fear of being shot. The jerky in his pack has been soaked. He feels he is a safe distance from those town monsters.

Vigilante hangs back at the stream watching the hiker treading his way unsteadily along a thin, slippery line where the stream meets land. Once he slips almost falling on broken glass. He scrambles up the embankment with determination to stay upright.

Luckily, his clothes and boots were bought from an upscale outfitter. Unlike the dead boys' thin bloodstained moccasins. These boots are light and well designed for even this rugged terrain. They will quickly dry. Reaching the road, he takes them off carefully tying them together with their laces. Roman, his guardian angel is nowhere around.

Hanging from his neck, the boots bounce against his back. Sandals from his backpack give him the traction to make it up the across the road and to the restaurant. He bangs towards hot coffee and food. The servers are used to seeing trail weary hikers here. No one gives him a second glance. Vigilante beseeches the universe.

"Where   is   Roman?"

Reaching relative safety within the building, Hiker stares through the window at Vigilante. For a moment, he imagines he sees someone, then nothing. He shrugs it off, but comically tips his cap as if to say goodbye. Vigilante waves back, but the moment has passed. He sits down to rest before ordering his meal trying to relax after coffee. But cramps from the water he swallowed propel him to the restroom.

Following Hiker from Buzzardville was easy for Vigilante. *"Where else could he go?"* Looking for Roman, Vigilante soon reaches the foot of Main Street. Halfway up the hill he spots the hikers' angel, hovering in front of the saloon. Roman slyly pretends not to see Vigilante. Infuriated, the echo moves close to the angels' face and pushes gutter air upwards. *"Ok, Ok, I see you!"* He shouts. *"So, what do you want?"* Vigilante shouts back. *"Go do your damned job!"* *"Your responsibility sits a mile down the river pooping his brains out!"*

The angel floats sheepishly down the street cajoling, *"You may not know this, but way-way back I was your mothers' angel."* *"This guy is just my latest assignment."* The echo screams, *"I don't care if you were the guardian angel to all twelve apostles; get your ass down there!"* He can't resist adding *"I didn't have a mother...you damn fool, I was hatched!"* Roman laughs, *"You were not hatched."* *"You   are   your   own   mother!"*

Moving quickly down Main Street the angel replies over his shoulder, *"So much for your great wisdom, wise guy, angels don't have asses either. "And even if you were hatched, it's all way more complicated   than   you   think!"*

Vigilante has little conscious memory of his parents, having never met them. Still he hopes to accomplish much more than either of them. He responds, *"I don't care who or what you were or, if you do or don't have a backside."* *"You're just a drunk!"*

He does know he is the progeny of two echo spirits whose marriage was a spontaneous event preceded by a short fiery courtship best described as a hot pursuit. Although he is far downstream, the angel continues trying to ingratiate himself, *"Your mother was an echo spirit who was dormant for a very long time."* *"Spirit, your father, was her last hope to exist as you are now."*

Hearing nothing from Vigilante, he tries to seize the advantage. *"Your screw-up with the hunter is really bad. Stop trying to be a guardian angel."* *"Do what an echo does best; straighten out your mess!"* Roman adds forgetting his own incompetence. *"We do the baby sitting."* Vigilante recovers from the shock of being his own mother and blasts downriver with an even stronger gust of wind responding- *"Save your bullcrap for judgment day!"*

With a reproachful backwards glance, the angel flows downstream and says no more. Still the echo has learned more than he knew before of Spirit and Gin. Vigilante shudders, *"This is way too much information for one poor echo."*

The hikers' guardian angel is secretly proud of Vigilante. Spirit, the echoes' father, burst forth as an echo in an extremely difficult way. It was more like a thud. For some reason, first generation echoes often start out with amnesia. Spirit was way beyond oblivion; he was completely disoriented and extremely unaware. Roman chuckles to himself, *"He actually believed he had to ride on a snail!"*

Gin, just the opposite, was just one of a long line of native American spirits. None of her peers still function as echoes. Her personality was so robust her sisters were more concerned with escaping from her than celebrating her marriage. It took every bit of their skill to make her appealing to Spirit when they first met at the campfire. One reason she said so little was she knew she was always argumentative. Vigilante inherited her sarcastic attitude.

Spirit and Gin were two desperate echo spirits who held one another up just long enough to keep from sinking. Their salvation was Vigilante. Echoes are roughly comparable to black holes in space in that they continually compress eventually fading until they marry.

Vigilante is much stronger than Spirit and Gin combined. He eventually too may fade. But he doesn't dwell on negative thoughts. Abruptly his resolve surges and he is up and moving. He has arrived at a half-adult, half-child stage, similar to a human teenager. Roman has Vigilante at a disadvantage because he knows everything about him. And he doesn't like the fact this twerp of an echo spirit knows he's a drunk.

Now Vigilante feels like the kid who has just wrecked the family car. He wants to forget and chalk it off to experience. But from his exchange of insults with Roman he's now more aware of himself. In hindsight it's become clear neither he nor Hunter was ready for the boys' confidence upgrade. Roman chuckles to himself. *"And he hasn't even met Dumbass yet."*

Instead of losing a drivers' license, something else this boy didn't have, his penalty was his life. Vigilante didn't see obvious warning signs. The hunters' hand to mouth style of living was a big hinderance. When danger warnings came neither know how to slow things down. Vigilante lost control; the boy died.

Vigilante decides he must get far from Buzzardville. He will find an even worse place…a place so wrong it's impossible to make things worse. Listening to graveyard gossip, he hears of a place that bad. He heads in the direction of *Wallow*, a city notoriously fitting his requirements.

Arriving at dusk, he looks for something he might do to make things better in Wallow. Vigilante combs through filthy city streets looking for anyone in trouble. *"I will be a virtual medieval knight slaying dragons."* Hesitancy isn't an option in Wallow to even the small degree. This place has become a cesspool of evil.

Small towns, even Buzzardville, strive to become righteous. Here in Wallow, wrong is right. The hunter and even his father were saints by comparison. The Buzzardvillain are good people hating evil. Wallow ridicules good as a weakness. People in Wallow aren't born evil. Its' sick culture passes it down to each newborn.

Vigilante flows down the city's streets hoping to challenge its' misery. Howling sirens and flashing blue lights saturate the night. He eagerly turns into an alley whose rusted sign proclaims *Lizard*. A jaded ghost warns him not to enter. It flees shrieking hideously into the Wallow gloom.

He finds evil in all of the vile creatures inhabiting the Lizard. Rotten fiends with rotten deeds flourish with its' rats undertaking the devils' drudgery. Only the rats are innocent. Through them he quickly learns these monsters tempt even the purest of spirits.

Vigilante flows into the darkness fending off evil from all sides.

Because some are still half-living they may wish to be raised back to virtue. But this is not for Vigilante. He is no ones' guardian angel. He has decided his new mission is to bring justice. One such, a fallen angel he comes upon, sobs - *"Be wary of seduction by imposters haunting this alley, for they crave your power."* As Vigilante passes, this very same false mentor attempts to capture him, but the echo is never exactly where he seems to be. These intrusions happen several more times as he makes his way towards something moving. He simply pushes through them.

He swears to himself and to God that no human, spirit or devil will ever leave him so unaware. Not to the degree he was with that poor lad. Regardless of his past failure, despair won't stop him. Failure here would make his self-ordained mission a failure as well. He flows down Lizard through a spiderweb of lost souls. He is determined only to avenge wrongs and never to lead again. He comes across seducers, thugs and rogues of all manner. Without pity, he passes through their confusion. He moves on down the dirty Lizard.

Abruptly, his senses are jolted by sounds of pain. This pitiful cries draw him to three human forms. Abruptly he is in front of two huge thugs beating a weak old man. Much like the thugs who ambushed Hiker. they punch and kick the helpless one. Both take turns smashing him then standing him back up only to hit him until he falls. In hopeless Lizard Alley no vicious dog or guardian angel will save him. Vigilante watches momentarily. Then gathers his willpower not to freeze as when the boy was shot.

They mock the wretch and laugh. His eyes roll in his head; he cannot see. Vigilante remembers hearing somewhere about the hikers' torment when he was attacked and thinks- *"This is how it must have been!"*

Blood is all over his face; his cheeks are cut. It runs in black lines down the center of the concrete alley. Even huge rats shudder and scurry away. Repeatedly his body rolls in the grime and slime. They hoot at him... They do everything they can think of to hurt him. It isn't just a mugging; it's brutal savagery.

Vigilantes' disgust with their blood sport excites his first blind rage. Their regular blows surge in potency because they are young, strong and their victim is an old weak man. They batter without mercy. An echo spirit has no need of gun or knife. Mind-force is his weapon…the only one he needs.

They sense a presence; one they can't see. Now alert to someone or something near, their eyes flare white then blood red with fear. They try hard to stop punching with the same determination as before. They want to stop, not out of mercy, but cannot. Each is now the target of the other. Compulsively they hit one another. Kicks and punches rain into their faces and upon each other's' bodies. No matter how hard they try they can't stop hurting each another.

Rising from the filthy concrete alley, the battered bum is dumbfounded. He watches in astonishment as thugs who moments ago beat him… now attack one another. Regaining his voice, their victim chuckles *"I wouldn't hurt a fly; I'm a nice guy" "But, I'm only human. You two are funnier'n hell!"* He thinks of hitting them then worries they'll kill him the next time.

They try hard but can't hit him. Furiously, they cover each other in blood. The gleeful victim now mocks their hideous laughing and retrieves their money along with the fifty cents they took from him. As a final touch, he rips every stitch of clothes from their bodies leaving them naked. All of Lizard's fiends gather to mock these fools.

Vigilante escorts the newly joyful bloody victim back up the Lizard floating unseen. They look back; the two naked opponents continue destruction. The fear in their eyes stays fixed not on their escaping prey, but upon Vigilante's long shadow caste from the streetlight up the alley. Horrible fear of this specter prods them to fight on. Their eyes project the hatred of hyenas craving revenge. They are now the victims of their evil.

The echo and the former victim leave Lizard turning in opposite directions as they reach the main thoroughfare. Experience has taught Vigilante not to remain with those he tries to help longer than necessary. Arriving at the next corner the man dumps the emptied wallets and clothing into a sewer. He pockets their money. Vigilante watches disgusted but is wiser for having seen. He reasons some who cry out for mercy may themselves not be merciful.

Those bloody two still down in Lizard Alley can do nothing except pound one another. Exhausted, they both are unconscious. After one comes to, his punching and kicking resumes until the other one hits him back. The echo somehow put a behavior loop into their minds. He watches a familiar form several blocks away buy drugs. It's the one he rescued from the alley getting high at his assailants' expense.

Two bitter days later, a sanitation worker finds them in the alley. He notifies the police. They are apprehended and carried to a nearby place of healing and charity. A week later, by wretched coincidence, both are taken to the same hearing. Their brawl resumes until both are dragged away in straightjackets punching at nothing and cursing The Lord. The Lord didn't curse them; their own evil did.

Both lost a lot of skin and blood. Later, with wounds treated and healing, they are returned to court. It is decided that both are still too unstable in mind to be tried. After some time and far apart their minds seem to heal. Each behaves as a model patient in separate mental institutions. Their charges are dropped. If they ever meet again, who knows what will happen? The echo doesn't know or care. Satisfied he muses: "*It worked out well...maybe I am a success.* "

The former victim, once an addict, will never be the same. Drying out with help, he returns to college and studies to become a prison teacher. He will even offer anger management to violent offenders. He fanaticizes, "*My, wouldn't a reunion with those two be fun?*" The meanness of an alley named Lizard will always be with him.

Vigilante now understands there is too much evil here in Wallow for hundreds like him to solve. He leaves in frustration gradually working his way to the big *City of Baltimore.* Something deep in his mind is pulling him to the place called *the city of charm.* Maybe here he can assist mercy and justice with success...

A dark winged creature in Baltimore once appeared before the eyes of the living by the pen of the great Edgar Allen Poe, whose *The Raven* maintains dual presences. One haunts libraries, the other sports.

Vigilante Spirit

11

Charm City

Vigilante is drawn to Baltimore by an unfathomable compulsion. It inspires him to experience its' spirits. He is destined see much more. Here in Charm City, this spirit will meet the most stunning creature of his existence.

High over Baltimore's inner harbor two sentries are watchful, yet tranquil. Wings folded neatly, they observe the nefarious human and spirit goings-on in a city some feel has lost some of its' charm. Still hope remains for this old town.

The building looks like an old Bromo Seltzer bottle. A venerable clock beneath them strikes midnight . From atop its' grey tower they observe Baltimore's day workers drift into deeper sleep. Should anyone look up at the sky through their bedroom window they might only see a raven. For only she is visible, not her companion. This odd pair share a magical reality living mortals can't perceive.

Both tower clock hands point up to heaven. *"Midnight!"* cries the raven.

Midnight opens the domain of protectors and predators. The fight is on; good and the evil engage battling out their rolls in the passage of life and death. Frantic hours await dawn; now is the time guardian angels are vital. In deep night innocents are their most vulnerable. Demons abound. Those prowling *Charm City* search for naked souls.

Looking down on all are these winged sentries. One is the angel, the other the very raven who saw Will Gold splinter into Vigilante's father. The angel, Lucien waits patiently for Vigilante; she is very curious. Hopefully, her radiance will serve as a magnetic force, a light drawing him near. Though, not yet sensing his presence, she knows he's coming very soon. Lucien and raven wait as time moves on.

Lucien has finely tuned intuition about those she finds of interest. Hers is a vital quality of protectors. The avian assistant endures a rather miserable existence. She atones her fatal distraction of the instant Will Gold perished. This wasn't a simple failure. Her adversary was more powerful. Even so, she suffers remorse for a defeat which was beyond her ability to prevent. If life isn't fair, neither is immortality.

Her lapse of duty as poor Will washed over the edge with so little warning can't be forgotten because his demise was supposedly preventable. Resting at the highest point of the city, the two mutely witness the sounds and sights on the streets below.

Their focus is abruptly drawn to the distress of another guardian directly across the harbor. While his responsibility isn't normally their problem, any desperate plea for help becomes the affair of all nearby spirits. A frantic angel is trying to guide its' client through a fall from a balcony. This angel can't revive his clients' consciousness to avert his limp body from becoming an unrecognizable splotch on the pavement.

Lucien and her assistant soar swiftly in his direction. But not in time to save him from falling. This is his moment to pass into destiny. Though they can't change his destiny, hopefully he can be slightly deflected from smashing into the sidewalk.

Using their combined will the three exert a bending force. The angle of his body slants away from the building. Striking harbor water from this height and velocity still is as brutal as if he hit the hard concrete. He needs to twist his body to have an open casket.

At once, another incoming spirit wakens him just enough to slightly angle his dive. He enters the water at barely the suitable angle to cheat death. His body is intact. The man's angel is grateful for the assistance.

Quickly his situation worsens. He struggles and screams for help. A floodlight from an approaching boat finds him. Still the man still cannot survive. For he doesn't know how to swim and inhales too much harbor water to float. His head goes under. Water fills his lungs before his rescuers can reach him. The angels' mission is a success because the mans' body is intact although he drowns. Even so, his guardian angels' assignment is far from over.

For this guardians' charge, a charitable person, bequeathed his body to medicine long ago. His body is retrieved from the water and shortly will find its' berth in the anatomy lab of a teaching hospital several blocks from here. After his viewing at a funeral home, Angel Michael will accompany him through the next stages. Then will stay at his side for as long as he is in the hospital. anatomy lab.

So strong was her focus on this man, Lucien didn't sense the identity of another. Vigilante was the spirit who awakened him as he hit the water. Unfortunately, the man suffered the panic of drowning, A regrettable necessity if he was to be recognizable postmortem. The raven is more alert and suspects the new angels' identity but doesn't speak. Lucien belatedly wonders if it Vigilante is the mysterious spirit.

Michael looks for the spirit to thank him, but he's gone. The raven says nothing and sulks. Then she sarcastically croaks, *"I realize part of my new job was to help find that damned spirit!"* Certain of the answer now, Lucien smiles but also says nothing.

Several block away, Vigilante turns from this good deed and returns studying the problems he came to pursue. He's restless in his commitment to improve wherever he wanders. Turning viciousness back on the wicked is his mission choice, he shouts to unseen demons, *"Bring it on!"* Without searching hard for targets, he practices by intervening in minor situations but not so harsh as the punching loop he devised back in wretched Lizard Alley.

Ghosts who lived and died here are still proud of their city. But Baltimore has evolved however as Poe's raven once said, will be *"Never More."* Over time, much has happened. Today it's a refuge for spirits, demons and others of many stripes. Baltimore is the nearest these old-school apparitions will ever get to heaven. At times, their needs and those of living people are in conflict. For those who are alive, the cramped nature of old-world construction is a major hindrance to just getting around. living souls need more separation from one another just to keep from colliding.

The oldest brick rowhouses are newer than many of the ghosts haunting these long blocks. Spirits and ghosts abound in the old ethnic neighborhoods. They're populated with ghosts who would rather stay than go to heaven. Generations, of both divine and the unholy collide with the living. Every ghost believes it runs the neighborhood and many do. Some even go so far as to surreptitiously drop bricks, or entire houses onto intruders.

Vigilante is the only echo spirit active here now. Earlier echoes, long ago dimmed-out to a level almost beyond recovery. Still they wait patiently. He wants nothing to do with any of the dormant echoes. Their plight doesn't appeal to his generous side. Passing near one just sitting on a bench he mutters, *"This just isn't natural."* He stops thinking about dormant echoes entirely after one yells at him, *"If you think you are natural?" "Humbug!"*

When the uproar of bullying comes to him, Vigilante picks only those he deems worthy of his eclectic talent. Enough serious maliciousness erupts to keep him busy. Gradually, his loneliness deepens. Other spirits avoid him as he did the hapless dormant echo.

Failing to be sympathetic to a distressed echo leaves him oblivious to his own vulnerability.

In addition, Vigilante is conceited. He doesn't comprehend he is merely a second-generation projection from the mind of a human. A mind mutated in such a way as to initiate an echo spirit. Because all echoes eventually fade away most ghosts and angels just refuse to believe in them.

His personality flaw has been noted by those around him. This causes a popularity problem. Growing increasingly isolated, Vigilante reasons, *"At my rate of progress I too will soon fade away." "I've got to improve."* The dormant echo manages to yell, *"Fat chance!"* before fading again.

Ghostly beings dislike anything they can't understand. Agnostic and atheistic ghosts still carry the bias they held when they were among the living. Echoes exist in a problematic dimension. If others believe in echoes at all they just don't like them.

Since coming to Baltimore, the nearest Vigilante has been to angels, was to sense their fading shadows or to hear telepathic fragments. They've shielded themselves almost as though he were human. Some angels are curious because he simply isn't native to this eerie community. Except for Lucien who's very interested but can't seem to find him.

As for how the angels feel about themselves, they may not all like one another, yet have a sense of who does or doesn't belong. Angels are a curious lot much like that of Eve when she found the forbidden apple so irresistible. Although he can't see them, Vigilante knows he's being watched.

Surprisingly, guardian angels are often incompatible with others of their kind. Some even have a love-hate tolerance aside from the fallen versus loyal angel schism. Most immortals share a common gift of high intelligence although each exists in a slightly different manner.

When the raven reported her distraction by a demonic raven on that terrible day the dam broke, Lucien counseled her saying, *"Always be on the lookout for that evil fallen angel." "He will never stop trying to cause you trouble."* Adding, *"It's horrible for the fallen angels, depending on how the demonic one feels about their plight." "Unlike echo spirits, fallen angels are never dormant." "They constantly spread their evil."*

Vigilante isn't as complicated as an angel. Perhaps an echo exists mainly to find a mate as was with his parents? It was the case with his mother and to a lesser degree with his father as well. Although clever, Vigilante inherited barely a basic survival instinct. He chooses to do more than follow an instinct to *just marry*. Consequently, his adventures are more exciting. His curiosity of the others in his dimension, and a certain angels' interest will soon erase desire to remain a loner. Reaching out to help others will trigger a cycle in which others reach out to him as well.

He explores Baltimore's old streets even haunted empty houses where people once lived. Long gone ghosts of women return each morning to scrub the vacant homes' white marble steps. These marble monuments remain a tribute to hard working people who took pride in them. Those steps say, *"We may be poor, but we are a clean and decent family!" "Respect us, for we respect ourselves."*

Many of those marble steps remain white and shining well past their owners
lifetime. Proud knees ached with pain as time and toil caused them to fail. Those proud handstrokes of marble step heroines are engraved forever within these white stone blocks.

Not all among the quick or dead in this city have such pride. Living sad souls coexist with old ghosts and angels in cold dark red brick. As for those who have passed, their bodies though no longer alive, prefer this short haunt to eternity anywhere else.

Lucien is increasingly obsessed with desire to find Vigilante. He was so near when he intervened for that poor soul. The one just accepted by the anatomy lab. Again, she commands her raven to locate him. Relentlessly, her weary assistant flies ever tighter patterns over the city. She does find her nemesis within a new crow.

As her search is appearing to be fruitless, a familiar evil form appears below. Loafing on a porch roof across from a bar it fails to see her swoop down. Instantly the demon crows' eyes are plucked from its head. They roll unceremoniously down to the street into a storm drain. This crow disintegrates back into the next dimension and is gone. Two evil eyes will glare at the sky until the next heavy rain, then who knows or cares where they will go? But the raven now sees who this demon was stalking…a very sad girl.

Whether Vigilante is being drawn to this very place by chance or by some remote instinct is uncertain…

Drifting down a strangely familiar street he peers into its' many bars. Suddenly, he comes upon a face so cold he simply stops in horror. He stares rudely fascinated by her lack of splendor. Oddly, the person behind the face is a barmaid in the very prime of youth. Her hair is red; her skin is as white as linen. Yet her fixed expression bears a hideous scowl. It's as bitter as the face of a demon from the poor side of hades. With one glance she frightens an intruding rat. It runs away in terror. Vigilante is shocked to realize that she is an innocent. He is spellbound.

In misery she rinses dishes and glasses in dirty water hidden from view. But no one who comes here would care. This innocent endures constant abuse from a revolting bar manager. One who is toothless having lost them in a brawl. Her blackened eye and dirty hair might have been found upon a stray cur. She hisses at the innocent one through bruised lips. *"Damn you, girl, get your backside over here and mop up this puke!"*

The innocent one nods in submission and begins swinging a filthy slop mop across a splintered bare wooden floor. She stoops to pick up a stool the regurgitating drunk knocked over on his way out. Her inner spirit hides from this misery, but her mind cannot.

Music belches from the cracked juke box. It's barely audible amidst a standing fog of stale tobacco and reefer smoke. From a dry tinny speaker, a long-gone country singer moans over the room. "*My dog got fed and now he's dead and ... oh Lawd what am I gonna do?*" A heavy hand slaps the young barmaids' rear end. She jumps aside and makes a threatening motion with the mop. The hairy hand slaps her hard, this time across her face. She rolls into the corner like a broken toy. Seeing this, Vigilante is enraged.

She pushes him away. Her groper abruptly slips falling backwards striking the puke bucket. It tumbles slopping its' dirty water into his face. A seedy barfly stifles any expression of his amusement for her attacker is the deadly *Strangler.*

In this seedy bar, the reason for his name is fearfully understood. He jumps to his feet dripping soapy green slime; Strangler advances on the prostrate girl kicking at her with a steel toed boot as big as her head. Her bloody face caves in.

Before Vigilante can inspire self-destructive behavior, as he did in Lizard Alley, Stranglers' hard boot swings again this time breaking the girls' jaw. A sickening crunch of crushed bone. It's one he's often heard and tells Strangler to become scarce before the cops show up. They are never very far from this degenerate den. The girl crawls on her elbows and knees towards the back room hoping to wash the blood from her face. Merciful oblivion relieves her pain.

Her assailant makes it down to the corner and halfway across the street without seeing a huge black tractor with a brilliant chrome skull hood ornament bearing down. It exterminates Strangler from this world like roadkill. Strangler dies screaming, *"I'll kill everyone!"* He passes but his stain on the earth persists...

His angry ghost craves revenge. It struggles to resist its' satanic destiny. Revenge oozes from his twisted corpse and fuels his ghost even as it leaves his lifeless body. The truck hit and killed the Strangler dead. Even in death his spirit evades the ultimate damnation due all who prey upon innocence.

12

Devils to angels

Seeing his unpaid tab, the barkeep wench gripes- *"Aw crap, that bastard stiffed me for his beer!"* The barfly is amused and jokes, "That *was great! Do it all again!* Vigilante focuses on his mind. The barfly stops being amused as he rolls through the door onto a fire hydrant.

The injured girl on the floor regains consciousness. She comes to, crawls aimlessly like a sick kitten. Then blacks out again. No one cares or shows concern. The barkeep, her mother, finally thinks lucidly long enough to call for help. Responding to the 911, an ambulance collects her. Its' screaming siren clears her pathway to a downtown hospital.

No one accompanies her and no one cares except the bar hag who yells outside to the barfly, *"Now I'm left to clean up her mess!"*

Her cold-concern is only for herself. She will rarely think again of her daughter. It's Vigilante's first gift to the girl.

This bitter woman's humanity burned out long ago when her dirty needle track marks became lost in the tattoos on her arms and legs. She has only a vague memory of the face of the man who fathered her child and doesn't care. She does like his child support checks she receives. All of the child support went for her drug addiction. Subsequently nothing was left for the care of the child she conceived on a drunken encounter long ago. Her last resolution, *"I'll dock her; she owes me money for not finishing her shift!"*

Bar regulars file in past the one who witnessed this horror who is still sprawled over his fire hydrant. Some ask where the girl is... This horror will tell them with crocodile tears. *"She quit and took off without telling anyone." "After all I did for that ingrate, she done me like this; It ain't right!"*

The so-called *"ingrate"* has been delivered from her chains of evil. Her mother will never see her again. If she ever should, she won't recognize her own daughter. The girl has arrived and is wheeled into the emergency room.

This trauma center is ready for everything people do to hurt themselves or others. Through its' doors come souls whose lives would be lost without these medical heroes. Burdened, yet always vigilant, this staff is always optimistically professional even in worst cases.

The girls' battered and bloody body fits this picture perfectly. She is so badly hurt, no one bothers to ask about health insurance. Legions of others have preceded her; more will follow. Asking anything of her now is hopeless because her jaw is fractured.

Seemingly no one came with her. It's evident to the staff she has no one. Helpless and alone, she can't move her lips to beg for water. It hurts too much to try. Other than her thirst, she doesn't know anything to say. Her cracked skull leaves her unable to remember. With the worst headache, imaginable she expects to die. Then, someone unseen ever so gently touches a moistened swab to her lips.

These greeting her know nothing about her except she needs them. The usual thin white plastic bracelet on her thin white arm from the EMT is her only proof she's real. And no one here knows her identity, including her...

If Vigilante has his way, there will be joy and this girl will soon be reborn to become the person she could have been. Despite her past, she has the faultless soul of an infant.

In stark contrast is her scarred little body whose very existence is threatened. Vigilante wants her to live as never before and vows. *"She will be much more than this!"*

Hearing his anguish, the hospital angels take pity. Some days there is joy even in this somber place of mercy. Everyone, even these angels rejoice in these divine moments when a life can be saved.

His focus on her does not waiver. But he's become aware of others around them. The spirit is amazed to see how many angels are working throughout this large area. There are more working here than he has seen since arriving in the city including everywhere else along the way. *"They allow me to see them!"*

No wonder. The big secret at this and most other hospitals is one no one openly admits. Nurses scream to themselves when no one else can hear, *"We are crawling with angels!"* Why the cover-up? The answer lies in labor and turf.

This angel scandal is one all hospital administrators find impossible to acknowledge. Because angels are silent volunteers, they don't appear on payrolls. This hospitals' administrator thinks, *"Let Mercy over on St. Paul be the first to tell the world they have angels!"* They might get away with it because most hospitals here were started by benevolent or religious groups.

It's one thing to pray to the Lord, but a whole different thing to admit His servants really are close by. Some time ago, an old priest from an uptown church was told about this hypocrisy during a parishioners' confession. He prayed for guidance. The priest claims the Lord just said, *"Those are my angels; your clients are the living."*

Before the good shepherd could divulge this revelation to his parishioners, it was the priests' turn to move on to a better world. Upon arriving in heaven, the answer became obvious. He is distracted. By habit, he reaches for a cigarette and hears, *"Smoking isn't allowed in heaven, father."* *"Why?"* He asks. The voice laughs at the question explaining, *"You've come to the wrong place for fire."* *"Is smoking limited to the netherworld?"* hoping he isn't there. His mentor laughs, *"Everyone down there is allowed to smoke, and everyone has a light.*" What makes it hell is- nothing that can be smoked gets past the gates.

After one beer too many on her bowling night a head nurse mumbles just one word- *"Angels!"* Observing this indiscretion, her best friend confiscates her car keys. Slumping in the backseat of the car the tipsy nurse grumbles, *"Not one angel ever showed me a RN certification." "I studied hard, and it took me a really long time to become a nurse."* Her friend warns giggling, *"Keep talking like that and they'll certify you… as nuts!"*

The tipsy one ignores her and rambles on, *"I can only guess what the union would think about all of that scab labor… even if they really are angels." "We'd go on strike and not come back until somebody figured out how to make them damned angels join the union."*

Then, *"How would you make angels pay their union dues?"* After sobering up from her bizarre outburst, after that on ER bowling nights, she just sips diet soda, keeps her mouth shut, and focuses on knocking down the pins down the alley. Her friend never again brings up the subject. From that night on she has pretended not to see any   angels.

Settling in the Emergency Room, the girl stirs in her sedated sleep. Vigilante moves even closer to her. He hasn't left her side since she was rolled into the ambulance. An even more serious arrival momentarily draws everyone away from this patient.

A nurse who examined her when she came in is relieved to notice, *"At least she no longer smells like beer vomit."* Vigilante wouldn't know if she did. But he suspects if he hadn't dimmed even their calloused senses some of the mortal kind here may be hesitant to come near her.

Another angel moistens her lips. The nurse sees a thin shiny line of moisture move across the girls' lips. Looking away she tries to pretend it didn't happen. These are the times when there's a moment of magic. Even in this stronghold of somber mercy angels rejoice in these wonderful moments when they know a life has been saved. Still pretending to themselves there's no angels, the nurses are happy for this patient.

Everyone pitches in. Her cleaner body is complemented by a more normal antiseptic scent. Even in her wretched daily life she always tried to be as clean as possible under miserable conditions. Now her battered body is much cleaner.

When she was wheeled in, at first the attendants breathed very slowly trying not to inhale her aroma. Carefully wearing latex gloves one gently cleaned her body and another dressed her wounds. A specialist arrives to examine her facial injuries. He is thorough, and his expression gives no hint of his deep sympathy. Her facial bones are   broken.

Resting now, in a somewhat mercifully sedated state, her dreamy thoughts quietly drift into a green valley somewhere between the mountains and the sea. It's a place she has never seen. Soon she will have completely forgotten a past where her surrounds were like an endlessly refilled cesspool. Incredibly this girl was trapped in misery by that nasty witch who was her mother. One who never should have been.

From this time, only a single mortal, the plastic surgeon who just left, will see her as she existed coming into the ER. Due to the severity of her head injuries her past is absent. All bad memories are gone forever. Her new protectors will see to it neither she nor anyone else will know her as the poor wretch she was from the moment   she   was   born.

As a person who is no-one, she's alive, but her existence is very dreamlike. She would be pleased to realize this light blue hospital gown and her reddish blonde hair nicely contrast. Nothing about her offers the slightest clue she is alone without a family or friend. Or so it may seem to these mortals. Angels and the echo watch her new mortal vitality infuse her being.

At some point, late at night her hair becomes nicely shampooed and scented. Those with unseen hands have looked upon her with merciful compassion. She has lived humbly; they love her innocent soul. Celestial fingers bless and heal her poor being. Her expression softens.

These immortal benefactors are a wisp beyond the touch of humans and dwell in an inexplicable dimension. While her injuries are real, her internal transformation is complete. A hidden hand submits the story of her death to the *Baltimore Sun*. Neighbors of the bar will pretend to be shocked. Vigilante realizes that it's the pen of angels for she lives.

Next, these conspirators scheme to craft her new physical being. A hospital records mix-up moves her to a private room. Vigilante remains with her, completely disregarding the fact she isn't his mission. A powerful impulse to help her has taken over his being.

However, it is one that he doesn't try to understand. Pains she feel stab him in jagged purple daggers. He senses everything and is no longer just an avenging spirit. Instead, he is becoming a loving being with sympathy for another.

Deep in his emerging commitment, he's jolted to see two stunning eyes peer back at him from the other side of the bed. When the nurse left the room, he thought he was alone with the girl. He has no idea how long those dark eyes have been on him. She's seemingly an angel. But one who's different and far more interesting than those down in the ER.

Since arriving, Vigilante has seen many angels in this hospital. But having one this spectacular staring directly at him just isn't the same. She is the first one to directly speak to him. Gradually like of flowering bud, she allows him to see her splendor. Quietly introducing herself, *"I am Lucien."* He is overwhelmed. This angel is radiantly magnificent. Existing in their own clandestine world, guardian angels seldom communicate with any sort of spirits. The guardians are extremely important to human souls in the hierarchy of angels. Aware of his transfixed state, she murmurs, *"I am here to know you and to help this sweet person."* Continuing, *"Your concern for her is wonderful."*

Lucien smiles. He's bathed in its' warmth. Then she asks him, *"Why is this pathetic creature suddenly worthy of your concern?"* ... feigning a lack of understanding why Vigilante cares for the girl. She tests him.

Vigilante struggles to answer even as his thoughts are transferred to her mind. He admits, *"I admit I've been told before this sort of thing isn't my job!"* Her eyes express incredulity. But she's inwardly amused.

Thinking she doesn't get what he's saying, he shouts without audible sound, *"I'm here for the duration!"* *"She needs more help than anyone has ever been willing to give her."*
He's shocked by his own words. The angel understands but lets the subject drop.

Lucien analyses his commitment. His perception of Lucien becomes one of a girl similar in most respects to the one on the bed between them. From Vigilante's perspective. Lucien is a beautiful version of the sedated victims' soul. But in contrast to this homely girls' reddish tresses, Lucien is a beautiful silver blonde.

Before Lucien allowed herself to become visible to Vigilante, she folded her wings tightly because she sensed they would make him feel uneasy. For her own reasons, she wants him to be completely at ease. They passed closely last night at the inner harbor rescue attempt, and she almost lost him.

Vigilante challenges. *"Why was she allowed to reach this pathetic state?"* Lucien explains, *"My vocation is to follow my assigned soul until they completely pass from this world."* She continues, *"There are many who are so much worse off."* She shields her inner thought. *"Your grandfather's indifference to his child is why she's laying here."*

Then soothingly, *"Guardians are more concerned with seeing our clients have a favorable hereafter than how they fare alive."* Life is very short in comparison to eternity." He persists. *"Where have you been all of her life?"* *"She really needed help a long time before this happened."* *"For her, hereafter wasn't in doubt."* *"If some intervention had happened early ...."*

Rather than answer, Lucien simply stops him with a mysterious expression in her eyes. He senses he is jumping to an incorrect conclusions. She has stopped him from asking more than she is willing to explain. To maintain a polite state of cordiality Lucien answers gently. *"There are not as many guardian angels as one might think."*

"There are considerably fewer angels now than at the beginning of time." They both realize that she is obfuscating. *"Just the baby boom alone created a whole lot more work."* Pointing Vigilante's attention to the girls' soul, *"For all of the turmoil her soul remains pure; she needed very little help."* *"Her worldly life, the responsibility of her parent, was a living hell!"*

She sticks to her explanation. *"Today, humans so outnumber angels that only those who plead for help from a guardian angel may ever receive this service."* She shocks him with: *"For reasons known only at the top level some souls don't get one even then."* He realizes he is too mesmerized to say anything. He tries to hide any misgivings. Both recognize she has charmed him until he is nearly limp and mute. It's useless to resist; she senses his every thought.

Smiling wickedly, Lucien continues to charm. *"We can create her a better future!"* Explaining, *"We are removing the filthy demonic bar and her witch of a mother from her past and replacing it with a wonderful myth."* Unnecessarily, he explains he has already removed those   stains   of   past   from   the   girls'   mind.

Lucien pretends to be impressed. She is vastly more cognizant of this situation than he might imagine. She knows echo spirits are mostly electrical vitality coupled with powerful but sadly waning existence particles. Graciously, she expresses comradeship, concluding seductively with, *"Perhaps this is why we are going to work so well together."*

Lucien proposes a plan to hack the hospital computer and explains which Lucien data she wants him to change. Because Vigilante is a simple honest being, he isn't happy with anything so unethical. But at this point he is so enamored he will do almost anything to keep her happy and to keep their relationship working. *"If in doing this, it will solidify a new identity for this poor girl, it's worthwhile."*

Making the girl forget was just a temporary fix. Now he admits to himself, just wiping out her past would have led her nowhere. He thinks it's funny that even with their great powers, guardian angels can't hack a hospitals' patient management system. A human mind or its' echo can hack computers without difficulty.

Mysteriously, even though Vigilante never has used a computer, he instinctively knows this is feasible for him as an echo spirit. Humanity is endowed with a taste for mischief found usually among the fallen angels. Those are the dissidents who lost an ancient heavenly battle.

He is numbly obedient. But wonders, *"If Lucien feels it's beneath her station to even try to hack this hospitals' records, shouldn't I be insulted?"* But Vigilante can't feel anything except fascination for her. He rationalizes, *"Doing this for a truly noble cause can't be completely bad."* Vigilante can't hear the general sigh of disagreement in the wind. So, he doesn't know how to interpret her momentary look of discomfort.

Vigilante has allowed himself to be persuaded into accepting the notion to do good he must also do something obviously unethical. In another realm, a judgmental mind reasons: *"It wasn't Vigilantes' responsibility to shepherd this poor girl as he has."* *"And it certainly isn't an angels' job to conspire with an echo to alter the records of the hospital."* *" Hospitals are a force for good... hmm!"*

Within this patients' hospital record, an application sends the girls' information to a distant server and back again. The firewall just doesn't recognize this kind of mischief. So, nothing in the application blocks this intrusion. The girls' record is also edited to create an event that will change the life of one Jane Doe. At midnight, her present and future are forever revised, not just in hospital records, but in every database on and beyond the cloud.

Echo hacking works very efficiently. His changes are not something anyone could discover from the input. Time, for just this patient, stands still momentarily This patient seems to die; then seems to be born complete with a backdated original birth certificate. She's matured into womanhood instantly. All this and she isn't even an   echo.

Her new profile is complete. Everything about her digital existence from her name and health insurance to her parentage evolves to an ideal state. From 12:01 am on, even those who treated her when she arrived see her new being. The nurse who visited earlier will forget as well. Emergency Room angels hold an instant staff meeting and reluctantly decide to go along with the lessor of evils...then forget they met.

Lucien's fantastic scheme occurs on schedule. She dons the sexiest nurse's uniform and wheels the girl to an even nicer room.

It's one reserved for patients of the head of plastic surgery. Few staff members are still around. Only the new nurse and her dozing patient are on the elevator.

No one sees her patient. Charts and records change noiselessly. A security camera controlled from within a station scans the private duty nurse from head to toe repeatedly without pausing for more than a glance at the patient. It won't matter because in the morning the night shift will sorrowfully report the recording was accidently erased. A security guard will take a day off to deal with his confusion.

In her plush new room, the eyes of each nurse, doctor and staff entering are immediately drawn to the beautiful white petals of a flower from a bouquet left by the angel. Each picks up a flower. As they look in on her they see a beautiful human replacing in their minds any residual image. All images are now in harmony.

Next morning, her new surgeon is summoned by the Director and told of a very generous contributor to the hospital requiring urgent attention. He quietly enters her room. Experienced fingers gently remove her bloody dressings. By necessity, her new facial illusion isn't repeated for him. The surgeons' tight forehead wrinkles in shock at the level of damage to her face. He feels challenged to restore and create beauty.

Only his trained eyes still see the reality of her pathetic facial remnant. Although she can't understand him, he promises to return her to the beauty of the angelic photo by her tray. It is his only template for her cosmetic reconstruction. He raises his eyes towards heaven confirming his vow. Beads of perspiration appear upon his brow. *"Lord willing, she will be my masterpiece!"*

Somewhere in the great beyond the Lord is thought to have enjoyed hearing the surgeons' comment to a good purpose and wills it done.

Lucien smiles at her co-conspirator with a kind but firm expression then bids Vigilante to be on his way. *"Come back when she won't need my attention so badly."* They both look at the new photo of the guardian angel on the dresser. And she prays silently for the skill of the surgeon. Prayer heard; mischief forgiven.

This hospital suite overlooks an interior garden within the wing. After surgeries they want patients to awaken to its' cultured beauty. The combined efforts of a guardian angel and an echo spirit have erased her bad memories. A lifetime of insults causing her perpetual scowl soon disappears.

Just as the father of a newborn is often banished from the delivery room so Vigilante is now banished from these rooms where the surgeon is creating beauty. The surgeons' goal: a young girls' metamorphosis from ugly caterpillar to the loveliest butterfly…

"If God is willing…once she heals."

After hours of surgery and recovery, Lucien's' mesmerizing smile, now on a human face illuminates the cosmetic wing. Everyone is overwhelmed by its' magnificence, including some of Lucien's' few angel friends. The girl is now uniquely beautiful for hers is the face of a blonde angel upon a redhead.

Lucien needs to admit nothing to Vigilante of her previous absence from the girls' life He is completely stricken with love; she is as well. But he must not know for she would become vulnerable. Helplessness isn't something she can afford.

But once Vigilante is away, again she asks the Lord for asks forgiveness for her deceptions. She is relieved to feel the warmth of understanding from above.

Prior to the necessity of surgeons' art in making the girl beautiful, Lucien understood there was another way for the girl to improve from homely to beautiful. If the injuries from the Strangler hadn't occurred, the girl could have lost her scowl by relaxing her mind. But she was in an impossible situation back at the bar. Her mothers' ugliness reflected upon her. Mental relaxation wasn't possible.

As her body heals so does her mind. The girl gains the poise, confidence and a legacy owed to a wealthy beloved child. Blissfully Lucien is aware her value to this person had considerable help from a humble spirit, a mere echo. Now, like those who are human, she longs for one who is forbidden ...this same insignificant spirit. He is madly smitten. And she is more attracted to him than he can possibly imagine.

Now without a single memory of her past the girl is consumed by waves of enthusiasm for living. Her hurt little body heals to the full radiance of beauty and health. In her newly enhanced reality, she was always beautiful, well-off and complains to her amused nurses, *"I can't wait to get out of this antiseptic hell hole!"*

Her high morale is reflected in her dreams as well. She dreams of the things she learns from watching the television on the wall. Her true past never happened. Lucien and Vigilantes' goal has been achieved.

But in fleeting moments, she wonders why she cannot remember anything before she came here. Luckily, it doesn't take much to distract her. She presses a button next to her bed.

"May I have some vanilla ice cream please?" Her nurse replies, *"Yes, but you have to get out of bed today! Doctors' orders!"* And such is the way of even the best hospital.

As much as Lucien appreciates Vigilantes' concern for this girl, there are limits. It is evident when Lucien insists, he leave for a while. He agrees saying, *"I'll be back in a few hours."* He does whatever she says and doesn't question her motives. She giggles to herself. *"What am I to do with him?"* Then she inwardly frowns with the realization their absurd infatuation must end. Their beings just cannot mesh; only she has a body. She pouts to herself, *"I have serious responsibilities."*

Like a lost dog, Vigilante uses his banishment to wander around the urban hospital campus. His soon finds a supernatural vagrant with a similar degree of intoxication as some of the humans slumped on a bench across from the hospital.

"This is really astounding." He thinks openly. *"Angel, what are you doing sitting around like a bum?"* Without looking up, the drunks' slurred voice mumbles, *"Go screw yourself, you wannabe!"* Recalling Roman, the hikers' guardian angel, he wonders if all male guardians are alcoholics. And this one has just told me to do WHAT to myself?

Indignantly the spirit hovers over the angel and using his own strength of mind rolls the trash mouthed angel out into the street. Dodging traffic, the angel sobers up enough to shove the spirit against a human wino. Neither is deterred and it's on...

The spirit fights his way back to the angel. They roll around in and above the busy street. It's obvious to the gathering crowd of cheering ghostly spectators that neither really knows what they're doing. It almost seems like a pillow fight

This pugilistic event may be the first in history between echoes and angels. It ends in a draw as neither has the slightest idea how to fight with one another. Even less do they know how to fight with any other ethereal spirit. Both have spent too much time watching karate movies on hospital TVs.

When Vigilante grabs at the angel, feathers fly out of its' hidden wings momentarily visible to the living as they evaporate. Drivers coming down the street are temporarily blinded. To prevent human carnage, Vigilante turns on the windshield washers of those passing.

This creates outrage from those with guardian angels worrying about the confused drivers. Trying to disguise this supernatural event one starts a rain shower. The echo really has nothing for the angel to grab onto, but by sheer force of willpower the angel scores multiple blows. Vigilante increasingly spreads out like a deflating hot air balloon and simply flops back and forth up and down the street.

Other angel spectators watching the fight become so excited with the fight they start having it out with one another. Soggy melting feathers create such a diversion that gridlock occurs. Baltimore traffic is disrupted throughout the city. Two TV channels mistakenly report another water main break. Traffic is at a standstill. But no one sends a film crew. There's nothing to see when a motorist takes a picture with her cellphone.

Tomorrow a station will report, *"Something unexplained happened."* Another will say later, *"Pillow fights just aren't in our news budget."*

Lucien watching from the girls' room focuses on an old water main. Obligingly it starts gushing. *"If they bother, the news media could offer a plausible public explanation."* she decides. *"There is no way the man upstairs wants human beings to figure out those good angels are having a brawl!"* The angels down in ER just roll their eyes. Then, *"How could Vigilante start this much trouble so fast?"*

Several *fallen* angels float up from East Baltimore Street, just to watch. Now they wish they hadn't fallen, so they could join in the fun. But no one up there, or down there, lets that happen again…at least not today.

Like their human counterparts these non-angelic brawlers tire completely and soon just hover over the curb. Finally, the sobered angel explains to Vigilante. *"It's so damn boring in General Anatomy. We're so tired of sucking up old fumes that we just let ourselves go with it and get a buzz on."*

"What do you say, angel wannabee, lets' go get a beer down at the harbor!" The echo is about to admit he has no idea how to drink a beer. Instead he grunts in a macho tone *"Yeah dude…whatever!"*

Lucien laughs so hard she rolls out of the hospital window. Vigilante pushes her back up the wall. *"By the way dude, my name is Vigilante, not wannabee."* Looking back up a Lucien, still in Baltimorese macho lingo, he screams up at her, *"Catch ya' later hon!"*

At a nearby pub a cherub brags, *"Yesterday my buddy waited for a medical student to bend over then had his cadaver pinch him on his you know what!"* Everyone laughs; male bonding occurs. Vigilante shoves an imaginary but weary hand towards the exhausted angel and tells him his name. The angel shakes where he feels his hand should be saying, *"I'm Mike."*

The echo betrays his ignorance of the who's who of heavenly creatures by asking incredulously, *"Michael the Archangel ...?"*

This is all he gets out before everyone roars laughing *"How in your wildest imaginings can you imagine Michael the Archangel would rumble with you in the middle of Green Street?"* With that Mike begins swooping and doing barrel rolls like an insane bird over the bar.

Vigilante Spirit

13

Twin troubles

Vigilante and Mike are interrupted by the appearance of another guardian angel, a friend of Mike. Listening to them unobserved, he hopes Vigilant will be the right one to help him with a really big problem. This is a leap of faith because he isn't sure echoes in general aren't just elements of imagination. Vigilante is so desperate for approval from angels he listens.

He explains to Vigilante, and every other angel in earshot, he's assigned to twin brothers with opposite but complementary occupational abilities. They don't know they are twins, or even that the other exists having been adopted at birth. Both have major financial problems. Their families are hurting. He asks for Vigilantes' unconventional help.

Before leaving, Mike and the new guy decide to engage in a friendly bout of wing wrestle. Mike loses and slips backwards through the plate glass window. All parking meters in Baltimore run in reverse for an hour. This loss in revenues could make the city reduce city police overtime.

This cause a problem. As honest angels they must compensate the city for this loss of vital revenue. Mike and his buddies will be working on this problem for years. Their silliness is too much for Vigilante.

He feels he has been away from Lucien and the girl long enough for whatever the doctor is doing to be completed and floats unevenly back to the hospital. Lucien feigns displeasure but without hesitation tries to hug him. He decides if brawling with an angel in the street was weird, then being virtually hugged by this particular angel is truly sublime.

This mutual attraction is distracting to both Vigilante and Lucien. Being in love is wonderful but worrisome. *"Romance with an angel isn't the main purpose of my existence...or is it?"* He doesn't know how to get back to his true mission. Both have assumed the role as the girls' protector; he thought he was the only one who could save her. His thoughts are interrupted when he realizes Lucien is staring at him.

The girls' progression from disaster to promise is now guided by Lucien. He reasons she must be the girls' guardian angel. But when he tries to learn more, Lucien clams up, and he has no closure. In a masochistic way, he likes just dangling on her string. *"It's a pretty nice string to be on."*

Still Vigilante frets. Fortunately, an opportunity to serve others comes from Mike, admittedly an unlikely mission supporter. At this point he's open for suggestions. Almost anything is better than wasting away without being useful.

Mikes' buddy from the pub still wants his help. Vigilante and Lucien talk it over; she accepts the idea. Lucien admits, *"It's obvious our time together is moving you away from your mission."* His infatuation for both her and the girl are rendering him immobile.

Sensitive to his dilemma, last night Lucien warned, *"Just keep doing nothing and soon you'll become nothing."* She had concluded by reciting the obvious, *"For you nothing is forever."* *"Echoes literally fizzle out!"* She didn't add the obvious- echo spirits are without hope for heaven or hell. Instead she softly murmured, *"Make whatever time you have here count."*

Lucien looks inquisitively asking, *"Why do you think this girl worries you so much?"* He admits that he doesn't know responding, *"Why do you ask?"* He just gets another one of her penetrating stares. Lucien's' mysterious attitude bothers him. When he presses her for an explanation, she simply smiles mysteriously. His persistent curiosity tickles her wing tips. She no longer hides them.

From his perspective, Lucien's concern about his future helps him understand why he is in love. Even so, he has an innate sense of his limited energy. It's a bomb waiting to go off within him. But, like humans, it isn't alarmingly obvious …until time is just about gone.

Mike and the other guardian angel want him to work on a problem very different from his past works. There are two lost brothers in need of one another. Both are really good carpenters. But neither has what it takes to be successful in working without the others' skills.

"If they worked together," according to their guardian angel, *"they could succeed brilliantly."* Unfortunately, neither knows the other even exists. This makes the process of getting them together thorny.

He focuses on the brothers and soon outlines a scheme to Lucien. Thrilled at his determination to do something…anything, Lucien smiles brightly. A bit too powerfully, for at nearby BWI Marshall, takeoffs and landings are delayed due to lightning in the area.

He explains to Lucien, *"This isn't about destroying thugs or saving innocents... but it's closer to what I should be doing... than watching you babysit."* Vigilante hopes if he unites the hapless brothers, Lucien's peers will respect him.

She stares blankly at him and doesn't speak. It's important for Vigilante to realize his obsession about angel respect as a peer is something he must grow out of on his own. Because it's irrelevant whether other angels like him, or not.

He wonders why she won't let him know what she's thinking. *"Maybe she isn't thinking anything."* Then then with awe, he looks at the girl then at Lucien. *"They are so beautiful."* He's slightly amused as he really notices for the first time that Lucien and the girl are identical. Of course, only Lucien has wings.

Sometimes Lucien seems to love him. But, he knows, many of Mikes' angel associates either think he isn't real or that he doesn't belong. Vigilante is in a very weird mindset. He reasons, to keep Lucien he must be accepted by her peers. To that end, he suspects a friendly conspiracy inspired by either Mike alone or even Lucien and Mike. He sees more than a little coincidence in their sudden need for his help.

Perhaps his recent pub episode with Mike was just subterfuge. This thought has him feeling somewhat used. If so, it was enjoyable. Leading up to meeting these angels, most of his past was gruesome and not much fun. Recalling Buzzardville, he despises the horrible episode. Once again, reflecting on his inadequacy, he feels guilty and   sulks.

Understanding his insecurities, but not entirely sympathetic, Lucien chides, *"If you really want to be with us why even associate with those guys over in the Anatomy Lab?"* Sheepishly Vigilante admits to her that they make him feel important because they think he is valuable. Lucien smirks as though seeing him for the first time and shrugs *"Whatever!"* She needn't say more. Now he feels like *crap, "whatever crap is…"*

Typical of most men in similar situations, waves of misery wash all over his being. He shouts to the universe, *"WOMEN! HUH!"* He decides, *"No matter what I say, nothing comes out right to suit her!"* From the heights of heaven to the pits of hell one huge male chorus booms- *"AMEN!!"*

Communal telepathy deprives their relationship of the slightest privacy. There just aren't secrets in their dimension. He dreams of making love with her; but how to is something unimaginable.

Anything he thinks of immediately results in giggles from angels, devils, ghosts and demons from everywhere...sometimes even from Lucien. She points out his major shortcoming: *"You don't have a body."* No sooner does he conceive a plan when a demonic chorus mimics her, reminding him, *"You don't have a ... ya-ha!"*

From across the street his newly found friend Mike teases, *"Vigilante is angel whipped! Vigilante is a WOOS!"* Now he feels totally embarrassed. Worse he has no idea whatsoever what a *WOOS* is any more than he understood the word *crap*. They who know won't tell; they who don't know can't tell. One demon quips, *"'EM-BARE ASSED!"* Lucien chokes with shame and amusement.

Vigilante shuts Mike and his cohorts up by threatening in a serious tone to *"come over there and wake up all of those damned cadavers!"* Mike is doubtful any echo can; Vigilante laughs nastily. His tone scares everyone in Anatomy. Lucien and Vigilante hear a ruckus as the other guardian angels stifle Mikes' sarcastic retorts. One yells out- *"Don't pay attention to him, he's been sniffing*

Vigilante laughs because although he doesn't believe in zombies, he suspects Mike might. Because guardian angels can't help but watch all those old horror movies, they're liable to believe anything. Whether Vigilante can completely reanimate cadavers, no one's sure. And no one wants to find out either.

They convince Mike to be quiet. Soon there is dead silence across the universe except for an occasional giggle. Vigilante feels he's finally a part of a social group and at the same time he's a bit embarrassed. *"At least I'm not lonely."* Lucien, who really believes in zombies wants to prove they exist by waking up some of those over in Anatomy. But admits she doesn't know how. So she lets loose.

Not to let the fun die, she starts agitating the Anatomy Lab angels. Lucien mightily launches a ticked-off brain sneer across Green Street at Mike. Fortunately, her aim is off. She might have cooked everyone, students, angels and wannabe zombies. A bored old cadaver's ghost yells back across to Lucien *"Becoming a zombie sounds like fun!"*

Her next shot flips Mike and the ghost into the labs' preservative vat. Totally disoriented, Mike floats down the hall and breaks into the cookie machine. *"Preservative stuff gives me the munchies!"* He gobbles the sweets and unleashes a colossal *"Hoo-Rah!"*, nearly deafening every immortal in the city.

An even mightier voice from somewhere in the great beyond orders them all *"Shut up before you do awaken the dead."* Creatures of this dimension don't sleep. Still, they need meditation for much the same reason as mortals. Quickly, it's quiet on both sides of the street.

Despite everything he has done, some angels still refuse to believe Vigilante is real. They still think he's only a hallucination. Everyone agrees whatever else, he's crazy and likeable. Lots of people don't believe in ghosts; some ghosts don't believe in people either. There's confusion within both realms. Oddly, most angels believe in both. Who would ever guess? It's weird. And what zombies believe in, is anyone's guess.

Vigilante is tired of this nonsense and is anxious to get started on the brothers. But he must wait for the right moment to implement his plan. Meanwhile under Lucien progress concerning the girls' future is moving forward.

Within a day of her operation the newly beautiful one is sympathetically told by the somber hospital chaplain her father has been reported missing. *"There was a boating accident."* *"His body hasn't been found"* *"The boat was located overturned several miles downstream from where it had been last seen."*

The hospital chaplain pauses for her reaction. He attributes her passivity to her recent ordeal *"There is no new information from authorities after three days of searching"* Clearing his throat he touches her hand. *"You've been unconscious all of that time."* The girl feels guilty because she doesn't remember enough to feel the sorrow expected of her. She knows she was terribly injured in an accident and attributes her apathy to the fact she can't remember her fathers' face.

Back in Elkridge, there is still no sign of Will Gold dead or alive. Nothing warrants continuing the search for his body. Firmly set in his daughters' reality, he was her loving and caring father. With this reasoning, genuine tears of grief fall from still puffy but pretty eyes. Now her grief is real...

Receiving grief counselling, she admits to having no memories prior to waking up here in the hospital wing. The psychiatrist suggests encouragingly. *"Your memories will probably return slowly over time."* Lucien sighs to Vigilante, *"I hope not!"*

They do not want suggestions planted in her mind. Soon the shrink receives a call to respond to a nasty barmaid trying to visit her boyfriend in the morgue. He leaves but won't remember this patient. The girl finds a small black bible in a drawer and seeks consolation in prayer. The cover is engraved with a simple cross. She will consult it frequently for the rest of her life.

Vigilante instinctively hates misleading the girl about her father. Still he just can't
bring himself to openly challenge these fabrications. They soothe the girl, and this path makes Lucien happy. Worse of all, he did most of the dirty work to get the girl to arrive at her present degree of disillusion. Real memories are the last thing she needs.

Hoping to clear his mind he sets out to help Mikes' buddy with the separated brothers. It dawns on him too, if the ghosts and angels are right about his strictly imaginary existence, he can never descend into hell. *"They can't have it both ways."* But, for now it's time to deal with the brothers. He finds them basking in their misery.

Barely west of Baltimore a rustic stone mill survives as a tavern. It rests beside an ancient stream. It's been here for so long no one remembers when it didn't. Its' time as a mill vanished from living memory more than a century ago.

This well-worn rustic den of alcoholic consumption serves as a beacon for any wanderers in want of collective wooziness. Although not very quiet, it is vastly more refined than the den of horrors from whence Lucien's charge was transported.

Two strong men facing one another across the wide oak bar have more in common than is evident to either. At first, they stare at blank spaces on the wall not seeing the other one. This one tilts Bud and munches on salty bar nuts. The opposite sucks on a Coors and scarfs up soggy fries. Just beneath the surface both are uneasy because the money spent here is badly needed to pay bills at home. Both are irritable.

On any normal night, each might have simply nodded and passed a comment about the *Ravens* or the *Orioles*. Tonight, money worries stirred with alcohol changes both. Looking across the bar each sees his own face as one might expect of identical twins. With a little tickle from Vigilante tonight each drinker sees the other make mimicking faces. Both become insulted.

Glaring, grunting and cursing, soon they are on the floor punching and pulling whiskers. Then the Bud drinking brother knees his Coors sibling in his groin. Hunks of hair are yanked from one head and then a bloody lip and nose follow on the other brother. The bartender summons *Mule* the bouncer. Both fly out of the door at the same time by one big man with huge arms... Mules' gentle admonition, "*Y' all hurry back when Y'all get sober Y'hear?*"

By a bad coincidence each came in a Ford F-150. As if on a jobsite, they left the doors unlocked and keys in the ignition. And the pickups sit nose to nose on the loose gravel. With a little persuasion from Vigilant each brother stumbles into a pickup and slams the door defiantly. Both turn on headlights. Each comes on with high beam. Both brothers feel the blinding headlights are a further insult. Seething raging burns all over.

Each jams his gear into reverse then grinds forward. Like stags they crash repeatedly into one another. Neither knows why. It just must be done to maintain manhood. Metal crunches with the sounds all motorists normally find sickening. But it's a wonderful tune for auto body shops. It's like music that renders their cash registers orgasmic.

Finally, they have demolished one another until neither can stand the pain of one more crash. Giving one another a final one finger victory salute, they turn away. Neither fears losing, but it would be embarrassing to run out of gas. Both have used their gas money to buy beer. Each honestly believes with or without gas or even many working parts his faithful pickup will take him home. But each worries, *"I can't drop too many more parts."*

Totally exhausted they both rattle home. Between beers and concussion, neither remembers the way home, but their F-150s do. With help from a spirit and an angel they each arrive at the different driveways, the one where these pickups are accustomed to park. Having arrived with manhood restored by combat, each falls amorously into bed. Their wives expect the worse and aren't disappointed. In the morning, each awakens in amazement. For both drove the wrong wreck to a total strangers' home.

Yet their wives look the same...almost. Vigilante and the angel both crack up shamefully at the benevolent mischief wrought on these simple-minded brothers. *"Honey, did you do something new with your h a i r?"* and then *"Oh – oh!"*

Self-preservation and reasoning sets into both households a few hours later. They are together now at the instigation of their wives. The twins each carry a photo of their deceased mother. One son grew up in an adopted family; the other was left back in the orphanage. Both were very young when their mom, a single-parent, died. They were baptized at the church near to the school where she taught.

The wives are not sisters, but each is a blonde with a ponytail. They exchange their wrecks. The hung-over brothers won't look the other in the eyes. Their wives do the talking. So, neither realizes their exact resemblance. Both wives immediately see it though, and both also cry out in harmony, *"OH MY GOD!"* The wives suspected something was different last night in the dark. They chalked it off to the beer and bragging about how each kicked some guy's butt.

But these wicked imps really unraveled the mystery of brotherhood for far more obvious reasons. These two men, even though identical, were not created exactly equal. And few people in this world ever are in the greater scheme of things.

Rather than allow the product of their mischief to cause the brothers to drunkenly crash on the way home the spirit-angel team guided them each home…but each to the home of the other brother. Each woke up in the other brothers' bed.

For some time both wives claimed ownership of *"Hefty"* the Coors drinking brother. The one wrong wife finally tearfully retrieves her Bud man. *"Let's go home "Shorty!"* The echo and the angels have worked their magic brilliantly and each is satisfied they are on track with their mission.

But, for the Echo, having supported and successfully completed his role in their reconciliation, this sidebar to his existence is over. His attention returns to the girl and his angel. After a short period of recovery from injuries caused by a *mysterious car accident* the girl's beauty is described by other women as *"cute"* and by men as downright *"foxy."*

The new beauty nears the time of her release. The staff delights in having their pictures taken with this bubbly kid. Several young doctors are particularly attentive. One offers to make a follow-up home visit *just to see how you are recuperating.* They bask in the reflected glow of her doctors' success. Her surgeon has taken leave deciding he is the greatest cosmetic surgeon anywhere because of the miracle his skill has performed. *"My masterpiece leaves the hospital as a proud self-confident young woman."*

This young woman sees herself as very wealthy. One who always has known wealth and luxury. In truth, she presently has very little pocket money though she stands to inherit the estate of the late lost William Gold, III. She doesn't understand she is experiencing a cash flow crisis. Fortunately, her medical bills are covered under her fathers' plan, a detail taken care of by Vigilante without asking Lucien.

Hospital angels know a lot about the illegal drug trade because they see addicts constantly being admitted. The girls' new personal checking account now grows overnight by the deposits of angels imitating Robin Hood. ER angels have been running all over Baltimore lifting involuntary donations from the least angelic.

A new drug war kicks into full stride. Enjoying being bad for a good cause, the angels make mischief on those who peddle to addicts in dark recesses of the city. They gather money by pilfering the pockets of drug dealers. They really justify these thefts because it seems the only way to balance the loss of humanity due to drugs. As usual, the bewildered dope dealers take revenge on one another.

Late night deposits flow into a local bank. Each angelic deposit includes a deposit slip with exquisite handwriting. Angels have refined their handwriting over thousands of years. It also helped them when they were assigned to teaching nuns. Those sisters and others so painstakingly guided the tiny fingers of students through the fine discipline of cursive handwriting.

Something even worse happens to the dealers. Their customers become receptive to divine influence. Soon they experience a transition of habit from drugs to The Lord. It is as though every church becomes magnetic overnight. Once hooked on Him, few will ever make another drug buy. *"Getting high on the love of Our Lord!"*

These funds somehow find their way into the new pink leather checkbook just inside of her new handbag. No one in their wildest dreams will ever suspect hospital angels are creating such chaos. One winged thief quips. *"What could they do if they do figure it out… conduct an exorcism?"*

Guardian Angels have a miserable social life compared to most other angels. Because they spend centuries of their existence serving as caregivers. Often as not, they are the only intelligent beings minding those who should be guided by both parents. Obviously, they are not always successful. For better or worse, they stay with their assigned people for a lifetime. Longer even for those who've given their bodies to science.

Lucien and Vigilante take Mike and several hospital angels to an excellent restaurant in Baltimore's' Greek Town. Choosing to be mysterious at first Mike won't explain why guardian angels stay with their clients after death in the Anatomy lab.

After sniffing several shots of ouzo Mike spills all. *"Although these guardian angels have completed assignments, the General Anatomy angels must remain near their lifeless assignments until they are buried or cremated."* One of the hospital angels just says, *"Why so much concern for the dead?"* Vigilante suggests, *"miracle drugs?"*

Mike grins, *"Our normally conservative ethics can be jaded by the preservative fumes at the lab.* "Then laughs at himself for being woozy from sniffing the Greek liquor. *"To be brutally honest my friends at the anatomy lab stay as intoxicated as any angel can become."* Mike pauses for dramatic effect. *"If the truth were told, we believe the Boss has us standing by in case anyone tries any of that zombie nonsense."* Lucien asks in her soft most coercive tone, *"Mike, are you admitting there really are zombies?"*

Mike replies, *"I 've never seen the dead walking"*. *"Why else would a couple of dozen really scarce guardians be on this assignment?"* Rather than question *The Boss*, everyone changes the subject and soon decide to go home.

Lucien and Vigilante leave as well. On the float back to the hospital they say nothing about the zombie discussion out of concern for eavesdropping. Vigilante makes a point to repeat compliments overheard about the kindness of the angels and their support for the girls' need for ready cash. *"They had no trouble understanding the girls' immediate need for cash."* *"They did it and I'm glad!"* A glow of pride over this praise reflects from those in question.

The following afternoon there is another party. Every angel parties at some favorite pub. Vigilante is invited but can't go…he is truly angel whipped. With little to do until their next charges are assigned the partygoers wobble around the streets of Baltimore singing at the top of their lungs. Only the dogs of Baltimore can hear their chorus; they howl back.

Drug dealers inspired these angels to be horribly vengeful.... a departure from the traditional nurturing and sometimes punishing relationship of angels to humans.

ER Angels may fight with other angels, but not with humans. This well-known fact is proving to be a major advantage to the angels. The dealers never consider the existence of angels, so can't imagine the angels are robbing them. Lifting cash from the drug dealers is so easy it's weird. Then it goes from weird to nearly sadistic.

Battles between dealers and angels are one-sided. A preacher sadly turned addict then dealer, finally blurts, *"Angels are stealing my money."* He spreads the word. For several weeks, dealers run around wildly waving butterfly nets trying to catch thieving angels. The normally overwhelmed Baltimore City Police Department is delighted to hold the net waivers for mental evaluation.

Soon more dealers are talking to shrinks than ever in charm city history. It's a wonderful time for the shrinks. Soon shrinks are seeing other shrinks and talking about angels. They all conclude there's no such thing.

But duty calls. The angel shortage forces them back to their regular duties and things return to miserable in the city. The ER hospital angels are used to nurturing the sick, but not in even well-meaning mischief. Shortly the involuntary contributions run out. Fortunately, the goal of financing the girls' entry into society has been met and exceeded.

The moment of her discharge arrives. Conveyed by wheelchair to a curb where a uniformed chauffeur holds open a door, she's so glad to be leaving the hospital she doesn't notice his dark and sunken eyes. He whispers warmly, *"Welcome home Miss Gold."* Smiling wistfully behind the bill of his cap he propels the black limo away from the city.

Neither talks much. Thus, neither needs to admit this is their first encounter. It will be the only time they meet during her lifetime. Vigilante and Lucien sit in the seat facing her. Vigilante muses, *"I wonder if zombies are real?"* The driver coughs politely. The girl asks if he's Ok. He demurs, *"Nothing serious madam."* Lucien nudges Vigilante to shut up. Their driver is a zombie.

Home for Miss Gold is her late fathers' antebellum house high above the river. Her heartless mother was one of very few short-term consorts of her dead father. Will Gold once described his experience as, *"a horrible one-night stand..."* Never mentioned by her mother, his daughter couldn't have imagined this mansion exists.

Until now, its' only inhabitant besides the reclusive mister Gold, has been Hilda, his housekeeper. Since Will died she's been stealing everything she can. Upon learning of his demise, Hilda immediately caught a cab and left with his silverware on an international flight from nearby BWI Marshall. She has no intention of ever returning because of her misdeed.

Bittersweet Hilda knows she will be prosecuted if anyone discovers she's pilfered and is carrying the family silverware, along with two rare paintings. Her bags contain more than enough Gold family wealth to travel a long way. For now, her crime seems unnoticed.

Hilda's theft is minuscule compared to the daughters' inheritance. But, in time she will lose much more than she stole from an orphan. Especially, one who believes she belongs here. For some reason Hilda can't remember Will's daughters name. If she had been straight with the girl there is no doubt each would have recalled a long and wonderful relationship on the hill… or so says the angels. Hilda has outfoxed herself, but someone else will sort it all out. Vigilante and Lucien decide to jog Hilda's memory in the wrong direction.

The angelic amnesia protecting the girl includes Hilda. When the former housekeeper forgets to pick up her luggage at the airport, it will find its' way back to this old house on the hill. This is the only address on the luggage tags.

As soon as Hilda's' flight takes off another force of evil follows the trail here. It seems that the angels were right about the walking dead. The girls' wretched mother arrived at the hospital morgue at this morning. She was strangled unsuccessfully while identifying Strangler's remains. His corpse experienced a post-mortem spasm as she tried to remove his ring.

Enjoying the living room of the mansion, Lucien jokes to Vigilante about the confounded drug peddlers. She quips, *"When good angels and spirits work together, no tombstone is left unturned."* But they haven't thought of everything …. for an evils spirit is near. His coming imperils the newest heiress on the hill.

14

Chaos

Raven waits patiently upon a chimney rim. Nothing distracts her vigil. At last, she spies someone below. She takes to flight circling over his weary form below. Having confirmed this observation her task is done. Seeing nothing more, she returns to Lucien. The angel is pleased her romantic plot to help these two young people is working.

Attacked and rescued one day, chased and escaped the next, Hiker boots trudge wearily as the daylight fades. Each footstep passes the one before. Anxious to be away from where he's been. With no clue what lies ahead. He hopes his luck will improve.

But Vigilante's fate is going the other way, for Lucien is uneasy. Her relationship with the echo is at an impasse.

Lucien is irate as Vigilante announces *Angela* is the girls' new name. She demands to know, *"How did she become Angela?"*

Vigilante simply shrugs like any man who can't explain to the woman in his life why he did something displeasing. *"I created her new identity in the hospital records because I knew the name she was assigned by the hospital would raise too many questions." "No one would believe it."* Lucien just rolls her eyes. *"So, without telling me, you just named her Angela?"*

"Vigilante, do you have the slightest idea of how complicated it's going to be to resolve this?" He countered, *"She accepted Angela as her name without hesitation when she saw it on the hospital papers."* Lucien exclaims, *"The girl has no reason to think she wasn't always Angela!" "She would have believed anything you put down!"* The crazy names he might have given her strike them so funny her anger dissipates, and they laugh until they are exhausted. Still gives her a chilling feeling; he's way out of control.

Lucian tries to pout, *"So, now she will always be Angela?"* She lets her wings droop to emphasize the seriousness. It doesn't matter now if he sees her wings down. While at the same time, she realizes he cannot understand the global effect of each tiny transformation. And this really isn't his fault for he's merely an echo.

Angela's' new name change triggers massive monkey business among immortals. They struggle to move every document, including her birth certificate, from city to county records. Even to nearby St. Augustine's where Angela Gold suddenly becomes a lifetime parishioner. Unfortunately, the little child who now is Angela, wasn't baptized. And that doesn't mesh with Lucien's scheme for two mortals who still haven't met.

Baptism is vital for documentation in the church records. This would be impossible except for the kind intervention of a sainted priest who once served at this parish. He makes just one demand: Angela's hospital bills, before and after she received her new name, must be paid in full. After more furious activity by the ghostly lawyers, Angela's bill is paid. An anonymous donation was also made to the hospital to pay for her other personality.

Once satisfied of restitution, the priest stays just long enough to perform the essential ceremony. He delivers his blessing on some old souls just beyond the valley and then is gone. He returns from time to time for here are where his friendships will always remain.

Roman and Lucien become her godparents. Dressed in human garb, sans wings, they pick her up in a car. It's remarkably like the one that brought her home from the hospital. Naïvely she accepts they know her and attribute her confusion to *"that terrible accident."* Angela accepts the idea it leaves her mind foggy.

Angela wonders why both leave as soon as she arrives home from church. Still she is in thankful awe of her recovery from her accident. As for baptism, even in her darkest hours with her mother she always longed to be christened but felt unworthy. Guiltlessly today she accepted the Lord and is glad. Vigilante wasn't invited.

This house, including land and the lake, along with other wealth accumulated by her father have become Angela's. Will Golds' other properties and investments are showering down upon her. Albeit, with the assistance of several ghostly lawyers whose purgatory is the old Ellicott City courthouse. Sadly, the richness of a true lifetime relationship was lost to the girl and her father by the casual nature of her birth and the selfishness of both biological parents.

Soon to arrive in her accounts are the proceeds from the selloff of securities Will Gold triggered while plummeting over the dam. The upshot of this is Angela has no financial worries. When her father triggered the sale of his holdings the stock market dropped harder than even poor Will. The market regained its losses within weeks. Poor Will Gold was less resilient and never can rebound.

And who of the spirit dimension could ever imagine an echo in love with a guardian angel can exist anywhere? The hikers' alcoholic angel adds to the general confusion. But at least Roman was useful today by serving as godfather for Angela. Although guardian angels have good intentions, they have little time available for the duties of a godfather.

A mysterious hand guides Hiker down an invisible path to Angela. Invisible to their godchild again, there two confused angels belatedly discuss their duties as her godparents. However, accommodating, the old priest wasn't about to allow any echo to become her godfather. Although Vigilante has performed well for Angela, he stands to run out of vitality way too soon.

Vigilante is perplexed because neither of the girls' parents are still alive. This means her godparents are obliged to see her through sacraments such as matrimony. He wonders how Lucien can be her guardian angel and her godmother as well. Lucien just gives him one of her imperious stares. Their matrimony goal sent Raven up the trail to check on the youth. Vigilante chuckles, *"Boy, you are in for a surprise!"*

It bothers him that Roman and Lucien may be together at Angela's permanently. Vigilante doesn't like Roman. It's true, they had the common objective of saving Hiker back at Buzzardville. Their mutual interest could have led to friendship if it weren't for their confrontation over Roman's poor response to Hiker's danger. Then he remembers his own failure with Hunter and is miserable. Lucien finds herself torn between romance with Vigilante and her godmother commitment. One that includes working with Roman in the visible human dimension.

Roman remembers Vigilante only too well and usually pretends he isn't around. He would love to deny he has a substance problem and doesn't need this spirit to remind him. In a dimension where everyone hears your innermost thoughts, Vigilante is a thorn in his side, or might be if Roman acknowledges him.

Worse yet, Roman has a suave air. Vigilante knows full and well slick Roman has a certain way that could appeal to women, maybe even Lucien. Once she teasingly smiled at Roman. Coquettishly Lucien scolded, *"Vigilante... you are jealous!"* Vigilante just swallowed his feelings. Although the angels can block their thoughts from him, he hasn't learned this skill. Both read his innermost thoughts.

All three become intensely focused on Angela and Hiker; they are about to meet. A knock on the big front door gets the girl's attention. She opens the door. Angela's face lights up with a beautiful smile for the first time ever. Stammering weakly, Hiker motions to an outside spigot asking for permission to fill his canteen. His weary and battered condition strikes a chord of sympathy within her. She wonders why. Yet for the first time, Angela meets someone she instantly likes. *"This is going to be fun!"* Lucien giggles. Roman dances in triumph. Vigilante's jealousy gives way to their enthusiasm. He's caught up in their happy mood.

Angela pities the exhausted youth ushering him into her home towards the kitchen. She insists on feeding him a tuna sandwich and tea. He politely tries to decline, *"You're much too kind..."* But he's too weary to do anything other than accept her gracious hospitality. Angela asks polite questions. Soon she's listening to his misadventures.

When he tries to learn more about Angela, she honestly states, *"I suppose I was born and lived in this house all of my life." "The only thing interesting that happened to me is my recent car accident." "It happened so suddenly; I can't remember anything." "They say I had a very bad concussion."*

Although pleased by her progress, Lucien worries that Angela could have dark nightmares from her past. Some still may remain deep within her mind. She also knows this precious person is the byproduct of less than even a one-night stand. In her sleep, some words coming from her mouth just aren't from an innocent mind.

Amidst this joy, a dissonant question occurs to the echo. *"How was Angela, as an unbaptized infant, assigned Lucien to be her guardian angel?"* Jolted, Lucien turns away from Vigilante. Even unspoken this very question in his mind makes everything impossible. She closes her mind vowing never to let him hear her thoughts.

Vigilante perceives from her attitude his doubts have jeopardized their relationship. Realizing the magnitude of his blunder, if he had a heart, it would have just broken. Within her inner being, Lucien shrinks in utter shame, *"I'm a complete hypocrite."*

How poor Angela was conceived: on a lonely night about twenty years ago, Will Gold rode downtown after too much to drink at a nearby bar. Randy Will rolled his new Harley to the bar someone in the first bar told him was really wild. Normally geeky Will was a sitting duck for the city bar harpies including a prostitute who became her mother. Back out his home bar Will would brag, *"...went downtown and sowed some wild oats"* If she hadn't picked his wallet, the pregnant prostitute wouldn't have known where to find him for child support.

His onetime and only loss of inhibition led Will to have a child with a stone-cold hearted prostitute. Unbelievably, their quick encounter produced a great child...one he never bothered to know. And Angela has nothing to remember Will ...only this estate.

Leaving the Harley outside of any bar in that neighborhood wasn't the same as leaving the bike outside of his favorite nearby biker bar. The *Strangler* made it disappear and the barmaid distracted Will as Strangler pushed it around the corner. Will lost both ways.

Fortunately for Will that night, he still had enough cash stuffed in his jeans for a cab to take him home. That Harley became the best possession of a notorious thug branded by bar regulars as Strangler based on this thugs' preference for murder.

The barmaid became pregnant after just one encounter with Will. She had no way of knowing who the father was but tracked Will down from his drivers license. After bearing his unwanted child and claiming child support they never connected again.

As time passed the prostitute grew increasingly bitter and worse. Without guilt or hesitation, she put their daughter to work in her own trade. The girl was passed from drunk to drunk. Each one was lower on the human compassion hierarchy until she hit rock bottom. She was passed to the Strangler.

The girl resisted as best she could. As punishment she was reduced to swamping bar filth until the moment when an ambulance carried her to the E R. Wild oats Will Gold did nothing to rescue her from the hell where he planted his seed. But his final testament recognized her rightful inheritance. When the dam broke it became too late for him. Death and his daughters' legacy were his terminal achievements.

Over their first breakfast and many to come, Angela's nurturing helps Hiker to fully heal from his ordeals. When he talks about his mishaps, she reassures him. *"Being mugged, then shot at, any reasonable person might think- somebody's out to get me."* Angela's sympathetic warmth is just the remedy to soothe him. In return she has a decent man to call her own. Both are very interested.

Vigilante tries frantically to regain Lucien's affection. Not a chance, with Hiker now in the picture. Even worse, with Roman his guardian angel, it's hopeless. Her focus is matchmaking towards the production of their wedding. It absorbs her, it's as though Vigilante really doesn't exist. Roman points out to Vigilante the futility of remaining at the house. Roman has his own designs and Vigilante isn't   included.

As for angels, earthly sex is unlikely because of their rather aesthetic nature. Angels may not need sex to reproduce. Sex is an option though. Lucien surely couldn't produce offspring with an echo. Regardless of speculation, no one, except angels and the Lord, know exactly how angels reproduce. Guardian Angels are obliged to stay focused on their assignments…usually one person or two as was the case of those twins. They have little time for much else.

 Before their breakup, Vigilante asked Lucien, *"Just how are angels created?"* Uncomfortable discussing something he had no need to know, rather than answer, she parried and attacked, *"Most angels aren't sure if echo spirits really exist!"*

Lucien explained, *"Angels perceive your being as someone's imagination escaping under extreme stress."* Vigilante argued, *"But Lucien, that's like saying all spirits stay dry by walking between the raindrops."* Then condescendingly admitting, *"Some days even I have a hard time understanding why I exist."* It seemed trivial then, but not now. He forgot his original question. Lucien was pleased to sandbag him so easily.

Mike showing Vigilante how to drink beer by absorbing bubbles was an unparalleled breach of the angel behavior code. Everything about the way angels operate is highly classified. Worse yet, because they are incompatible, angels and echoes aren't supposed to hang out. Another reason, sooner or later someone's feelings get hurt.

The night Vigilante returned to the hospital room intoxicated, Lucien was disappointed with him. It was the first of several times. Things are clearer as he analyzes what went wrong and how to regain her affection. He recalls how cold she was. And wonders if it was his prying thoughts and nothing else. Nothing brings her back to him. He assumes she has been won over by Roman.

Spitefully, he consciously thinks about Roman's substance addiction hoping to jade his image. Vigilante hopes it will spoil things for Roman. He immaturely thinks, *"Roman's just a drunk with wings."* Roman hears and fumes. To his chagrin Lucien laughs hysterically. But Vigilante is blocked from their thoughts and can't hear.

Nothing makes a difference. Vigilantes' love for her is hopeless. Now, he feels there is nothing they have in common other than their mutual concern for Angela's welfare. The echo thinks silently, but unwittingly to every other ghost and angel nearby *"I have fallen for an angel who knows I'm real and still she breaks my heart."* A sympathetic moan rolls down the Patapsco Valley.

To shut him up rather than compassion, Roman focuses fully at Vigilante saying *"Kid, you couldn't feel this much pain if you weren't real."* The echo must admit grudgingly if compassion is the essence of guardian angels, obviously, Lucien doesn't feel any for him. *"I have been dumped!"*

Vigilante worries Angela will disappoint Lucien once she realizes she's so wealthy. He muses … *"Not only a great inheritance but all of that angel-mischief money."* Roman softly, *"Vigilante, Angela* isn't your problem any longer." "Whatever is destined to happen will happen; we are here." Then once again gently, "Your mission is no longer on this hill." "You really have a mission…it's just not here."

Lacking anything else, Vigilante commands his perceived competitor to return Lucien's' affection. Roman gives up on him. He turns away flowing into a room where Hiker and Angela sit staring into one an others' eyes. Roman chuckles to Lucien's' delight "I can't turn my back on my idiot boy for a minute; now he's got a girlfriend."

The angels aren't really paying attention to Angela as she hears something at the door. Opening it, she's greeted by an extremely tired dog who also has found them. Whatever drew Dog to this house on the hill lies only in its' mind. Hiker is happy. Angela has never had a dog and is ecstatic.

Both smart and stupid dogs just follow people they like. Even enlightened dogs don't know why. But Roman is pleased because it gives him a familiar force to use if his charge gets into trouble again. Vigilante doesn't plant the idea in Dog but would be happy if the dog bites Roman. Lucien wonders whether she can make Dog bite Roman. "Cut it out!" cries Roman.

After Dog rescued Hiker, they spent an evening by a campfire. Then splitting up both assumed they'd never again meet. It was the night Vigilantes' parents met. Neither dog nor youth could imagine they would reconnect at some old house. The slaughter in the meadow happened before Vigilante existed. Obviously, he couldn't inspire this reunion. Some things happen for reasons best understood by scheming angels.

Roman trusts the animal, but Lucien is apprehensive. She sees Dog as potentially dangerous to Angela when the couple inevitably has an argument. Whenever possible she places herself between the canine and Angela. This makes Dog feel uneasy; her defensive postures make him nervous and prone to flopping out on the front porch.

He sees himself a free creature who shouldn't be possessed by people or spirits. *"I'm my own good dog and nobody's dumbass!"* Perhaps he's right because he's much more enlightened than any other pup. As smart wears off, someday soon, he'll just lay there calculating whether or where to bite Roman and Lucien. But he truly loves the two humans inside.

Hikers' guardian angel is growing out of his totally passive role. Roman calls Dog back into the kitchen. Dog is considering sinking his teeth into the angel when the boy comes into the room. Hiker and the dog are one. Dogs' wagging tail has a mind of its' own. Angela leans over petting him, Lucien winces in alarm. Hiker gets gives him a leftover. Boy and girl fingers touch; neither moves away. Dog, Lucien, and even Roman approve.

Vigilante is moving towards the river. Without knowing of this coming together, Vigilante understands he has been entirely eclipsed in the household. He decides to spare himself further pain. Lucien, Roman and even the dog acknowledges his exit with sympathy and silent respect. *"Only in the mystical world!"* Vigilante thinks cynically. The angels smile knowingly. The dog tries to smile too but can't remember how.

The echo gives a lonely sad look back. Then a loving hurt *"Good luck my love!"* towards where he thinks Lucien may be. Vigilante floats down the hill out of view from the house, stopping just short of the river. The raven warns, *"Danger, danger!"*

Down where the road meets the riverside a seemingly mild old gent squats upon a short wooden stool facing down the path. He mouths a weird old flute creating a haunting tune. He doesn't seem to notice something evil coming directly at him.

Everyone else does. Ghosts and spirits turn away in fear from the specter. Vigilante would have ignored it except the figure coming towards them is familiar. If Vigilante had one, his body would him have shaken in anger for the approaching ghostly figure is the malevolent Strangler's ghost. He isn't fooled by the new appearance of Angela on the hill, he's coming for revenge.

The little musician is disarmingly pleasant. The Strangler sees just a harmless old ghost with snowy hair and a thin goatee. He sings softly playing an old tune and seems unconcerned. As the Strangler draws near the gent croons the time-worn spiritual, *"Swing low sweet chariot coming for to carry me home..."* His soothing voice hums in a low moan as the Stranglers' ghost arrives trying to turn in the direction of the house.

Strangler ghost snarls at what he perceives as a helpless old man, *"Fool, get outa my way!"* *"Who do you think you are?"* Condescendingly the little man sneers back

"Gee. you devil!" *"My name is Gee!"* *"I am the Grim Reaper!"*

The blocked figure takes hold of Gees' neck with his choke hold.

From his emaciated body, Gee suddenly extends his own muscular hand directly at his attacker. He clamps its' neck in a deadly clutch. Strangler's apparition fades slightly.

As the pale shrinking specter of Strangler flattens trying to get away, Gee squeezes so hard the demons' evil pallor dwindles to a sickly green, then white-on-white. Gee drags the sagging carcass down into the river. A dense curtain of fog parts revealing a mighty sailing ship. Its' boarding ramp drops to receive them.

Dragging the demonic ghost with one hand, he looks over one shoulder and waves. Vigilante waves back with a friendly *up-yours* one finger gesture. Gee isn't insulted. He understands that Vigilante feels cheated of his own opportunity to destroy this evil demon forever. Smiling Gee looks back at Vigilante explaining he isn't an ordinary angel.

"My first name starts with G. They call me the Grim Reaper." *"So you can just call me Gee,"* The good ship slides ever so smoothly down the river. It rides upon a perpetual tide of its' own for a short distance. Then it dips forward into the depths beneath the water, a river long ago silted in and lost to ships of any size.

The mighty ship's hoisted sail is fully extended. Pressure from a mystical breeze forces its' bow down. It buries the vessel from keel down to the topsail. Gracefully it tilts up one last time then disappears beneath the gravel and muck of a bottomless course to infinity.

Finally, this soul reaches his ultimate port of final and complete despair. From a long-gone chestnut tree, Lucien's ghostly black raven screams another, *"Nevermore!"* Then it escorts the ship into the netherworld. All is quiet. All is still, on its' course down to hell.

Vigilante flows curiously over the spot down where they disappeared. The great vessel left neither wake nor trace of passing. Once more, the river is just a country stream. Perceiving nothing else around, Vigilante feels he is completely alone. In due time he will learn he's very wrong. Clyde will be unhappy until he finds his true   love.

Vigilante Spirit

15

Discovery

Sad and alone, Vigilante follows the stream down through twisted fingers of the Patapsco. Winding with ancient memory of an abandoned port this old river leads into the Chesapeake Bay. Waters feed this thread as it joins a parade of streams and rivers marching to the Atlantic. But Vigilante isn't interested in the vast world ocean. To heal he needs respite from his passion for his lovely Lucien.

Along the way, lonely ghosts reach out in consolation. Whispering sad tales of loves long lost they wish him well. For some it's their lust for nearby buried treasure. Yet neither ghost nor spirit may wield a shovel. And none could spend a coin or wear a gem.

Poor souls beg for just a word of kindness. Dark fog and despair thrive amidst the river reeds. The echo lets himself flow away down the bay to a new start he longs for, to escape the loss of Lucien.

The Bay is calm; the echo isn't... rejection sinks in. They had nothing in common except their desire to save Angela. He wonders whether Lucien always knew their relationship for what it was... an impossibility. *"If she did, I didn't!"* He fumes, *"Why was she so heartless?"*

He flows out with the receding tide finally accepting the insanity of their relationship. It might feel better if he knew Lucien misses even the love they had. She feels terrible for the cold way she brushed him off. *"If only there was another way to let him down gently."* His curiosity concerns things she doesn't dare answer.

Lucien slips into her very quiet state. One so deep once it caused her to delegate duties she should have personally handled. Things haven't been right since. Her protégé was distracted at a critical moment. Remembering, she has it take wing to watch over Vigilante.

Even though Angela's home is full of happiness, Lucien feels alone. She could have company easily if she just encouraged this amorous guardian angel. Roman might be suitable if she wasn't disgusted by him. She tolerates Roman just enough to allow him to watch over his charge… from an old woodshed.

"If I had good sense, I wouldn't have revealed myself to Vigilante in the first place.." Now he wants more than she can give. His time as an energized echo is barely a thread compared to hers. He wouldn't have imagined she existed before she made contact. Contact was bad for us both. She sighs, *"…or was it?"* Then there's *his horrible persistence to know things."*

She tried reasoning with him when he wanted greater intimacy, *"A gigantic reason for our apparent chastity is we have no bodies." "At least, nothing compatible."* When she argued, *"Can humans or echoes possibly achieve the emotional energy of angels?"* He ignored her logic and refused to accept s reality in which he must remain celibate. Nothing he tried worked. The angels dimension is as distinct from an echo's as is his from the living.

Vigilante's mind keeps repeating the same things. So deep are his thoughts, he doesn't notice the raven soaring high overhead. Ruminating, *"I'm nothing more than her imaginary blip."* Then angrily, *"I was a chump!"* From the big white house overlooking the Patapsco faint sobbing becomes a moan. Despair deafens him; Vigilante can't feel her pain. Her soft sobbing is unheard. He senses nothing.

The echo glides slowly down the Chesapeake on the ebbing tide without a plan or destination. He regrets his past arrogance. Then vows to someone above to renounce conceit and ego forever. Even with no audible response, relief bathes him. His humility lessens his torment.

Focusing up at the sky for a moment he sees a black floppy winged blackbird being stalked by a hungry osprey. The predator is ready to pounce then suddenly forgets what its' doing. This seriously confused osprey retreats to a pole nest on the Magothy River. Vigilante gives it less thought than anyone might when swatting a fly.

But this little intervention rekindles his sense of mission. *"Determination and staying focused on good works may make me forget everything else."* Relief from rejection trickles in like drops of mist. These are as fine as the dew in the dawn. They are mere droplets of love falling mutely from the heart of an angel.

Probing her for vulnerability, Roman cajoles Lucien with mock sympathy, *"Tis a cold mean blade that cuts without mercy into ones' being..."* Lucien retorts bluntly, *"Mind your own blade."* Whose *booze are you sniffing now?" "Hiker says his Jack Daniels is flat."* *"Why doesn't it surprise me? "Roman, You are a disgrace."*

Oblivious to Angela, Hiker empties most of his whiskey glass into the kitchen sink. Back in college, he ran cross country where he drank only water. Neither knows why Angela compulsively refills his whiskey. Lucien is too busy mourning her own breakup to notice Angela's return to her old barmaid reflex. Surprisingly, Angela doesn't drink anything except iced tea.

Roman is delighted because this way a steady flow of the fine whisky arrives weekly. Its' always signaled by a knock on the side door. All the great old bottles he found secreted in tree stumps and other odd places outside have evaporated. With his help, the little remaining in each became bubbles he sniffed.

This rogue resolves not to be deprived of his addiction. After sniffing the Blackjack flat, he's once again busted by Angela. He sniffs wistfully in the direction of the Jim Beam. Lucien shoves him back into his woodshed and advises she won't let him out unless he stops sniffing booze. Trying to win her over, he whimpers theatrically from between the rake and hoe *"True torment is love disengaged."* She just flips him off.

With each wave he follows down the bay the echo flows further away. Vigilante decides both the love and the rejection he experienced with her have in some way helped him to mature. Still nursing his ego, he remains resentful. But the further from her the less is his depression.

This is as much progress for him as it was for his father when he left the swamp in a dogs' jaws. As his self-respect stabilizes, he's once more an able echo. Newly invigorated he bounces over the waves. *"I'm over her!"* From above a cloud the raven cries, *"Angela*

Flexing mental muscle, he cries his challenge for the entire world to hear, *"I am a force majeure!"* Then somewhat remembering his need for humility he returns to his senses. He realizes he only knows the phrase *"force majeure"* from something he read in Angela's library… Puzzled, he remembers turning the pages with his fingers and thinks *"That doesn't make any sense." "I hadn't been there before and don't have fingers."*

He starts to put this thought from his mind. Then, he decides it's worthwhile. *"How did I know to look there?"* He shrugs it off as a delusion. Then, *"Obviously, I can't turn pages with fingers I don't have, any more than I can make love with something else I also don't have." "That woman has driven me nuts!"*

A chuckle comes from a ghost beneath him. Vigilante realizes with embarrassment he's being delusional. Still, he knows that he learned to see beauty and virtue during his time with Lucien. Before her he saw only evil and stupidity. Both vices always seemed to appear without his need to look hard. Since Lucien and the other angels now he understands mercy.

He liked having a real home with Lucien. Vigilante hopes to make new friends and have another place to call home, even though it couldn't be as good. Before Lucien he was content to be anywhere he happened to exist, except for filthy Lizard alley. Now, such a hostile existence is unthinkable.

As with any young person leaving his parents' home, he's looking for his place in the world. Maybe even someone to talk to again. He remarks to a passing seagull, *"Having friends is wonderful."* The bird completely ignores him, except for an open beaked screech. To a gull, only catching the next bite of food is wonderful. Gulls only talk to gulls; they scream rudely at everyone else.

He muses. *"How stupid of Will Gold to have lived without love."* The thought startles him. *"Why am I thinking about that loser?"* He rejects further worthless thoughts of anything so remote from his reality. His focus returns to exploring.

Moving further south, well past Annapolis, Vigilante notices a curious but drowned island not far from the eastern shore. For all its' vast area the Chesapeake is not always deep. A sunken house grabs his attention. The chimney is the highest point on the island. It's barely deeper than the very lowest of tides.

With much of the same architecture as Angela's big house, it stands submerged like one of those little white ceramics one sees at the bottom of a goldfish bowl. Once eastern shore tidy, now it's rustic eerie. The structure will never again be suitable for air breathing creatures. But it's just fine for marine life and spirits.

He claims the island and names it *Oriole*. This is just one of countless numbers of drowned islands gradually slipping gently beneath the waves. He inspects it with the businesslike assessment of someone buying property on land. An annoyed terrapin scampers out of his way.

Its'17th century understated grace wows him. He becomes aware that he is thinking like a human rather than a spirit. Although somewhat amused, he doesn't particularly like the idea of being human. As he hovers just over the sunken garden he consciously thinks imperiously, *"So this is how a fish lives?"* The thought of being a fish or a turtle amuses him even more. He pretends to chase after an eel; it doesn't recognize him as a predator but wriggles away just in case.

The big houses' heyday was long gone well before the bay swallowed Oriole. As time passes and waters continue rising it recedes deeper. Now it hides even its' once proud white widows-walk over a wing facing west. No widow now walks its' planks, so only its' architecture bears witness to the uncertainty of a seafarers return. Centuries of tall sailing ships and these sailors lie far beneath the sea. Many widows walked in vain.

Of course, the basement submerged first. Now it rests under yards of silt. The echo brightens, *"Nothing could be better!"* His attitude improves and getting here has relaxed him. His mind beams for the first time since leaving Lucien.

A mighty locked front door guards the house from any who might break in from the front. A big key turned in the rusty lock by the last mortal to evacuate still hangs in a safe spot where a shed stood. Its' oxide streak now coats the board. It's true, Vigilante could easily flow right through, but he finds it more convenient to enter from the rear because the back door is completely gone. Inexplicably, he wishes to behave like a gentleman. Something has bestowed proper manners upon this spirit.

Now he uses doors and likes the mortal manner of going through them even though no one here appreciates this refinement. He chuckles. *"Flowing through these venerable walls seems uncivilized."*

The once grand furniture is seriously encrusted with marine life. No owner of this manor ever moved anything out. It's all still here.

The old servants left everything behind. It was a matter of life and death to steal from their dangerous employer. So, it went nowhere. It wasn't moved to higher land onshore and no one dared to salvage it either.

And so except for barnacles and worms undeterred by rising tides, things are where they were when big door was last closed. Sheets and pillows on the beds included. Once white linens are tinted in oyster shell grey with bits of marine life growing through. Vigilante mumbles, *"Because Lucien would hate this place... I love it!"*

Suddenly a shadowy figure confronts Vigilante. It's the ghost of a pirate. This sad relic of a dead picaroon is a very amateurish haunter. Most old, abandoned houses are haunted to some degree. As a challenger, this one isn't even the most forceful ghost Vigilante has come across. Compared to the nightmares in the city this guy isn't very scary.

He makes a feeble to frighten Vigilante away with a show of his nastiest eeriness.

Sorry to say, this ones' pirate face is not frightening. Vigilante feels sorry for him. To make him feel better about moving in without permission he tries to pretend he's afraid. It seems to work. The ghost is encouraged. He digs deep for louder and meaner. *"I am the cruelest picaroon who ever lived."* Vigilante can tell from the juvenile way he expresses himself this so-called picaroon was only half-grown when he died.

To make a point of staking this house as his territory, the ghost mimics the force of a pirates' rage. He doesn't want this spirit or anything else here. Completely out of scary ideas he tries to push Vigilante. But echo spirits don't have anything to push.

Vigilante decides, *"It could be awhile before I have a sane conversation with this goof."* The ghost tries to bully him by engulfing his space. Instead of backing off Vigilante short circuits the ghostly aura. Mystical sparks are as bright as lightning. This scares the devil out of the ghost, so he retreats out of reach.

Finally, Vigilante has enough. It doesn't make the ghost feel safer when Vigilante breaks up laughing. The ghost shamefully disappears into his hideout. Vigilante pretends not to know where he is hiding. Gradually stillness returns as his nervousness subsides. The big house is quiet except for occasional shivering coming from the hideout.

Vigilante knows he's here but ignores him. *"Just too many much eviler ghosts are all around the bay to be concerned."* Vigilante worries, *"This sad kid is a useless defender and could even need my help."* Forgetting the telepathy of his mind, with unintended disdain, the echo has insulted a likely consumer of his reason for being.

Hanging out with angels hasn't helped Vigilante's skill of thinking quietly. Ghost *Clyde* is very annoyed. Vigilante knows his name because Clyde thinks and talks. He talks to himself and floats around in his hiding place addressing himself as Clyde. He says, *"Clyde, go chase that bastard out of here!"* Then, answers himself with, *"Yes, I'm going to do it; I'm going to do it..."* *"Yes, I'm going to... just not right now."* Clyde isn't schizophrenic. He's just been alone in his haunt way too long.

Clyde wasn't a terrible pirate. Although he associated with real picaroons, he was just their stooge. But he really believed he was one of them. Since drowning he just haunts his not so secret place in the kitchen cupboard. In life, he was so low key the servants never knew he lived in the cupboard. Having anyone know he's in there is a new and frightening experience.

They usually pretend not to see one another. Vigilante finds him amusing but misses intelligent conversation. This is too solitary to suit the echo. So, he decides to get to know the ghost better.

The pseudo-picaroon and estranged echo are an odd pair of bachelors. Real picaroons were considered by even their friends to be among the fiercest of their day. This deluded ghost hasn't even been able to chase crabs from his pantry hideout. Even tiny minnows nibble on him. But Vigilante wants to think only positive thought and keeps his thinking to himself. As usual things are about to change.

Little does either realize a gigantic challenge to their existence will soon descend upon them and this part of the bay. Oddly, it's coming from a small ship that has run aground at the end of the old carriage road. For the past week, Vigilante and Clyde have enjoyed undisturbed mutual disdain. This annoying vessel became stuck here after an unusually high tide receded.

Vigilante hopes it will simply refloat itself and be gone on the next high tide. Neither ghost nor spirit cares enough to discuss how to get rid of it. But both are thinking openly without concern for privacy. Clyde hums simple mindedly as if he's reciting a nursery rhyme, *"Tides in, tides out... ship's in the garden!"*

Both assign the ship a low priority. And for the echo, tomorrow is a workday. Just after dawn he makes his way back up the bay to Baltimore. He hears a sigh of relief from the ghost in the cupboard as he leaves. To prevent confusion, he thinks aloud, *"I'm coming back later."*

Dogs are being maimed and tortured in the city. Vigilante feels their pain all of the way to Oriole Island. *"Helpless animals forced to fight one another as a blood sport becomes my affair."* He pities them. They are domestic animals bred to respond to every whim of their human masters. *"It raises my hackles... Or would if I had hackles..."*

"Domestic dogs can't protect themselves from human cruelty the way wolves can." He informs his angel buddy Mike on the way up Greene Street. *"They are killers because fighting is how they're trained."* Mike is sympathetic but remains in his calm lab without budging. He replies, *"Sorry, dogs don't have priority; people do."* *"If you want help with the souls of those watching the dogfight let us know."* The echo replies, *"They can't have souls!"*

Shocked by Mike's indifference, Vigilante has seen too much pain in his journeys to stop for the argument he just heard. He recalls a phrase from one of Mike' guardian angel buddies *"Don't sweat the small stuff."* He doesn't like the idea because the world is full of important small stuff. He stays on task quickly arriving at the brick row house where the dogfights are underway.

Outside of the run-down house, he senses extremely strong pain vibrations. Moving through the wall instead of the door, he comes to a ring where one pit-bull is destroying its' weaker opponent. The winners' bloody fangs have already sliced long red gashes in the face and neck of the loser. Powerful jaws grind at its' throat in a death grip. The stricken dog gurgles its' death rattle. Vigilante focuses on both dogs; to the dismay of the crowd it's suddenly released by the apparent winner.

Without warning both dogs suddenly charge those watching. The underdog joins the winner. The simple barrier separating pit-bulls and those betting goes down. Biting spectators is the new blood sport.

It's a dogs' day! They tear and slash even their trainers. Soft people skin tears and bleeds easier than the dogs'. Spectators trip, knocking down others scrambling to escape. Throwing a bottle and his money at a dog, one cries out, *"Money be damned; I'm outa' here!"* Powerful jaws grip arms and legs. Flesh rips off as they run. Under such enormous pressure from those leaving the door jams. Avenging dogs block them from the back door. The front door explodes off of its' hinges.

Torn and bleeding spectators crash outside onto the pavement. They are herded towards an old cemetery. Someone manages to call 911. Long minutes pass. Wailing sirens signal the arrival of police and an ambulance. The caller was so hysterical the operator thought he was having a baby. Vigilante flows out of the splintered doorway pleased he's improving Baltimore. He mutters, *"This house was pure evil!"*

Spirits must be able to instantly calculate fine measurements and distances. Shifting quickly through dimensions requires absolute precision. His ability is obvious as the echo encourages those who were victims to pursue their tormentors. The dogs herd them into a place where only the dead usually retreat. Everyone makes it under, over or through the iron gate.

Bolting across old Greenmount cemetery they manage to agitate the ghost of presidential assassin John W. Booth. The evil ghost moans something unintelligible and retreats into his secret grave. Without pausing the dogs try to bite him too, but he's too slippery.

Exhausted overcome gamblers flee for their lives. With their legs fueled by searing fear, they run and run. Each one is just one step in front of teeth, and then he isn't. They wish they'd gone to see someone's new puppy instead of these monsters. Gamblers race on until the teeth find them.

The two-leg stride of those fleeing in front compared to the speed of the four-legged ones gives those with the most legs in this man-dog race a huge advantage. Even, with no bets down, any who might have won money on the dog fight are losing more than cash. The dogs rip hunks off backsides easily keeping pace.

With magical energy, dogs and runners cover diminishing distance until what had been a one-step lead becomes a half-step then quarter-step. One by one, exhaustion rules. The slowest gamblers are chewed apart and drop for scavengers from the sky.to find them. In the morning, a reporter sarcastically writes a headline. It reads: *Bloody Trails of Bloody Tails*.

Hideous screams ring out as each dog wins his race. The caught scream, *"Oh Jesus, Oh Lord, please make it go away...!" I'll be good Lord!"* No comment from above; just two guardian angels were assigned to all pursued. Betting on the outcome, one jokes about his charge. *"This's the first time he's ever prayed!"*

No one seems to hear; no one seems to care. Some run all the way out to the county with jaws attached. A victorious angel proclaims, *"That was a great race!"* As proven mankillers, these dogs eventually will be caught and hauled to the pound. Every dog would have been humanely euthanized had they not figured out how to open their cages.

Those in charge of the pound are convinced as the dogs escaped they saw them smiling. Each will stalk their surviving tormentors for the rest of their short lives. These dogs only do what predators always do... they follow the scent of fear.

Vigilante has little sympathy for those pursued. His concern is for those chasing. He fully realizes the ultimate cost of their emancipation. Maneaters just aren't tolerated. It's a death sentence.

Vigilante Spirit

16

Turmoil

There is no place for these vicious pitbulls in the city or out in the wilderness.

Fighting dogs are misbred to lose their gentle nature. Vigilante believes the privilege to use animals imposes man with responsibility to treat them with mercy. Just as our Lord is the master of man, we are masters of beasts… unless our Lord decides otherwise. Vigilante knows these dogs will be killed when caught …but not today.

Along his way back to Oriole, he visits a popular restaurant in the inner harbor. Amazingly the wealthiest miser in town walks in and orders crab cakes for everyone in the city's homeless shelters. The only one more surprised than the waiter is the miser. Vigilante's mission today won a double header from outside of the baseball park.

"Today was a success." He liberated victimized dogs and persuaded a stingy miser to be charitable. About his mission, "W*hy?"* one might ask. The question rarely occurs to Vigilante because he knows why. *"Serving is satisfying!"* Vigilante is back on track with renewed self-confidence he's on mission.

The Chesapeake Bay Bridge looms high overhead. As the sun sets on the bay, lots of sailboats tack home through the haze. Nearly alone, Vigilante flows southward past Annapolis to his new home. Anywhere without Lucien is sad. He can't resist thinking of her. She remains on his mind although he tries to shake her off. The sun setting on the Bay is exotic. The beauty of the sunset reminds him of her.

In sensuous lethargy, Vigilante fantasizes a tender intimate moment with her. It crosses all of the natural boundaries separating spirits and angels. In his self-indulgent fantasy, they are as one. Words mortals might say are needless. His imagination makes their union complete. Powerful emotion explodes without those hateful limitations of not having physical being. Potent energies blast back up into the Patapsco in an all-encompassing gale. Lucien is captured in his wave.

This passionate force releases vitality akin to the potency of a black hole in the cosmos. Its' marvel is perceived by nearby mortals as continuous lightning rolling through the sky. But to the two whose experience this is, it is wildly private. Normally for Vigilante, a dream is just a dream; only reality is real. And for him, it's his moment and no one else's. *"I'm a simple echo." "Who else notices, but me?"* Then the raven floating on a cloud above says, *"That's what you think!" "You've just singed my feathers!"* Witnessing this experience the raven wills to change her own being.

Had Vigilante looked back, or wasn't so self-absorbed, he might have seen that gale resulting from his odyssey…one felt immensely back at the house on the hill. But he doesn't.

At the house on the hill, a shocked angel Roman scarfs up Hikers' whiskey mist and voluntarily retreats into the safety of the woodshed. For a tiny blissful moment, Lucien hovers above the house in sheer delight. The echo's moment passes; he will rarely think of her again…until he does ...

Dawns' first sunlight brightens the long green eastern shoreline. Gradually golden rays filter down illuminating Oriole. An ominous shadow reveals the vessel now stuck to the roof of a barn. The quiet beauty of morning starkly contrasts with sounds of discord onboard. Sunlight reveals one side of the vessel. Thuds of anger within bleed through its' hull and reach two who are listening below.

The ships' stern is nearly free. Still, no one onboard is alert enough to hoist sail and be gone. So, distracted are the crew, stowaways and captive, they fail to heed the rising tide. The ship drifts a bit and runs aground once more.

Vigilante was slightly annoyed last evening as he passed it on his way down to his new quarters. He decided he will investigate after some much-needed rest. Then he entered an exhausted slumber-like state and was oblivious to everything.

Before descending into oblivion, he was momentarily aware of the quiet within Oriole. And he wondered why Clyde was so still. The ghost said and thought nothing, nary a cordial hiss or boo. Weird vibrations from the ship overhead indicated something wrong. But, too tired to think about another thing he decided, *"It'll wait for tomorrow."*

Vigilante isn't worried Clyde might throw him out while in his restful state. Its' become apparent to both; the other isn't leaving soon.

Vigilantes' final thought as he drifted off was *"Maybe the problem will just float away..."* Mercifully, his mind drifts peacefully into a gentler relaxed state. Soon dreaming, he is in a boat trailing a fishing line without bait. Its' side scrapes along a wire and then... *poof!*

The nightmare awakens him. His mind returns to reality. It's a new day and he's here on Oriole with a weird ghost. From his pantry lair Clyde isn't so peaceful. For he remembers outlaws like those up in the ship only too well.

Typical bachelors, Clyde and Vigilante haven't tried to make Oriole more presentable. Little wonder; neither plans to have guests…ever. Were a female echo to see how messy Vigilante keeps his space, none would consider this slob. And ghosts are even worse. They await either heaven or hell, in Clyde's case, most likely the latter. So, appearances don't bother Clyde. But now with trouble so near he's so worried he rushes around trying to straighten things; stuff that won't budge. The ghost imagines his habitat as an unusually tidy haunt. One that might attract demons or worse, human curiosity. Neither causes much clutter. Just existing they typical messy bachelors. Fate has goings-on about to happen that will change both forever

Their initial hostility is gone and now is mutually understood to be ridiculous. Whenever prankish shock waves come from Vigilante now, they have become amusing to Clyde. Sometimes he lets loose with an equally evil but harmless display. Mostly they just wave as they pass. Both realize it's useless to try spook the other.

He senses something awry about the ship, something beyond everything he has encountered. Vigilante isn't looking for another job of the kind best left to angels. Not, after the Buzzardville fiasco. He winces at the recollection.

As Vigilante becomes fully alert, he focuses on Clyde. He senses the ghost is as pensive as when Vigilante dozed off. Clyde is probing everything up on the grounded ship. He senses a female captive. Clyde becomes aware of Vigilantes' developing concern and now is glad he came to Oriole. The way the ghost sees things shaping up, he needs heavy muscle.

But above all else, Clyde has personal worries for he is suspended in time. He dreads facing his destiny. He believes at any time it will be his turn for eternal punishment. He worries this period of agonized waiting for hell is just retribution for past misdeeds.

He decided Vigilante was a fighter when he quipped to Clyde several days ago, *"One of my best friendships started out with a punch in the nose."* The ghost remembered his own youth and recalled his own fights with guys who became friends. They aren't so different. But Clyde wonders how an echo spirit ever had a nose.

Vigilante scans the stranded ship and thinks *"Pirates."* Clyde adds ... *"and Picaroons!"* The ghosts and demons onboard don't see them. They fail to look beneath the ships' hull. It's just as well. But could if they tried. They fail to comprehend anything except their rotten lust and intoxication. Probing deeper, the echo and ghost detect hellacious confusion, turmoil and evil on evil.

For the time being, they just watch and eavesdrop. For neither can imagine how to deal with a gang that consists of both ghostly and living pirates. They grasp they are listening to complete evil. Clyde's' thoughts point Vigilante to the innocent female captive on the ship. Picaroons dead and alive are drunkenly carousing and fighting just overhead. They've kidnapped her.

This bizarre pair of misfits wants to *attack those bums!* But before getting into a fight with the picaroons Vigilante realizes he needs to learn a whole lot more about Clyde.

They compare strategies. Nether has ever tried to develop a boarding strategy. In fact Clyde never actually went with his fellow pirates on a raid.

Small talk helps to give any rescue from the ship time to evolve into something more manageable. Ordinarily echoes and ghosts don't care to just babble on. Clyde probes, *"Where did you grow up?"* Clyde is embarrassed to realize the echo is at a loss for words. All Vigilante can sputter is *"I didn't grow up."* Clyde can't stop the echo from reading his thoughts...

"Oh, woe is me!" *"My partner in this fight was hatched just like a little bird!"* Afraid he's about to break out laughing, the ghost forces himself not to think about Vigilante as a baby chick. He focuses on feeling empathy instead. It doesn't work, the humor of his birth hits Vigilante as well. They only stop laughing when they realize they're making so much noise they can attract attention from the pirates.

Oblivious of his own momentary embarrassment, Vigilante's curiously asks, *"How did you get stuck here?"* The ghost replies politely, *"I lived here before the tides swallowed our island."* *"I worked down there."* Clyde points to a barely visible hatch in the pantry floor. Vigilante is surprised. He thought he'd discovered everything about this old house. *Down there...* is new to him.

"What's down there?" Rather than answer, Clyde leads the way down the hatch following a stairway beneath the pantry. They flow through a long descending tunnel into a large area. The echo follows the ghost into a vast room greater than the house stretching beneath the bay as well as to the western edge of the original island.

The immense treasure in this room is evident even in the dim gloom. It's an astonishing testimony to the value of the booty pirated from great sailing ships of Clyde's era and before. Everything of great value from the rich of a past era surrounds them as they move among the pieces.

Gold bars, kegs and many bottles of wine, coins, fine art, diamonds and lesser gems were haphazardly stashed within this timeless bubble beneath the bay. Here is a vast store of pirated wealth quite easily within the reach of all who float upon the Chesapeake, if only they knew where to look. Forgetting the upcoming challenge for the moment, Clyde articulates in a tone much like a guide. *"Caches like this still exist throughout the world and remain hidden until they are found."* Vigilante is impressed but doesn't understand why. *"This room is different."* Clyde reveals-

"Air is trapped here." Pointing west, *"There we have a concealed underwater entrance."*

He explains calmly, *"This treasure all came through the underwater access, it's one that can't be seen outside."* *"It was well away from the eyes of them from whom it was hidden."* *"And, from the eyes of them what might want to pinch it back."* *"No one up in the house knew we were down here."*

Pausing… then continuing his explanation, in a lower strained voice. *"Coming back one time, I did not reach the entrance by the end of the right tide."* *"I drowned just outside."* *"If the people upstairs knew all of this treasure was down here maybe it would be gone with them."* This is the most he's said since they've been speaking to one another. It all comes out in one long burst of shrill desolation. *"No one knew where to look for me!"*
"I've never had a Christian burial."

Oriole Island is close to the border between Maryland and Virginia. Neither States' watermen saw much value to this wasting island. They were mostly concerned with fighting over who had rights to the oysters. Clyde mournfully repeats. *"No one even looked."* Vigilante replies," *None could stop this island from sinking."*

Vigilante consoles Clyde with the idea– *"Maybe no one came back because any who might know you were here with their treasure all died."* Pirates often were hung, their heads impaled on posts, as a warning to others. Few may have tried to recover Clyde' body after he could no longer tell anyone where the treasure is hidden.

Clyde continues *"The master of this house must have gone straight to hades and never became stuck between here and there like me."* Returning to the problem at hand, Vigilante worries whether the *"old master"* is among those pirates in the stranded ship. Thinking, *"Maybe he came back to reclaim his lost booty."*

Clyde savors his sins. He confesses, *"I'm trapped by my guilt of being a party to the piracy." "I was their storekeeper and traded their booty on shore."* He knows he pandered to those who were evil. The ghost kicks a pile of furs preserved in this cool dryer part of the cellar.

Spectral fangs snarl back and bite at him. Then, seeming to recall they too are deceased, all fall back into place like so many tabby cats. The sad picaroon blurts out... *"It did not seem wrong back* then." "As time passed, the stealing of this, and the killing they did to get it, forever cursed my soul." Sourly, Vigilante asks about Clyde's own murderous deeds. "No Sir, I never robbed, beat or killed anyone!"

Vigilante reasons to him, "By the ethics of your time and place Clyde, you only did what many here did to survive." Clyde s beats himself up wailing, "Even after I knew it was blood money I still did their bidding..." "One of 'em trying to store booty was too greedy." "Like me, his skull and bones lay out there with a chest heavy with gold coins." "Sorry to say, I didn't try to help him." Vigilante realizes Clyde is determined to be viewed as an evil picaroon.

He points his gnarly finger at piles of pirated goods spread throughout the room. "This is all mine; ho-ho I'm rich!" Both laugh at the notion of a rich ghost. Although this vault has been closed for centuries breathable air trapped here will very soon become very useful in a way that neither can foresee. They haven't forgotten their decision to battle those above but still haven't come up with a method.

Vigilante stares at paintings of once proud nobles. Rudely those lords and ladies glare back. They can see him. None would want to see an echo while alive. Now they see more than they care to. Pompous pairs of eyes stare from their canvas. In protest the face of each portrait closes its' eyes.

This precious art may as well be trash. For all of this is useless to ghost, echo and even those from whom it was taken. Everyone who touched this treasure was cursed in some way. His mission doesn't include them; they are already dead. He remarks to Clyde, *"Wealth can be misery."* Clyde agrees.

Ghost and echo each has slightly different capabilities to alter events in the world of the living. One can move physical objects and more. The other can motivate living creatures and persuade others to help. Both traits are about to be vital to the survival of a good person needing help.

The ship starts rocking; it's no longer stuck. Once more none onboard are alert; she should set sail. Still the ship flounders. Now it dances over rusted spikes of an iron fence. That these pirates tarry, surprises both ghost and spirit. Ideally this clash to come would take place some distance from Oriole. Finally prepared, they listen to running feet and loud cursing from the deck above.

A young pretty college student was oblivious of her peril when they kidnapped her from the beach over at Assateague. She remains living by sheer luck. In total dread her mind is completely engaged. She places her fist over her mouth and gags. Feigning sea sickness she suddenly turns towards the rail as though to heave. Not wanting to be in the way of her puke, her captors are caught off guard for just a moment too long.

Her feet pound furiously on the deck; she leaps over the rail. Her body hits the water hard. Sounds of her plunge booms just over Vigilante and Clyde. The girl plummets down into the unknown abyss of dark water. Her kidnappers finally react. *"She's getting away!"*

Sadistic flickers of anticipation from hell belatedly alert her guardian angel to the moment this poor wretch nearly drowns. Hers' is just another overworked guardian who rarely has time to think of this girl. Her angel is too far away but is aware the echo and ghost are near her.

The angel pleads to both to help. Vigilante inspires Clyde to action. The girls' dive is very close to an old rusty fence spike. Outstretched arms reach to save her with incredible speed for any ghost nearly two centuries old. His spontaneous move allows her to just miss impalement.

Clyde never experienced so much excitement as a picaroon. He sighs. *"She survives."* *"But, what happens next?"* Vigilante yells, *"Into the room Clyde, she needs to breathe!"* Belatedly, her kidnappers peer over the rail. They can see nothing beneath the waves. They are too late. Now Vigilante is fully into her rescue. His mission- he has them looking everywhere she isn't.

Christie hadn't the slightest clue where fate would carry her as she dove overboard. But jumping was her only chance. Drowning was better than captivity. Spotting a clear path to the rail, she leaped as far as she could. Sucking in as much air as her lungs could hold she plunged into the murky water.

Returning to the surface wasn't thinkable. So, she put her life in the hands of her maker. This was unique for Christie. Her relationship with the Almighty usually dangles between stressed to non-existent despite having a good upbringing.

Although near panic at what she perceived to be the strong downward current, she holds her breath. *"I'm going somewhere way too fast!"* Then wondering… *"Am I dead?"* Then the dim sunlight vanishes. A voice in her head answers, *"You'll see the sun again…but not today."*

Encouraged, she fights panic and holds her breath just long enough. The struggle is to survive. Her chest is about to rupture. She can't hold her breath any longer but does. When she feels her head is about to explode, she nearly gives in to drowning. Then… she lets her breath out and then in. *"Is this Air?"* *"It smells bad, but I'll take it!"*

Vigilante states the obvious. *"Now they want her dead!"* Ghost and echo managed to prevent her from drowning. She's gotten away faster than her captors onboard could react. Clyde dragged her into the hidden entrance. The captive is free.

She splutters coughing out the murky water. Vigilante points out, *"Swallowing a little bay water is better than drowning."* Clyde remembers swallowing way too much water when he drowned. He finds himself in complete agreement with the spirit.

Her captors perceive her loss with the sympathy one would a drowned rat. They're confused, but still resolve to retrieve her dead or alive. They can't see where she sank. But think she should have come up somewhere… One says, *"It's impossible: she can't escape!"* Vigilant continues casting confusion into their minds.

Vigilante Spirit

17

Christie and Clyde

A strong powerful resolve propelled Christie the instant she saw her escape solution. Getting past their grimy grabbing hands alone was improbable. Making it underwater to anywhere without drowning was more than she could have accomplished. Safely within the dim treasure room her cheeks shine with tears. She demands, *"I'm smart enough to know I didn't get here by myself."* *"Who saved me?"*

Hearing nothing is Ok for now, but the human psyche needs more. Two bodiless companions understand her physical needs. Food and water for example. After much effort on their cavern lighting problem, Clyde and Vigilante manage to generate just enough static electric creating enough of a spark to ignite an ancient torch. Maybe it hung on the back wall for over a century just waiting to shine for her. Food and water are more difficult to supply. She won't last long without both. They think hard.

Squatting, she relives her escape, *"They almost stopped me!"* Looking around, *"This is the weirdest place I've ever seen."* Still, she knows this is better than being up there; she's safe now. The enormity of the treasure surrounding her still hasn't sunk in. A part of it soon will.

The monster who kidnapped and took her aboard made a futile effort to stop her by clawing wildly at her hair. His greasy fist didn't close quickly enough but she's missing a small clump on top. And then Christie was over and beyond his reach.

She nervously shivers and rubs the salt from her eyes. *"I 'm safe... but where in the world am I?"* She yawns in exhaustion. In the gloomy flickering torchlight; her eyes close and the question fades into exhaustion wondering *"...that light...?"*

Soon, sound asleep, Christie is comfortable. But has no idea she is held within a cradle of ghostly arms, much less one who decides he's in love. Clyde catches Vigilante's chuckle and responds, *"The way I feel is more like a father, or grandfather and that's all."* Christie has scant sense of any presence except her own. The last thing she would imagine: a ghost and spirit rescued her. Vigilante doesn't tell Clyde about his own frustration with incompatible physical structures. *"Like me Clyde, you're going to learn the hard way."* Clyde is just happy. He smirks, *"Don't bother me with reality."*

Though asleep she relives her ordeal in nightmarish detail. Screaming inwardly, her legs spasm and jerk. Clyde sings softly. She's soothed by his tune; one she wouldn't hear if she were still awake. But one whose melody will haunt her forever.

This soothes her into a deeper dream sleep. But the terrors of the day overpower her. Dreams become nightmares. In the worst, her body is sucked into a whirlpool. Its' force carries her to a vantage point where she looks more closely at her former captors. From here she sees them in a way they cannot see themselves. Her captors themselves are slaves whose souls are lost. They are the helpless victims of their own evil. Christie cannot bring herself to pity them, or their souls. These living pirates are mere cattle to demonic soul-eaters.

These wretches are oblivious to their plight as demons feed on their souls. Each demon cuts and cannibalizes strips. It leaves the living carcass a mere skeleton of who it was just before. She cringes and now understands a greater reality. One even her former captors can't see. A human soul can be mere sustenance for those even worse. Evil feeds on its' own. Those scavengers devour fools whose souls are rotted and depraved. Evil feeds on its' own.

Watching their horrible souls consumed, Christie fearfully peers inward at herself. She is nearly blameless. *"Who would have thought they were devils?"* Seeing the place where she so recently was imprisoned from her dream vantage point, she is shocked to see something enormous. A gargantuan creature hovers over it all. Resembling a dragon more than anything other, its' putrid green figure engulfs the entire ship and crew. And it feeds upon those who feed upon the living.

The horrific head of a beast towers well above the topsail. Huge yellow eyes see all. Its head turns to where she hides. A foul mouth parts baring reptilian fangs. Its' forked tongue probes in her direction as though tasting something unseen in the mist. She prays this is only a nightmare; she tries to wake herself up by twisting her body. Clyde holds her tightly.

Her panic lessens. Now, this is just a comfortable resting place. There will be time to mull it over later. Using a quiet telepathy, Vigilante shields her mind from those searching for her. Her vision, although a dream, could otherwise be a beacon for evil ones dwelling in that slimy pirate ship bilge. The spirit and ghost saved a person neither knew existed. Remarkably comfortable, Christie now descends into a quieter sleep.

Then abruptly, her nightmare returns. She cannot move. No matter how hard she kicks, her legs simply quiver. Her body is again wet with perspiration. But the green reptilian cannot come after her, because to try would force it to leave the ship. This is fortunate for Christie. For if it came she could not escape, even if she could move. Gasping …her heart races.

Over and over, her mind rehashes her escape. Something grabs her leg, and she is drowning again. Instinctively she holds her breath; she relives the terror. Panicked she tries to keep her lips sealed to keep from drowning. But she cannot and the devils in the bilge try to take her.

Mercifully, this episode is over quickly when Clyde shakes her. She wakes up looking at the flickering torch. She moves closer to its' yellow flame for any warmth and security it may render.

Afraid to doze off again, the girl again wonders where she is. She yells, *"Is anyone here?"* Still no answer. The torchlight flickers. She peers through the gloom seeing a cold dark room with so many sparkles she imagines she's seeing fireflies. She coughs up the last of the salty bay water. A line from something she once heard comes to mind, *"Anything that doesn't kill me makes me stronger."*

She shrugs and thinks, *"It's a corny thought."* Still, the knowledge gives her comfort.

Even in this crazy place she appreciates her freedom. *"I escaped those lowlifes!"* For the rest of her life she will always remember her captors as *"those lowlifes."*

Christie's cracked lips part as she announces to no one, *"I'm thankful to be here despite how creepy this place is..."* The ghost and the echo spirit sigh in relief. Clyde whispers to Vigilante, *"Her name is Christie!"* The girl stops and listens to something. Thinking she hears something... but what? But all is quiet.

Inhaling the ancient musty air deeply, fully awake and out of immediate danger, her emotions let loose. She cries hysterically. Fortunately, her noise stays within this hollow mound, one to appear as a slight rise beyond the old house. Vigilante channels her sobbing away from the ship towards the shore. Onboard senses only perceive the cries of gulls circling above the mainmast. None notice a lone raven high above. Not even the dragon.

Still the kidnappers are raging angry over her escape. If or when she reports them to authorities, they will be rounded up and prosecuted for serious crimes. Because she got away, at any time, they could be tracked down or even shot. The cowards crave release from their fear of being punished.

Of course, they knew all along that if caught they would be charged with stealing the ship. Little do they realize a worse fate awaits them just below in the bilge. Smugly, ancient pirate fiends who inspired them to commit these crimes lay unconcerned. For those foul creatures fully understand their own destinies are carved in stone much harder than ships' ballast. Nothing will alter the damnation in store for them. They have no pity for those mortal souls on deck. They are wasted by their greed. The mortal kidnappers are the prey.

For this isn't just a maidens' nightmare. Those oblivious living pirates' brains burn with desire for the girl, if only to shed her blood. She is the only witness to her abduction. If they can find where she is hiding they will have her dead or alive… preferably dead.

They endlessly run frantically from bow to stern screaming, *"Get her! Get her! Kill the wench!"* Their ghostly mentors spur them on from the very brink of hell. *"Get her! Get her!"* Their quest is folly. For their judge is He who judges all. And they are the mere pawns of the rotten scum of the bilge.

No matter how hard they look, they cannot see down beneath the waves into the dark cavern where she is hidden. For Christie rests beneath the water of the Chesapeake safely within the picaroon cache of Oriole. And the scum can't get her.

Those bilge scum seek to taste her fear. But they sense nothing beyond the noise Vigilante puts into their depraved minds. And now, the girl is no longer afraid. She only feels calm. They who would eliminate her have no way of sensing her. For, serenity is one emotion none of them feel nor will ever feel again.

The mortal pirates are lost souls. They each are possessed by the worst pirates who ended up in the old Chesapeake. These living are so deluded they believe they are the real thing as did Clyde. Disgusted by them, Clyde quips to Vigilante. *"These pirates are stupid lowlifes!"* He likes that word; he just learned it today hearing the girls' thoughts.

The mortal pirates turn to their ultimate source of knowledge. They pick up their electronic devices and try to get answers. The image of today, but only for them, is a dancing red devil with horns and a pitchfork. The red fiery image constantly fades and reappears sneering at them. The leader yells *"Up yours!"* Instantly their screens go dark.

Then they light up again; the devil sneers … *"This search engine finds 1,755,100 sites all leading to **devils' revenge**."* Nothing else appears and the links don't work..

In desperation, several even more frantic than the rest are determined to locate and eliminate their former captive. They don wetsuits to descend to where the girl was last seen next to the rail. Although four start pulling on gear only three get their gear on and crash face first into the bay. And obviously the rail has moved as the ship off and afloat.

Water in the masks is finally blown out, but they are only able to see a few feet. When she went under, one recalls seeing her go into something. He swims in that direction; the others try to follow. Now no one can see the eroded underwater passage. They are frightened and distracted when they come across two human skeletons glare up at them.

At one point one is just outside but can't see the opening because of the overhanging debris. And his drunken drugged haze makes him sick. He retches underwater as the wave motion rocks him side to side ... motion sickness compounded by stupor. He bolts and gurgles *"I'm out of here!"* Unwisely he comes up too fast holding his breath in severe pain.

Once hauled back up onto the deck, he grabs a stashed grenade. Without thinking he pulls the pin and drops it over the side. Having it in the first place was only one dim-witted idea of many. His first was when this fool and his friends stole this vessel. The hand grenade was his own idea. It wasn't inspired by the bilge pirates. He fumes, *"I'll teach her a lesson she won't forget."*

The exploding force of the grenade is largely absorbed by the water but stirs up the muddy bottom even more. A few stunned or dead fish float to the surface. Worse yet another diver is still underwater not far from the entrance to the room. The shock wave hits him hard stunning him. He floats to the surface with ears and lungs bleeding.

Almost as an afterthought, another onboard uses a gaff to snag the stunned divers' wetsuit and drags him in over the rail. His shoulder is cut; he bleeds onto the deck from his nose. No one tends to his wound. Little beneath the surface of the water can be seen from above because of the stirred-up muck. But the shock moves the ship. Finally, it rolls completely away from Oriole and drifts aimlessly out in the bay.

Below on Oriole, Christie remains safe in the hidden room. The house blocks sound of the turmoil. When she feels the shock wave of the exploding grenade, she recoils in fear. The explosion hits hard but not nearly as rough for her as for those closer to the explosion.

Poor Clyde, after living, dying and haunting is in love. Even though it's the love of a parent ready to fight for his child. His valor won't be tested right now. For, none of the wannabee picaroons dares to enter the swirling muck stirred up by the explosion. At last the boat moves away from Oriole and sets sail. Even muffled sound travels a considerable distance underwater. It attracts the attention of a Coast Guard patrol.

In answer to the girls' hunger and thirst, Vigilante alerts her to the only beverage still fit to drink. Wonderfully aged wine, though nice, isn't a complete diet even though vegan and organic. Nothing bothers her once she gets a bottle open for she isn't used to alcohol. Christie drinks until she's completely numb.

Clyde and Vigilante watch over her more like babysitters than avenging spirit and pathetic picaroon. Vigilante joins with Clyde's resolve to defend her against further harm. The faraway sounds of confusion still reach them. From bow to stern the pirate vessel still resounds with howls and curses. Christie will sleep most of the next day.

With impending danger past, her rescuers fret over the destiny of this wine gulping woman-child. For this place is very dim and chilly. And no human can survive here for very long on even the finest wine. They search for food and fresh water. Food is abundant as they propel freshly killed fish through the opening into the cavern. The grenade served a better purpose than the pirates might imagine by providing fresh fish..

When the girl first saw the flicker of the torch, she worried it would soon burn out. Another concern of Vigilante and Clyde is the slow depletion of oxygen consumed by the burning flame. It is a worrisome situation. Each time Christie falls asleep they blow it out to conserve whatever remains.

They agree to only work on the torch when she's asleep. They think they can anticipate when she will wake up. As soon as she stirs they light it. They are getting better at lighting it after Clyde pressure the old torch holder to a lower spot on the wall. They try to make the process appear to be seamless. Even in her increasingly woozy state Christie giggles, *"Somethings crazy about a burning torch in an underwater room!"* She asks anyone who might hear in a groggy voice, *"Hello, hello. Is anybody here?"* When no one answers, she yells several more times and gives up.

Her companions grin at one another chuckling ...*" If Christie were scared up on the ship, she'd be terrified witless if she knew we were right beside her!"* For the first time, they both laugh. Their laughter sounds like that of a Halloween haunted house.

Still unsure whether she is safe or in danger Christie worries and fueled by wine becomes furious. Peering into the gloom she thinks whoever saved her is hiding... Growing very curious, she scrambles to her feet to find whoever is pranking her.

Discovering paintings, she wonders if she's in a museum. Her toe strikes a heavy box. It opens to fine silverware; she uses it to clean the fish she thinks she just caught. The torch flame serves a way to roast her catch.

She looks for water. Finding none, she amuses herself by opening old barrels. It is an idea Vigilante has planted in her; it releases more trapped air. Then the reality sinks in.

"I'm surrounded by millions in gold and jewelry." The gold discloses its nature as she rubs two large coins together; their identity is unmistakable in the torchlight.

Amazement sets in when she discovers every direction taken simply leads to another treasure room. With nothing better to do, she does what women love to do … she starts gathering up jewelry. Her throat is parched with thirst. Finally, she sees another wine bottle then finds a way to release the wine using a sharp pin to puncture its' cork. Several more gulps and her jewelry bonanza is over, at least for today. Christie has just become the most richly adorned woman on, near and beneath the Chesapeake Bay.

As the demonic ship moves down the bay, those aboard have increased their misery. Those fleeing south strive to forget a present reality that's not much fun. Every living wanabee pirate onboard has been infected with the will of a bilgewater ghost. Except the leader. That one has the distinction of being possessed by the evil echo emitted from the final mind burst of one more evil. It happened as Strangler's soul was going to hell.

Even as the Strangler's soul experiences perpetual torment, his evil echo has found its' way into this evil crew of lazy youths. They were easy. He found them laying around without the strength to protect themselves from becoming possessed. Once Stranglers' echo coerced the leader, it was an easy matter to broker a deal with the old pirate ghosts in the bowels of the ship. In mindless lockstep, these fools are doomed to eventually follow Stranglers' own demonic soul down into the abyss. Gee plans to get around to each one. They exist in murkiness far gloomier than that of the room beneath Oriole island.

Vigilante Spirit

18

Gee's dilemma

Backlog is why the bilgewater pirates haven't reached eternal damnation. Gee hasn't gotten around to catching and descending them. For if the truth were known, both the Grim Reaper and hell itself are seriously backlogged.

Michael is Gee's true name. He likes to be referred to by the initial of his vocation because so many other angels have the same name. Gee explains to the few bold enough to inquire- *"Why Gee?" "Because ... there's only one Gee!"* And Gee claims he isn't slow to carry souls off to hell. *"I'm just prudent."*

He grumbles, *"All of those souls to take and just one grim reaper to do all the taking!" "Some make it to heaven; lots of others go to the other."* Gee thinks it's more important to give priority to those going in the heavenly direction. Having tasted the agony of hell with clients so often he despises visiting even to drop souls off. *"The longer I wait the less hurting for them and me both."*

He's very aware that he is treading on thin ice with the Man upstairs. *"The Boss really hasn't bothered me much about it, but I sense lots of trouble coming down."* He rolls his eyes upward. And he knows literally it means shoving a whole load of souls down there in a hurry. *"Each one I take down adds to how long I'm there and it sure ain't heaven!"* Gee hopes the Lord is sympathetic.

Angel gossip has it Gee leaves drowned pirates in a sort of cold storage until it suits him to use their damnation to fill up any slack time. He claims it's his mystical management system. However, he express-ships any wrongdoer who he feels intentionally hurt people. He really enjoys using the *"big boat"* to take down monsters like Strangler. Great plunges like the one he took Stranglers' ghost down on in the river make his job worthwhile. *"Serving him justice puts fun into my job."*

In his rare talkative moods, he says to anyone who listens. *"When all of the old pirates are in hell, I'm looking forward to escorting ponzi-schemers." "They create poverty for widows and orphans."* These who hurt the weakest, he cons into believing they are saved. But, when their turn comes, they are delivered to the worst part of hell. For now Gee must settle for catching up on his backlogged pirates, *"... because the Big Guy says so..."*

Back on the pirate vessel, not even abuse from their ghostly mentors can dispel the confusion of the schoolboy picaroons.

Finally, one takes the helm and gives the orders to take a deceptive course. Disgustedly, they make haste and continually alter course as the Coast Guard boat appears on the horizon. Zigzagging makes their guilt obvious to anyone watching.

The Coast Guard spots them. Observing the ships' eccentric course, and having heard the grenade go off earlier, they chart an interception. Both boats are of similar size however the Coast Guard engine is massive. An officer radios a command to stop. No one onboard the pirate ship is listening.

Vigilante and Clyde observe it's doubtful if the pirates will ever find their way back to Oriole. With the Coast Guard chasing the pirates they just need to help Christie survive her rescue.

Finding drinking water for Christie is a ridiculous problem because water is all around. It's just not the right kind. Drinking wine all of the time is taking its' effect on her. And she says, *"I want to talk to someone...anyone."* Clyde and Vigilante are shocked. Clyde demands, *"We've got to get her home before she tries swim for it!"*

Christie is a digital age girl and the only thing she can say looking through the ancient treasure. *"There's got to be a damned cellphone somewhere in this mess!"* Then she finds an extremely old bottle with French words, *Chateau neuf du pape.* She tries to open it.

"I need a drink." It takes considerable effort, but she gets the bottle open and after a gulp, *"This is even better than the last ones!"* And she takes another gulp. Christie thinks her mother must think she's dead. Tears fill her swollen eyes.

"Not bad!" After several more gulps the aged yet still palatable blend combines with her exhaustion. She completely forgets she has a mother and falls asleep. Later, when she wakes up, before her hosts can react, she becomes alarmed. *"It's black in here; the torch is out!"*

Instantly the harried pair has it burning again. She decides, *"I'm either blind or having another nightmare."* Then she feels the open bottle in her hands and sips… and sips… She passes out and topples off of her feet so fast poor Clyde nearly misses catching her. Christie snores so loudly the skeletons outside inch away.

Meanwhile, two worried minds desperately try to figure out how to get her back to dry land. Clyde moans, *"This child is somewhere between prayer and confusion."* Once she discovered the wine, with only cave mushrooms and burnt fish to eat she went from a scared young thing to a boisterous alcoholic. She can't remember any songs, so she invents them and sings words she makes up. They ruminate in unison, *"She's driving me crazy!"*

Her terrible voice motivates both even more after she wakes up. Happily, she remembers some of the words- *"Proud Mary keeps on rolling... rolling down the rivah!"* They endure, and both bounce with it. It's completely new to Clyde.

Back when he was alive, after taking care of business in town, Clyde remembers enjoying the company of young ladies. All of that ended when he started making money for these thieves. Then the pirates wouldn't let him out of their sight, even when he went to town for them. They said it was for his own good. Vigilante remembers something about girls but can't remember what it was... except Lucien.

Christie becomes irrational repeating... *"Who were those lowlifes?"* Answers come into her mind from her protectors. They find it quite easy to inject thoughts into her wine-soaked mind. *"Modern day pirates; born again picaroons!"*

"They're under the influence of ghosts of Chesapeake pirates from centuries past." Although drunk, but not stupid, it dawns on

Christie her benefactors are somehow communicating with her. Clyde recalls his mother once telling him, *"The more anyone drinks the easier they hear people one cannot see."* Vigilante saw people on the streets and alleys of Baltimore do it. And there weren't real ghosts or spirits talking to those poor folks.

She tells these unknown communicators she knows that her captors have no scruples about what they did to her. *"They kidnapped and would have murdered me."* She says, *"I was just sunning on the beach and somehow ended up on the boat!"*

"They're all crazy evil!" "I was about to be sold to somebody overseas." "Any of them who wouldn't go along with it would have walked the plank!"

Nothing creates male bonding like a mutual quest. This challenge involves valor. It is as cooperative a venture as any centuries old ghost and young echo will ever undertake. And Christie's tenth drunken rendition of *Proud Mary* is the final straw.

They decide to attract the first Coast Guard vessel anywhere near the vicinity of Oriole Island. The one pursuing the pirates has drawn a backup. Belatedly Christie's guardian angel is arriving. Vigilante welcomes her even though the angel left her for dead when she didn't surface. Vigilante notes- *"Not a very bright angel, but maybe she will take over once we get this poor kid back into sunlight."*

He is correct. The angel arrives when Christie finds herself riding on a floating log cradling her hungover head. From this day, the girl will receive top priority from her angel.

A newscast the day following her rescue:

Twenty-year-old Christie Kelly missing from Pasadena, Maryland for more than two weeks was found early today clinging to driftwood in the Chesapeake Bay by a Coast Guard patrol 20 miles south of Annapolis. The young woman is believed to have been kidnapped. She says she escaped from a stolen vessel. Ms. Kelly claims to have been taken against her will from Assateague Island. However, a check of her blood alcohol level when rescued found she was well above the legal limit. The woman claims to have been to Davie Jones' Locker and to have seen his actual treasure. No legal limit has been established under Maryland law for operating driftwood while intoxicated. Therefore, no charges are pending.

In other news…

Sadly, all the fine old wine she consumed back on Oriole triggered alcoholism Christie will find hard to lose. Several old diamonds and gold coins mysteriously arrived from where they were hidden soon after returning to her parents' home. Instead of telling her mom, she took them to a jeweler. His mutually beneficial offer was accepted.

The jeweler bought several of her large mine cut diamonds for a fair price, but less than he might have paid otherwise. Both were satisfied. Now Christie has more money than she can prudently handle in her delicate state of mind. Any new consumption of rare old wines is restricted by her budget.

Fortunately for her liver and other tender parts, she reacted with determination to treat her alcoholism. This was with the nagging inspiration of both her mother and guardian angel. DUI citations awarded by the Maryland State Police made her problem real.

She finally confides with her family. Her mother listens to her whole story starting with her abduction by pirates. It moves on to the ship, the cavern and to the invisibles who rescued her. Then, of course to the wonderful wine she consumed. She complains now she can't afford a decent drink anywhere.

Still Christie says nothing about gold coins she has hidden. She sells more coins and puts the money wisely into an account to be used someday when someone is willing to marry her. Hearing her whole story her mom just sobs. She follows her moms' advice to get help.

Upon her release from a major addiction clinic, and completing a Twelve-Step program, she is now cured of sunbathing and expensive wine. Someday she hopes to marry someone who wants to grow spectacular wine grapes. Unfortunately, her diet has caused problems with her teeth. Redeeming antique coins go a long way in getting her new teeth.

She thinks her perfect husband would be someone she could work with to create a perfectly blended red comparable to those mysterious ones she knew within the hidden room and not just another ho-hum *Cabernet Franc*. Even so she vows never to taste a drop herself. She plans to just sniff the bouquet of the finished product. Her sponsor disagrees.

Christie denies believing in ghosts to her mother now as a sign she isn't crazy anymore…. but admits to her shrink, *"I really do…"* The shrink admits defeat and refers Christie to an exorcist. The main thing she feels she gained from rehab is she will never go to a beach again instead she takes scuba lessons.

The shrink tried to reason with her over the nearly unbelievable events she keeps pointing out to him whenever they have a session. She told him, *"I may have been almost terminally intoxicated when they rescued me, but I wasn't so out of it I hallucinated the treasures down in that place."*

Gradually the good doctor comes to believe her. In fact, so much so he steps out of his professional role and explains to her he can no longer retain her as his patient. In response to her demand for an explanation, he explains he is swamped with education debt. He is willing to do anything including joining her in an expedition to find the sunken treasure if she agrees. She not only accepts his offer she does a cartwheel around his office.

While neither of them has a scuba license, she helps him enroll in her class at the college. He can only sigh as he incurs even more debt for the class and equipment. Their roles are reversed as he questions, *"Where are we supposed to get the money for the boat and equipment to locate your magic treasure?"*

She just gives him a look intended to show she is a woman of wealth. By now, she has him convinced everything she says is both weird and authentic. He just sighs and nods. After a month, they both take their open water examination and have the basic knowledge needed to stay underwater for an hour without getting the bends or drowning.

A whole different adventure will await them if they find the treasure cave and try to bring more treasure out. Who knows? Maybe her luck will hold out. Meanwhile, other events must now happen before Oriole and its' treasure can be approached by someone so hated as this fugitive from pirate injustice. Some who would harm her are still around. Hopefully, they won't be around when she gets there.

19

Bilgewater pirates

"Clean out the Chesapeake!" Gee receives a firm order from High Command. This rare event isn't something to be taken lightly. It doesn't get clearer; he needn't ask for confirmation. Because now, the *Bilgewater pirates...* Gee's hates them... are trying to break out

and run amok on the high seas as they did in their day. The problem is urgent.

A demon of the nether world is inspiring these depraved beings.... a scavenger from the depths of hell. The same vile beast from Christie's nightmare, who feasts upon the lifeless souls of those who cannibalize living wanabee souls. It's one so emboldened as to have captured Christie an innocent on-shore. Add to this menagerie, the Strangler's echo stirring the pot.

Grumbling: *"After centuries of ignoring their evil souls, I'm expected to evict all of these damned ghosts all at once just like that!"* Gee doesn't know where to start. The Big Boss isn't pleased with his backtalk and pretends not to have heard. *"What was that Michael?"* Gee replies in fearful awe with humility upon hearing his formal name. Quickly improvising, *"With your permission Lord, I would ask two very strange creatures for help?"*

He senses permission is granted because he hasn't been destroyed. Gee wishes his boss said something like *"Do what it takes."* Completely aware of Gee's feeble effort to maneuver him, the Lord doesn't answer. Gee feels the Lord obviously feels to say any more is pointless. But Gee doesn't dare think out loud. One never knows when one more word is one too many.

Satisfied he's received some level of permission, if only tacit, Gee sets out to enlist the ghost and echo of Oriole. He hopes in the future he will always …well nearly always…be answered quickly by The Lord. He listens … the cosmos is deathly quiet.

Clyde and Vigilante would be astounded if they had any idea an epic undertaking is about to encompass them. And they would be shocked if they knew the notoriety they've achieved by their rescue of a pirates' captive. Vigilante understands Gee's sense of justice because he saw the capture of Stranglers' ghost. Guilt-ridden Clyde would be terrified to be anywhere near the grim reaper.

If Gee were a living breathing being, sighs of relief would come from his chest right now. It was at least a temporary reprieve because the Lord did not use the word *"privateer."* To remove every privateers' ghost in this roundup would be more than he could handle.

Even with mystical power, capturing and shipping so many would be nasty. The Chesapeake was home to privateers who took their legal license to attack merchant vessels for just cause to criminal levels. Privateers turned rogue benefited from the inability of major powers to protect their maritime merchant ships. He very quietly reminds himself, *"I'm only to transport them, not their judge."*

Hearing nothing from on high, Gee demurs, *"After all I'm no St. Peter."* Nothing escapes Him. The Lord chuckles at the Grim Reaper's retort, *"Yeah, you don't want to be St. Pete either!"* *"You try telling all of those damned souls they didn't make it through the pearly gates!"* *"Your job is a breeze in comparison!"* The Lord says nothing more, both Saint Peter and Gee know it's time to get down to the business at hand.

Transporting souls across dimensions consumes most of Gees' time even though each occurs in less than a nanosecond. Because Gee is basically sympathetic, he rarely enjoys his work. But he carries each soul dutifully without hesitation to their appropriate journey's end. Except for those like Strangler, he despises them so much he doesn't hesitate when he has to take them. It's how he missed an echo breaking away as he apprehended Strangler's soul. The grim reapers' work will finally end on resurrection day... *"A day I hope will come soon."*

It's also repetitious. There are so many paths possible for human beings to follow and so many trail markers available. Gee doesn't understand why so few are willing to stay on the right course. The rules are easy to remember; there are very few. Even children have memorized The Commandments since the time of Moses.

The damned are dragged down into hell screaming and clawing, as did the Strangler. Most have self-serving reasons for mistakes placing them among the damned. Gee shudders. Sorting legitimate privateers from the true monsters would be outrageously difficult. He reflects, *"Just like death row convicts, privateers appeal until St. Pete says, Enough!"*

"It's not my fault!" *"No one told me right from wrong!"* Gee hates that excuse, *"I fell in with bad company ... it's just not my fault!"* All arguments lead to his same response, *"The bad company was good company until it fell in with you!"* No one accepts responsibility for their own evil deeds. Gee always says, *"You had a free will to do or not to do wrong."*

Occasionally a soul demands to know- *"Where's mom?"* Less often, *"Where's dad?"* It's always a shock for the hell-bound to realize their terrible parents and some friends are in a better place than where they are going. *"Your parents and peers are where they deserved to go."*

Now down to business: the command to exorcise the Chesapeake. It's a gigantic challenge. Entrenched as they are, means these demons are going to be hard to catch. To a man, they will be kicked out of their twilight existence for one more horrible. They must recall, this is consistent with the deal they made with the devil when they terrorized honest seafarers.

It doesn't bother the Bilgewater pirates they corrupted this crew of brainless youth. Now their payment is due they hope to cheat the devil. Not to be cheated, the devil slipped his dragon like demon through the wall of hades. Gee doesn't need The Lord to tell him this scavenger demon must go down along with the picaroons.

Wistfully, he hopes the demon will just follow its' supper in the bilge down to hell. *"I've never exorcised anything as big and bad as this dragon demon."* From heaven's gate, he hears St. Peter in a cajoling tone he picked up from a guy from New York, *"You can do it baby... you can do it...".." Just hang in there!"* All of heaven roars with laughter at their hero's' humor. Having let nearly all of heaven through his gates, St. Pete is truly popular.

By collecting souls for the Lord and Satan as well, unfortunately Gee manages to serve both. He got into this mess due to his rather ill-timed neutral stance long ago. It was way back when the fallen angels left the house of the Lord. If he fails to complete this task, Gee worries he too might be sent down.

For Gee, *"Go to the devil"* isn't something he takes lightly. So, for this mission to be successful, Gee is using the crafty general contractors' strategy. He will *subcontract* sending Chesapeake pirates to hell. If the project is successful he'll receive the credit.

But Clyde and Vigilante must voluntarily enlist; he can't force them to do this. He can offer them nothing. For Clyde is a pirate, therefore a part of this cleanup. As for Vigilante, there's no salvation for an echo. Echoes eventually just fade away or marry. *"What perfect scapegoats!"* He must be completely honest with them because he's required to be perfectly ethical in matters of heaven and hell.

The embarrassment of a loss against the picaroons is unthinkable. Especially one in which they stay where they are. Honesty is heavy on Gee's mind as he approaches Oriole to enlist help. Having beaten the pirates out of Christie, he hopes Clyde and Vigilante are agile enough to help him keep his own feet out of the fire. They really impress Gee.

They are unique in their dimension. He believes they can complete this mission. Consider if you will, to even Gee, an echo is only a human minds' runaway program. Some ghosts who don't believe in God, also don't believe people are really alive. These ghosts see their past lives as an illusion. Gee hopes Clyde and Vigilante aren't that weird.

To some, only what they experience at a given moment is real. From Gee's perspective, *"Living people are the caterpillar waiting to become a butterfly."* But Gee understands if he fails he can't blame Clyde or Vigilante. It's his responsibility to help them to succeed. Then he recalls Vigilante once gave him *the finger* and realizes he must treat this echo carefully or else he won't enlist.

Within the silent treasure cavern, Clyde and Vigilante hear the now distant sounds of the pirate vessel, but not the ponderings of Gee except one word. For some reason, the word *privateer* was so emotionally voiced within Gee' mind that it blew forward to where he was headed. Quickly they try to anticipate why he's coming.

Vigilante doesn't know much about privateers. Clyde explains: *"Baltimore was once an epicenter of privateer operations."* *"In addition to those with license to capture enemy merchant vessels, other Baltimore businessmen promoted and benefitted from this nefarious enterprise."* *"Scores of scoundrels who never went to sea still reaped privateer plunder."*

Wound up, Clyde continues to explain. *"Innocent life and property were often taken without mercy."* *"Many privateer supporters believing the cause was just saw the practice as patriotism."* He adds with a weird sense of pride, *"We picaroons were more than just privateers, but we too began with the idea of loyalty and became corrupt."*

Vigilante muses, *"Maybe those souls motivated by pure patriotism are without the stain of sin?"* In a placating tone, he says, *"Could it be that both sides of all conflicts include some innocents?"* Clyde ponders the idea then cynically discards the idea.

Pausing outside to listen, Gee also has confidence in the echo because of the way he works with the guardian angels. *"Whoever heard of an echo trying to seduce a guardian angel?"* Vigilante's sheer audacity captures his imagination. *"Hmm... So, how to convince them to work for me?"* He abruptly appears in the treasure room. Clyde feels his presence and turns green.

Both decide, *"He's coming for me!"* Instantly both the echo and the ghost pounce all over Gee. But then Vigilante stops short when he realizes this is the guy who ferried Stranglers' ghost down into the bottom of the river. He holds the ghost back beseeching, *"Clyde, this guy's Ok!" "Give him a chance to tell us why he's here."* Clyde releases Gee, but says, *"I know why; he's here to take me down!"*

Soothingly Gee reassures him. *"Clyde, if I came to take you today you would be gone by now."* Clyde's' nerves relax, but he makes a mental note of the chilling word *"today." "Ok, so why are you here?"*

Seizing the moment, Gee makes his pitch, *"I want both of you to help me in eliminating the evil polluting the bilge in the ship that was here." "Unfortunately, I cannot grant either of you a good future existence, or even to remain as you are." "Please consider, this is your best chance to make this world better than it would be."* For Vigilante, it's all Gee needs to say. The idea of a brawl in which those who are the victims can fight back is a great challenge and it's *on mission.* It ignites him.

His enthusiasm is contagious. Clyde accepts the challenge. And yells, *"I never liked them anyway."* Those listening from the distant bilge thought Clyde would always be their flunky. They begin jeering and hissing venom. Grumbling no living being can hear permeates the bay. Even the dragon stops and roars in defiance.

Gee continues in his most persuasive tone, *"This isn't going to be easy because we will fight spirits, picaroon ghosts, mortal pirates...and something indescribable"* Living pirates are a big problem for me because the grim reaper may not slay the living.

Seeing their obvious disbelief of his statement, he denies the urban myth he kills people. *"No matter how deserving I don't touch anyone alive... "Obviously, some angels and demons don't have this restriction."*

Contritely Clyde confesses, *"I was part of a truly foul bunch."* *"Those picaroons in the bilge can't help but have the same nature as they had when they were alive."* Gee agrees without condescension, *"Consequently one is no nicer once dead."* *"They remain malevolent but down and out of the way."* *"They were cruel and bloody when they terrorized hapless communities."* *"Their evil continues even* now in a ghastly state." "Though dead and damned, now they think they have nothing to lose."

Clyde is somber; Vigilante is pumped and jumping for action. Gee boasts, "I'll take everything they still have left." "They didn't count on me ever coming because they're embedded with mortals." "They have a nasty surprise coming when you show up."

They continue to listen. Neither interrupts again as Gee continues. "Even Strangler's ghost was a cinch for me because that criminal was a dirty coward." "In life, he never came near anyone nearly as evil as he was."

"Strangler bumped himself off with a little help from the devil in himself." "And then he ran into the spirit of a guy whose Harley he once stole." Vigilante is so focused on the upcoming battle the remark doesn't sink in. He's bouncing up and down like a fighter waiting for the bell.

Gees' briefing is interrupted. Green haze illuminates the room. Momentarily, they mistake it for a divine presence. But then are alarmed as another ghost enters. The first to recognize this intruder is Clyde. He says, "Gentlemen we have the agony of being in the *company of my old master... Captain James Farthing was the last proprietor of Oriole Island."*

The intruder settles down with them and pleads with condescending graciousness. *"Before anyone harshly judges me let them consider that I was a victim of my circumstance here." "Oriole sat helplessly where great powers and pirates landed." "If I had challenged any of them I would have been a goner."* They listen as he explains and then Clyde speaks.

Clyde challenges his former master for the first time ever. *"Why was I kept in this dungeon and forced to do all of your dirty work?" "I came here as an innocent child and died with you just outside of this room." "Why have you never expressed even a thought of comfort or consolation to me for the centuries that I have remained here forsaken and in misery?"*

Captain Farthing looks at Clyde with sneering contempt and proclaims:

" Clyde, my boy, you were my bastard of an ignorant wench of the kitchen above." "Your very existence would have ruined my wonderful relationship with my dear wife the fine lady of this home,"

"I treated you with tolerance, unlike the contempt which I had for your harlot mother."

"I shipped her out with the next crew to come after she suckled you to the time of your weaning in this very room." "Neither of you were entitled to my compassion." "Consider yourself fortunate to have lived as well as you did."

"Sir!" Farthing addresses Gee... *"Would you not agree my sins are so trivial in nature that they and I should be granted full pardon?"*

Gee gives no more answer to Farthing's ghost than does St. Peter to his question a moment later. In what might have been the blink of an eye, if one remained within Farthings' skull, Gee and Farthing vanish and are gone. A nanosecond passes, only the grim reaper returns from hell.

Gee sourly remarks, *"Clyde's father should have remained down in the muck haunting the crabs and eels!"* Vigilante and Clyde rumble in unison *"Amen!"* Gee, ghost and echo chant *"...One down Lord!"* From afar, the wretched Bilgewater pirates curse them. The three don't speak of the obvious. Afterwards, none here will make mention of the Farthing matter. Quickly, their minds return to the upcoming battle. They plan their frontal attack for the morning. Gee mumbles, *"One down Lord."*

Clyde reserves any further anger for those onboard for when they are engaged in battle. They stalk the vessel. It's the *Copperhead*, named after a notorious native viper. He pledges it will be Farthing's old friends who will feel his bite.

Gee cautions them as to the nature of those to be vanquished. *"Be alert, remember, these are the most cruel and cowardly of all who plagued these waters."* Clyde feels shame. *"They were so appalling they earned contempt from both the kings' men and innocent colonials as well." Even their benefactors were disgusted."*

Intentionally pumping up his small band, Gee roars, *"They will all go to hell if I have to drag each of their rotten souls one at a time down that hole!"* Clyde and Vigilante gaze down a flaming vortex that opens. A sick gurgling moan issues from hell as though belching after swallowing the dirty Farthing soul. It resonates across the bay, Even the dragon winces in dread.

Destroying only deceased pirates actually applies to ghosts as well. Clyde is a human ghost. Consequently, the quick are off limits for him. Without a conscious thought, loud enough for him to hear, both Gee and Vigilante separately wonder if Clyde may have been the naivest individual ever to bear the picaroon label. Then Gee remembers *both* were derived from human beings but to prevent confusion   says   nothing.

All three head for battle upon Gee's mighty vessel. The El Muerte bears down upon the Copperhead without warning. The wanabee pirates can sense but can't see their danger. The Copperhead crew decides to outrun them. This isn't going to happen because Gee's huge ship was designed to conquer man o wars at great speed. Such trivial quarry as Copperhead can't outrun them. on the other hand, the Copperhead has outmaneuvered the faster Coast Guard pursuit in the fog.

His old companions barely comprehend their young storekeeper is coming at them so fortified with sheer vengeance. The damned bilgewaters release their grasp on the souls of the crew realizing they are being attacked by other immortals. *"They'll need everything they've got left for the battle."*

Bilgewaters haunting the human crew were desperate to stay close to human warmth because ghostly existence is sterile and cold.

Their anxiety and anger peak as the gap of blue water between the ships lessens. Ancient weapons are readied.

Nearby crabbers head for home mistaking the boom of El Muerte sails catching the wind for the thunder before a mighty gale. When they return, their traps will be full. Crabs dart into the false security of the wire traps to avoid whatever is going on. Ospreys deserting their nests also seek cover. The natural world knows something bad is about to happen.

Other sailing ships can't compare to the El Muerte. For it dominates the seas. The Coast Guard patrol boat lost track of the Copperhead. For its' radar image is blocked by Gee's ghostly vessel. Even radar can't see through ghost ships. Gee's comes about in front of the pirates becalming the wind in its' sails. The Copperhead tacks to regain the breeze. But this clears the radar image for the Coast Guard. They resume pursuit from afar.

The El Muerte, an ultimate predator, opens this eerie battle. Weaving back and forth Gee screams, *"The fight is on!"* In response, all turn to face his wrath. Gee clearly sees every bilgewater just in front of the El Muerte bow. He fires a virtual cannon shot straight and true through the pirate hoard. Though unseen by those among the living dimension it's a thunderclap and lighting strike at the heart of the vessel. The warning is mandatory. Only those living can repent; the rest are hopelessly hellbent. Instantly the Copperhead is becalmed and dead in the water.

The alive onboard are oblivious as the El Muerte cannonball is in the ghostly dimension as is the ship from whence it blew. The Bilgewater pirates in the hold clearly feel its' pain and know the battle is on. Grabbing ancient sabers and muskets they rush to repel the boarding party.

Only ghouls accept Gees' challenge. The rest of the Copperhead crew doesn't understand why they've stopped. Picaroon ghosts abandon their possessed wannabee pirates. Several try to get Copperhead underway by trying to push the living overboard. To no avail, although a strong breeze fills her sails The Copperhead doesn't move. The one who captured the girl grumbles bitterly, *"Grounded again, damn it!"*

Ancient ghostly cutlasses flash as if in flames as the three bilgewaters swing over boarding El Muerte. They slash and attack savagely attempting to resist their demise. Should they overcome

Gee, there will be no quarter asked or given. That prize would be a lasting testament to their fierce savagery.

The only echo spirit aboard Copperhead is that of Strangler. His ghost is in hell with his morbid soul. Vigilante slashes his echo into many pieces and slam-dunks nearly all into a vortex to the same destination with the Strangler's other pieces. Vigilante relishes this moment, but like Gee did back in the Patapsco, he misses the vortex with just the tiniest sliver of the final slice of Strangler's echo.

It does seem strange now, Vigilante learned karate watching cable television back at the house with Lucien. The rest of his opponents, ancient pirates, have never seen martial arts. Their ways were effective once, but no contest today. Vigilante is unbeatable as he propels Clyde's thrusts against even living wanabees.

Thugs on the backstreets of big city have also taught him technique. He fights effectively through Clyde and Gee. Their strategy session back on Oriole included sparring practice. Clyde's strikes are accurate.

It was impossible for these Bilgewater opponents to anticipate a battle with martial arts... They have no defense from an art never a part of their culture. They are defeated by Vigilantes' simple white belt moves. When he parries a thrust, the attacker is propelled directly into the vortex to hades. With each Bilgewater thrown into hell the mighty three chant- *"One more Lord!"*

Gee challenges the cowardly dragon. They stop chanting the score during the Grim Reaper's attack because this demon isn't on the list. Gee's specter is slashed apart from chin to heels and flies apart only to reassemble. Gee has the dragon just where he wants this slimy vulture. Nearly exhausted, Gee makes a move that dislodges the dragon from its' hold on the main mast.

The dragon refuses to follow its' prey down the vortex. It's repeatedly attacked by the mighty trio. They try to electrocute it using the Copperhead's meager system. Copperhead's electrical output is no match for the dragon as it slips free leaving the hell bourn and damned to their own misery. Without traction, it's sent sailing off over the eastern shore peninsula towards the ocean.

Clyde battles the wanabees visibly. These jaded mortals can't see the reaper or echo. No one can see the fleeing dragon. As for mortals, the Coast Guard simply keeps collecting drowning wanabees from the misty bay. The dragon has a new victim in sight.

Upon hearing a huge noise, akin to a jet breaking the sound barrier, Gee knows the dragon has left this bay for good. Believing the demon is gone. Gee says, *"Hopefully the hole in this dimension will close behind him quickly."* Gee plans to follow up later when he's not so busy as he says, *"dumping trash."*

As they pitched pirate ghosts into the swirling tunnel to hell the triumphant three count singing out, *"One more in hell Lord." "Then finally, they're all in hell Lord..."* Having completed the mission; the victorious trio is jubilant. As the conveyor to hell plunged on, it created lightning all of the way from Baltimore to Norfolk.

Onboard the pirate vessel the few mortal wannabee pirates not nearly drowned simply surrender to the wind with no idea of who to fight. Finally, the mist lifts and these few are greeted by the U.S. Coast Guard. The wanabees are fortunate to be alive.

The Coast Guard wonders how it lost the Copperhead. First, it was on radar and then it disappeared. Very confused former wanabees wish to be anywhere but in chains aboard the Coast Guard boat.

Gee Locks his attention on the hapless wanabees, Soon they are in front of a judge. The final phase of their capture is at hand.

They are charged on two counts. The Copperhead is stolen; these punks meet the description of a rescued girl describing her kidnappers.

Obviously, The Coast Guard doesn't sense or acknowledge the El Muerte, for it's of the realm of ghosts, angels and spirits. The Coast Guard is elated at their capture. It takes the stolen Copperhead in tow. The wanabee pirates are formally charged with boat theft and kidnapping rather than piracy.

Jubilantly, Vigilante and Clyde return to Oriole. Arriving, Clyde and Vigilante disembark.

Vigilante Spirit

20

Liberation

Once more the mighty El Muerte moves its' toxic cargo, The bow tilts down.... down into fathomless depths to a dimension beneath the deepest sea. Sooner than any would wish for, El Muerte and Gee will return to Oriole Island. Finally, the damned have descended to the destination of the devils. For these souls are lost forever. Except one...

The Grim Reaper is triumphant. Those diseased souls, once the worst of the Chesapeake, are where they belong. He returns to his normal routine of shuttling everyone from bankers to bandits to eternity. He cringes recalling the only incomplete element capable of ruining his great accomplishment. Unfortunately, he can't overlook this last task. The Boss's command, *"All of the pirates..."* He must deal with the Clyde.

Their battle won, Vigilante and Clyde are euphoric. They hover within a cove of their Oriole cavern savoring victory with satisfaction. Then the echo says. *"There's no tomorrow... for now!"* With his spontaneous utterance of *"for now"* he inadvertently revives the ghosts' anxiety.

Clyde's euphoria instantly plummets to hopelessness. A silent thought is far more difficult to invalidate than even a soft spoken one. Their imaginations run wild. They moan and groan but can't stop sharing images of poor Clyde burning and thrashing about in hell. Too much communication is a curse. Clyde prays for redemption: Vigilante is humbled because once more he is reminded an echo's prayer is without meaning.

They have little time to agonize because Gee appears. His role as a comrade in arms is over. Gee stands rigidly professional in his deadly role as the grim reaper. He offers a formal statement of gratitude for their help: *"Ghost Clyde Farthing and Vigilante Spirit, I will always be personally grateful to both of you for your assistance to me in doing the work of The Lord... however, His command was explicit."* Clyde realizes this is the first and last time anyone has recognized his surname is *"Farthing."*

Still formal, but in a softer sincere tone, *"You may recall I made no promise of clemency." "Do you recall that?"* All three recognize nearly apologetic questions need no reply. A moment of silence…no need for thought or spoken word. A slim bond of comradeship remains strong among these warriors. Just as well for each is too numb to fight the inevitable.

Poor Clyde has matured immensely since that first day when he and Vigilante tried to scare each other away from this place. Clyde is unnerved. Still he appreciates his only friends. *"Please accept my appreciation for allowing me to join you in the greatest adventure of both my life and afterlife." "Gee, if it has to be, let it be you." "At least I'm going to hell with a friend."* Adding, *"I appreciate your attachment of the Farthing name to mine." "I did not think my parents were married?"* Gee says, *"They weren't."" Your biological father was a bastard too."" So I took the Farthing name from him and deeded it you." "You are the only true Farthing now."* Vigilante decides it's too complicated and shrugs it off.

Clyde moves to the entrance saying, *"Let's go!"* Then adds, *" Before I change my mind and use some of Vigilante's fancy fighting on you... I just might kick your butt...if you have one."* Disregarding the dire nature of the moment, they laugh so hard the old torch on the wall is snuffed for the last time.

Almost sympathetically a bottle of bubbly pops its' cork in the corner. Vigilante shows the ghost and reaper what the Baltimore guardian angels taught him... how to sniff the bubbles. This delays Clyde's trip for a bit longer. Finally Gee and Clyde head out on their journey.

Gee compliments his passenger, *"Clyde, you are going out with style!" "None of that quick down the hole to hell crap the way your wretched father went." "You are going first class on El Muerte the way a significant hard case pirate travels."* Vigilante had shown them how to celebrate after each victory over the pirates. They give one final celebratory high-five.

As Clyde and Gee board the El Muerte, Vigilante starts fading considerably. His limited energy supply is running low. When he erupted in a blaze at birth his total energy allotment was generated. Recent exertions, such as the Copperhead incident have prematurely depleted his force. He knows of no way to generate more now, and it's nearly gone.

Watching from the helm, Gee's afraid Vigilante will be embarrassed by fading out in front of his buddies. He approaches Clyde in a gentle manner and places his hand on the sad old pirates' shoulder. *"We need to move on."*

Vigilante rambles incoherently as he fades, *"Clyde, because this may be the only time I've ever been anywhere with true friends...Good luck in hell... it's amazing I can't even go where you're going!"* He grieves that he is about to fade into nothingness surrounded by this dreary pirate treasure...and that he will never exist again.

Because echoes are just a by-product of human intelligence, much like a computer program, there is no paradise or hades for them. For heaven and hell are strictly the ultimate possibilities for human beings. Vigilante laments his legacy of nothingness...

"If only I could just pray..."

Clyde understands from centuries of confinement in this gloom that being here forever is even worse than the hell where Gee is taking him. The ghost communicates with his friends quietly savoring each remaining moment and wonders whether his body or his spirit could possibly hurt worse down below than it did here. For, the idea of eternal solitude in the largest storehouse of the wealth of this world is sheer hell for Vigilante Spirit..

The spirits' energy level dissipates even further. Vigilante somehow is remembering things he never knew. Something tells him *Spirit*, his father had pursued *Gin*, his mother. She was the very first possible mate who attracted Spirit. They were desperate spirits who clung together at the very end of their beings.

Vigilante never hurried to lose his independence. Now in these final moments he feels the nagging miserable loss of those wonderful moments with lovely Lucien. Gee and Clyde both moan at his delirium. At the same time, much like people watching a soap opera, his torment distracts them from their own.

Disregarding these happy and sad memories, he knows that his time in this world was a success. Having lost the angel he loved; he wouldn't have wished to marry anyone else. *"Why spoil things?"* This resolute mindset rests right behind the *"Do good"* mandate etched within.

He declares to the universe, *"I loved the angel Lucien and the sunlight that shone down upon her beauty."* Seeing his consciousness drift and nearly gone, Gee and the ghost quickly move away. Here in Oriole they all know the gloom of its' darkness becomes unbearable alone. And now the final moments for echo and ghost are nearly gone. The grim reaper is sad. Then a bolt of reality strikes the grim reaper. Clyde's parents weren't married, and his biological father is nameless and is filling the spot in hell reserved for Clyde. *"His transit documents are flawed!"* *"His father wasn't on the list and is as evil as any."*

As adventure and comradeship shared pass, Vigilante knows he is in his terminal fade. Because spirits can't shield their worries he unwittingly admits to all the angels, ghosts and spirits on the Chesapeake he's afraid of being… *"alone without Lucien!"*

Echoes never completely die. Unattached echoes, like soldiers of old, just fade forever... infinitely growing dimmer. He had no reserve for his tryst with Lucien and his battle with the pirates. Sparking and sparring have drained his vitality. If Vigilante had prudently just followed his directive, he could have retained enough strength to go on until something unforeseeable happened. Like countless foolish young men, he dallied.

His final thoughts return to the injustice befalling Clyde. Vigilante faintly croaks out at Gee, *"He fought for you!"* A backward glance from Gee makes the dying echo think his demand of clemency falls upon deaf ears. The ghost instantly understands he has overstepped his bounds.

Clyde smooths away any embarrassment Gee feels by saying to Gee *"I always knew my day to answer would come."* *"But our spirit friend here can benefit from some of my energy?"* The grim reaper concedes to the bequest with sarcasm, *"It is easy to be generous when you don't need it where you're going!"*

Gee immediately regrets his thought and is ashamed. Vigilante defends Clyde. *"How many others have ever faced pirate hell worrying about anyone except themselves?"* Gee realizes he's fighting a losing battle and has had enough. He gently moves Clyde from the worst area of the El Muerte. Old ghost and Vigilante bid a final sad farewell and on cue the mainsail of the ship to eternity once again captures the wind. Gee ignores Vigilante and grasps the huge ships' wheel.

Vigilante senses the bulging sails trap the wind and brusquely thrust the vessel forward. Like a lion, it leaps away from Oriole. The exotic beauty of this mystical relic of the seas is wasted on his cheerless apathy. As the bow stabs the mist its' thrust builds.

Vigilante awaits a final savage bow plunge. One carrying poor old Clyde into the abyss of hell. Grinding horribly this great vessel of destiny strains forward and slightly downward awaiting the power of the wind in its' sails… At this very moment, the ships wheel is wrenched from the hands of the reaper. The El Muerte tilts upwards exactly forty-five degrees. A greater power than the grim reaper has charted a far better journey for the mighty El Muerte.

Golden sunlight reflects from the gliding vessel. As it's bow rises heavenwards it takes with it a foaming spiral of glowing white haze. Supporting waves lift it into the clouds over Oriole. El Muerte rises in a silver column of froth. Clyde grasps his change in fortune. The tired old ghost kneels in prayer upon the deck as it slowly rises into the clouds.

His knees are bent in supplication but with his head is erect and proud. Giving thanks to The Lord for his redemption, his arms reach out to embrace his heavenly destination. In a few moments, only a trace remains over Oriole. A lone white gull soars within a rainbow.

A historically unique moment of mercy has happened as El Muerte conveys old Clyde to his deliverance. Although the echo is left behind he has stopped fading. With renewed strength Vigilante Spirit knows Clyde's gift of vital energy was passed to him. A grateful Vigilante is restored to his full measure as an echo spirit. If he chooses, he can go on to meet another. Or he can go once more as a lonely avenging spirit on missions to do good.

He peers upwards to where Gee and the old pirate passed into the clouds. So long as he can see their passing he can feel their warm glow of friendship. It's a new day for this echo.

Although happy, Vigilante is a very much wiser spirit. Again, he has missions to accomplish and love to pursue. Feeling almost foolish, Vigilante flows back up the bay to the mouth of the

Patapsco. It was there he last felt the light of the sun and the joy of love.

Approaching the big house, he is met by Dog. It sees Spirits' son and greets him. Dog sits before him on Angela's front porch. Understanding more than any dog should know he fails to sound an alarm. Vigilante understands Lucien is aware he's here; still she ignores him.

His fantasy of a reunion with Lucien crumbles; he feels clobbered by her again. Just behind the doors of the Gold house, Angela and Hiker are deeply in love. Vigilante is of no use to either now they have found each other. Their guardian angels, including the almost sober Roman, avoid thinking of him pretending he never existed. It stings him because he sees Lucian's' pretense. He is ticked off. *"This is deliberate because she knows I sees through her."* She pretends he is lost to her forever. *"Why?"* The answer comes from the least obvious source.

The dog follows him back down to the river wagging his tail and then turns back. Dog has a home and a family now. After leaving him dog trots back up the hill thinking, *"If he only knew what I know."* For once, a dog knows more than an echo. Dog looks out at the retreating echo from the porch; the dog woofs *"Ho ho, you can't guess what I know!"*

Vigilante echo hears it in the distance and decides *"That damn dog is way too smart!"* And hearing the dog laugh at him, he suspects there is something he doesn't know. *"I will worry about it another time."* I've learned my lesson and I'm free of them all: dog, lovers... and all the good folks in the house on the hill." Making a last ditch effort to get the pooch to tell, he yells, *"it's because I almost faded out and Clyde had to save me!"*

Dog snorts, cocks his leg on a daisy saying, *"Nope!"*

Vigilante flows back down to the river. Coming across two boys who aren't in school where they belong he stops to watch them fish. *"If they only knew just how close to the hole to hell they are they would hightail it out of here as fast as they could."*

Disgusted, Vigilante floats back along the river down towards the Chesapeake. Passing beneath the old viaduct, the futility of coming back sinks in. Any thought of visiting the house on the hill was absurd. He's so amused by the coincidence of these boys fishing at that very spot where Strangler was taken; he pauses to see if anything happens.

Vigilante Spirit

21

Passage

It's exactly where Gee seized Strangler's ghost and took it
abord. There's nothing to suggest it's an unusual or dangerous place.
Two hoys fishing from the riverbank bench are oblivious to
everything. Like generations of truants since the beginning of
modern education, fishing's more fun than school.

In their wildest dreams, nothing like the capture of a murderous fiends' soul would ever happen along this nice place. They lean back waiting for the fish to catch themselves. Their only concern: a truant officer might catch them playing hooky. Their plan: just throw back anything caught and run like hell through the sticker bushes. Same plan if anyone demands to see their nonexistent fishing licenses.

At the spot where Strangler's soul descended, there's no sign anything.. The sleek El Muerte left no trace as it passed through the silted riverbed. Vigilante recalls it happened exactly where the road meets this bench. He's amazed and wonders, *"How did they manage to be here?"* This spot is precisely where the truants' fishing lines enter the water. One feels a nibble, a crawfish toys with his bait.

He tries to set the hook; nothing's on the line including the worm. He slips another night crawler onto the hook and casts. By chance, his sinker hits that spot the ship passed through. He gets an enormous hit; his tackle is gone… the fishing rod is so hot he throws it in the river. The truants panic and run for school right through the thorns.

Another unseen spectator has been watching.

Watching Vigilante and the fleeing boys from a chimney, the raven muses, *"A path to hell is easier opened than closed."* Then flutters to a branch high above the echo. She's just come from telling Lucien her echo is back. The angel wants to keep things with Vigilante how they are and won't see him.

The echo moves on; something else follows. The dog sneaks along assuming he's invisible in the brush. It's clandestine stalking might have been shielded by the abundant riverside overgrowth. Except, its' wagging tail gives it away. Realizing he's spotted, Dog crashes down the hill barking. Vigilante is annoyed at this disrespect. *"What do you want?"* It glares at Vigilante as though he's crazy. He clears his throat with a raspy growl and says. *"I have news of interest to you."*

Dog announces, *"Hiker and Angela got hitched over at the church last week."* *"Not only did they pledge their eternal love before the altar, more importantly they promised I will always have a home with them."* Impatiently the echo asks, *"Why are you telling me?"* Dog explains, *"As their family watchdog, it's my job to warn you that you don't live here anymore."*

"So, stay away!" *"Who gave you so much authority?"* As Vigilante nicely scares the ticks from the animals' fur, Dog points out the obvious. *"We fetch newspapers and ducks when people are too tired or lazy to pick up their own."* *"We watch over them and their property by growling at our first sense of danger, though not necessarily theirs."* *"Therefore, I'm warning you I will do my duty as their watchdog and ..."*

The echo points out the obvious; he is not human. Dog decides Vigilante is extremely naive. But continues without emotion, *"This is how I now earn my living."* This insults the echo as it implies he's a threat to the newlyweds.

Annoyed with Dog's smug attitude, the echo replies, *"Maybe your name still should be Dumb Ass!"* Dog growls sarcastically, *"Oh, yeah?"* *"Look at you down here and me up there."* *I'm high, warm and dry."* *"You've been so wet since she dumped you, that you think you're a shark."* Vigilante laughs, *"Bite me!"*

Concluding all he planned to say, he barks a *get lost* *"Woof"* and trots back up to the house along a faint deer trail. Hearing his dog, Hiker peers out of a window. Turning back to where Angela lay sleeping, he climbs back into bed forgetting to let his dog in for the night. Dog flops on the front porch with resignation as his hungry ticks waddle back up the hill to him, *"It's going to be a long cold night   out   here!"*

Vigilante regrets the moment the words *Dumb Ass* crossed his mind. But it's clearly impossible to retract either insult. Its' sting has just cost him a canine friend. And, with no friends left anywhere he drifts further up the river. He reflects, *"Maybe Dog isn't so stupid after all."* Helplessly, its' exhausted ticks tumble back down the hill.

Moving along his mood improves. Vigilante's self-esteem soars when from both sides, he's greeted by a cheering white mist of ghosts. One explains they all watched his friend Clyde's salvation with enormous interest. Hopefully, his good luck will rub off on them.

No one thought old Clyde could make it upstairs; all thought he would follow the bilgewaters down to hell. These ghosts watched close up. with terror as Gee took Strangler from here Prior to Clyde's salvation. These ghosts didn't like the idea of echo spirits, not even heroic ones. But Vigilante is special.

As for why they are wearing sheets tonight, one explains that most ghosts like the sheet idea. It provides substance and decency on those rare occasions when they appear to people." *We really don't need to wear white sheets, but everyone imagines we wear them, so we do when we want to be noticed." "It's not really about trying to be ghost kosher; it's sort of our thing." "Sheets are ghost traditional."*

Vigilante starts receiving a spooky version of the old-time ticker tape parade. The contingent from over in Severn even brought bits of dryer lint to fling into the breeze overhead as he passes. In his honor, they project themselves against a swinging footbridge artistically. They call it their- *Arch of Triumph.*

He says, he's honored, and a bit astonished to learn he has their respect. Though not echo spirits, ghosts are as near to a peer group as an echo spirit has. Passing beneath their arch in heroic style he waves to all as a great dignitary. While savoring the moment, still he doesn't dally. This is nice of them, but as with the crew of the Copperhead, some of these won't make it upstairs. Misdeeds were done and will be accounted for in time.

He stays above the center of the narrowing river. The ghosts respectfully maintain a discrete distance, so he doesn't feel threatened. They could easily overwhelm him. In awe, they cheer as he passes. The contrast of this reception to the rejection he felt just downriver is bizarre. But these aren't self-important guardian angels. They are just poor souls desperately wanting to go to heaven.

Most were once nice people. He senses hostility from one though. He was the dope dealer mistakenly snuffed by his own. His former associates had money missing and thought he was skimming. It was during the confusion when the guardian angels played Robin Hood. Drug money vanished when the angels deposited their cash into Angela's checking account. This sorry fool died because they thought he took their money. Then of course by the time anyone realized the angels thievery it was too late for him.

Their funds neatly financed Angela's transition into her home on the hill. But this naked wretch is worse off for their deed. He will haunt this place for centuries before Gee bothers with him unless there's a fuel shortage in hell... which isn't likely.

Each recalls it well: the echo with glee, the doper with fury. Vigilante disrespects this peddler of addiction. It strikes him as hilarious this mixed-up ghost still thinks he's baring his teeth in a vicious snarl. The doper can't see himself and couldn't even if he had a mirror. Here he is as naked as the moment he was born. If he could he'd realize he is nude, and his missing teeth are in the sewer back at his old corner. Neither earthly necessity followed him to this moment..

Two ghostly nuns from the old convent up on the hill try to save his shameful figure further embarrassment. They signify at him sternly with feigned anger. And one snaps a wet towel stinging his bare virtual posterior. His fury turns to fear. Gee offered to take them up a long time ago. *"We aren't quite ready yet." "We'll let you know soon."* That was years ago.

Both sisters wield brass edged yardsticks, the symbolic staff of their   generations' nuns. But to be sure, a butt swat won't hurt him now nearly as much as it would when they were alive. This dopey specter hasn't been dead long enough to understand the folly of his threats or even theirs. Abruptly he realizes his naked toothless state. His imaginary fingers spread to protect his former private parts. He looks down and can't see anything.

It's downright funny to the echo because he knows these sisters fully realize their bluff. These pure and lovely souls of The Lord are intimidating just by their virtue. And this unhappy ghost will speed up his meeting with Gee unless he quickly adapts to his loss.

Vigilante reflects to the nuns and the doper, *"Sisters, should he dare to be rude the Grim Reaper will have him before he remembers where he lost his pants and false teeth."* The nuns smile knowingly and cover the fool with a sheet. His day will come.

Flowing away from their area, he exhibits his transparency of mission. To reward their kind thoughts of him, he lets them all emotionally share in the salvation of Clyde. He deliberately allows his thoughts to relive their collaboration in defeating the pirates. He need not embellish for the affair was more amazing than anything he can invent.

Those of the white mist love his tale of Clyde. For, although a picaroon and damned he made it to paradise. Every soul here laughs and cheers as he describes Clyde's' infatuation with Christie.

Vigilante overhears several ghosts plan to sneak over to a nearby inn. Many here were once fun-loving scamps who stayed a bit too long at life's' parties. Their sin was, they neglected responsibilities. But they had a great time.

With the exception of the toothless lad, Vigilante has captured everyone's admiration. In this dimension without privacy everyone wants to know him. Everyone but the one he hoped to see. Lucien stays home…

He shares his regret about Buzzardville with these admirers. *"How can I atone for my big disaster?"* His audience hums sympathetically, for most have also come with serious mistakes. With thoughts of contrition pouring from his penitent mind these have the consolation of knowing they aren't alone in their imperfections.

With lessened anxiety, they bid their goodbyes and return to their haunts. Some wanting to keep the party going search for someplace to party where ghosts might be welcome. The nuns tow the newly sheeted former belligerent up the hill by his new sheet. He'll wear sackcloth, rather than a sheet after today.

Even with this echo spirit nearby, many ghosts continue to believe life on earth is little more than a transitory state of soul. Thus, if people are unreal, an echo spirit can't be real either. It's perplexing to be a ghost. Because, in some small way Vigilante has helped them feel the potential of their redemption. He decides perhaps giving hope to these sad wanderers was also his mission. He flows farther up the river.

And finally, he turns away from the source of the Patapsco. A dog here left him sad; agreeable ghosts made him happy. Above in an overhanging tree. Vigilante sees only a sleepy looking raven, resting upon a branch. He gives it no mind and heads overland to a wretched town he loathes.

The echo comes to the bridge. It was here Hiker recently fled to the river. He has no reason to stop at Buzzardville. Vigilante is drawn to where the old barbers' son stands with fishing pole peering into the stream. The son still tries to figure out what happened the day their shop window was broken, that day they shot an innocent man. Guilt overcomes the echo.

Unexpectedly, the greatest largemouth bass to ever graced this stream eyes a washed-out worm reeking with Aqua Velva. Worm and hook seduce the bass. With terminal insanity, its' huge mouth sucks down hook, line and sinker.

For many decades, this bass, after preservation through the art of taxidermy will grace the Buzzardville barbers' wall. It will glare down upon each new generations' patrons. That hook once plated in gold shall hang from the huge lip of this aquatic beast. A lip on the face of a poor bass who still can't believe he bit that smelly hook.

Buzzardvillains will listen in awe to heroic tales of the battle and landing of this venerable bass. They will honor this legend of cunning and yes, even courage, in having conquered and landed the newly famous *Bass of Buzzardville*. Vigilante accomplishes one step of his restitution.

On to another, Vigilante follows the neglected old road to the chapel. He arrives at the weedy graveyard with its' forsaken stones. This place remains as dreary as it was back on the bad day Hunter grabbed his fathers' stash from beneath the altar stone. Vigilante searches for only one solitary soul.

He isn't hard to find; his resting place has considerably less weeds than other graves. But here is no stone bearing the sorrow of a lost loved one. Father-robber and hunter-son lay flat with nothing to do and nowhere good to go. Plain wooden posts poke up in gloomy contrast to neighboring old grey tombstones.

As for neighbors, the preacher and teacher, their legend might read: *Not one teardrop has fallen, nor one flower was lain, for either for many a year*. Regardless of their noble deeds, all are forgotten.

They who once mourned have come and gone. All rest silently from dusk until dawn. Except these two who never are still. Both have now read the great books of the other without accepting a single idea.

For the preacher and teacher, neither soul can progress from their purgatory until they compromise. Fruitlessly, they strive to answer timeless questions with useless and endless arguments. Like two old mules they bray back and forth. Each gnaws on any contrived new gem of logic behind clenched teeth. To this very minute neither opens his mind to the others' wisdom. with this constant struggle all others, who must hear, believe hearing them truly is hell.

How did this ever begin? No conversation between the two would have arisen were they not struck by a single bolt of lightning while passing a saloon from different directions. The bawdy establishment and these two all exploded in a single flash from the heavens.

Oddly, neither combatant has even seen the inside of a saloon. Ironically, parts meshed with their bodies when they and the saloon merged, including the nude lady over the bar and the poker chips. The explosion hit them so fast that when the teacher asked, *"What happened?"* The preacher screamed, *"It's Judgment Day!"* The other impulsively countered, *"It can't be there's no such thing!"* Vigilante decides their resurrection day will really be something phenomenal to see.

As one old-timer buried here grumbles, *"From the moment they were laid to rest 'til now this graveyard just hasn't been sane."* *"Only thing them birds agree on, is one's right when he's talkin' and the other'n is all wrong!"* Hunter and his father wonder whether hell is worse than listening to them argue with nowhere to hide.

The preachers' booming voice recites favorite phrases from Genesis by memory. *"In the beginning God created the heaven and the earth"* *"...And God said, "Let there be light: and there was light"* *"...And god called the firmament Heaven."*

The teacher haughtily retorts with Darwin's notion of evolution. Phrases of his argument are repeated in his righteous high-pitched whine, *"...it found its' way from the sea to walk on the land..."* *"natural selection"* *"common ancestor."*

Vigilante easily locates the hunters' new easily visible grave. Yet even he can't block out the teacher as he harangues the preacher. *"Mutations evolved becoming creatures of higher intelligence each surviving through coincidence and by chance evolved into the*

342

human animal." "Creation is a myth!" The preacher tries to roll his eyes but can't because he left them in his coffin. These arguments ran their course long ago with this pair, but their egos remain powerful even here. Neither will admit defeat or compromise.

The teacher turns away before the preacher can respond and then vanishes into a contemplative state within his coffin. He struggles constantly to prove the nonexistence of deity. Also, he refuses to accept the reality of his present existence. Trying to prove once and for all his lack of belief is scientifically true frustrates him because no evidence acceptable to either exists.

"This validates scientific method." He reassures himself, *"It's not real unless it can be scientifically proven."* Because it suits his atheist bias he disregards all evidence of deity from any sources, while somehow still feeling *"scientific."*

The preacher remains determined to save his adversary's soul while vehemently disagreeing with everything the teacher believes. When the teacher tries to hide, he pounds on the teachers' coffin. Once, his knocking continued for a year before the teacher said anything.

Finally response came in weak scholarly whimpers that can only come from the dead of soul. *"I'm busy grading test papers... Go away!"* The teacher lied; he answered just to hear his own voice. Vigilante thinks sarcastically, *"So here they are displaying their brilliance for all to hear forever." "How can I help the hunter with this much noise blurring my every thought?"*

Preacher dares the teacher to get out of his coffin and debate with him. *"The Word awaits you!" "Get out of that box of damnation right now and defend your position!"* A long silence and then before the demand could be repeated he teacher admits, *"My mind is whirling so fast from all of your nonsense that I can't get out!"* The preacher isn't surprised. He shouts, *"Give it up sinner and accept the Word of the Lord!" "Damn you Satan!"* Moans of fear come from several graves including Hunters' father. For their master must certainly be Satan. A soul asks Vigilante, *"Are you Satin?"* He politely replies, *"No Madam."*

Vigilante calls for help in his appeal for the poor young hunters' salvation. He decides to taunt a guardian angel; *"You are supposed to know how to do these things!"* He certainly can't ask Lucien. So, he projects his plea to his angel buddy Mike back in Baltimore. He projects, *"Your buddy owes me a favor from when I helped him with the twins.*" Acknowledging the debt, Mike still can't desert his client floating in General Anatomy. So, he passes the obligation to an ancient old school uncle.

Pride still won't let the teacher admit defeat. But, with these others showing up the truth is becoming obvious. He removes most of the poker chips and dusts off his tweed jacket. It was last worn the day his life ended. With the utmost poise, while trying to retain his dignity, he chins himself up using his gravestone. Pomposity served him well in school with disagreeable students. He murmurs with hollow sincerity to the preacher, "*If you need me, I will join you out of compassion for your solitude*"

The preacher looks at the teacher with absolute disbelief. "*The audacity of this snob…!*" He says nothing more, having momentarily decided silence is best. Neither acknowledges Vigilante during this phase of their arguments. They stiffen stiffer with sudden alarm. A fierce creature casts a shadow and drops down in their midst. "*My nephew said you need a hand.*" "*I'm here; what's up?*"

Everyone stares in fright at the newcomer. Ghosts in the graveyard, including the preacher and teacher are struck mute. Little wonder, he's a scary old-testament angel. Everyone here was already scared stiff and now are even more so at this specter. No one dares to think aloud.

Vigilante gets to the heart of the matter. *"Preacher and teacher... you each miss the point!"* They glare at his rudeness. *"I may be new to this, yet it is obvious that neither of you has enough knowledge to persuade the other."* Both frown at him.

This moment could have been a fraction of a nanosecond. They must overcome their differences. Out of fear of his angel muscle, rather than respect for this puny echo, they listen... Still each maintains a dignified posture loyal to their ideas and era. The echo explains their problem and for once they are quiet.

Vigilante scolds the teacher. *"Because you are all here, obviously there must be something after death."* The teacher fumes back, *"This is obviously a nightmare; I will wake up!"* The preacher responds. *"You, my brother, it's obvious you don't understand the science you profess."* The angel addresses the preacher, *"Believing God made everything, how can you not believe God created the wonders of science as well?"*

The preacher begrudgingly groans in agreement but isn't ready to credit any part of his victorious argument to anyone here. Still he is quiet. Because no one who has read The Old Testament messes with one of these terrifying old-school angels. The teacher suddenly gets the message.

The angel speaks soothingly. *"After exhausting all the knowledge, you gained when living, it only makes sense that each of you return to this debate once each has read the great books of your opponent."*

The preacher believes the end is near, likes the idea and promises to return before the end of the world. The teacher mistakenly thought the good books of the preacher would be a fast and easy read compared to the texts of science. Once again he gingerly accepts the dog-eared pages of the ghostly circuit riders' black bible… as though touching a hot coal.

But neither Vigilante nor this wise old-school angel thinks they should return to the rut they've endured for so long. In a deeply chilling voice, the angel gives them just one day to come to an agreement… *"or else!"*

They beg for more time, for once agreeing on something- their fear of this angel. He shows uncharacteristic mercy for an angel of his era by deporting them to Baltimore. The city is a place really needs of their combined talents. *"We have positions for any who are enlightened in Baltimore... are you interested?"*

He asks politely as though they really have a choice. Without hesitation, both jump at his offer. Replying simultaneously, *"It has to be better than here!"* He poses one condition: they can never repeat those old divisive arguments...

This opportunity to be constructive again makes the preacher and the teacher instant teammates. Whatever the job in Baltimore they agree they will approach it as a team. Vigilante says nothing; he just listens in awe failing to note they are both terrified. *"Who would have guessed old-school angels can be so diplomatic?"*

The angel briefs them in a businesslike manner as to what they need to do: *"These positions have been handled for some time by just one overworked angel whose time has come to retire." "You will take turns using the apparition of a saintly cleric who once lived within a large church located close to where you are going."*

"From the first time you speak to anyone, that person must never know you are two separate beings." "You are required to speak with only one voice." "Should any of your clients think differently, both of you will suffer the most extreme punishment possible." "Do I

make myself clear?" The old angel takes their petrified silence as their promise to speak in unity.

Finally, the teacher murmurs *"What are we supposed to do?"* The angel responds, *"Just be there; the job will become evident."* Not to be outdone, the old preacher begins to ask the same question. The angel stops him saying, *"Help all who seek wisdom."*

Shortly, they are sitting on benches in church yards on opposite corners of Cathedral Street in Baltimore. When one is approached on either side, the one approached is delivered an answer from both spoken in only a single answer. They believe they are cooperating. The old-school angel has filtered the serenity of the ages into their lips. Although millions pass by; few seek their wisdom.

But those who are truly worthy come. Their gaze will be drawn to a kindly cleric. They ask him about all they wish to understand. Then he will seem not to have been there. Each will be drawn to take their own mortality seriously... an extraordinary task for mere mortals.

As the angel bids farewell to the two newly employed ghosts. he explains, *"All mortals want everlasting life but must mend their minds and souls continually to achieve this wish, so as not to instead y attain the worst."*

It took a bit of wheeling and dealing for Vigilante and the angel to get these two good souls into a mode more useful than argument. Although new to diplomacy Vigilante can't imagine why anyone would believe this complex world would have happened without a central plan. Again he decides – *"People aren't very smart…"*

For some mysterious reason, Gee also decided to visit the church yard today. It turns out he also knows the old-school angel. They agree the old ways weren't always best.

Vigilante Spirit

22

Regeneration

Vigilante turns his attention to Hunter's grave. As usual, Hunter's father thinks only of himself. Quickly Vigilante shuts him down with, *"I'm only here for your son."* Without giving him further thought he turns to Gee. Realizing this, Gee just looks heavenwards and smiles in answer to the echoes' obvious petition for clemency. As always, a souls' ultimate destination is in the hands of someone above. Gee lets them know his visit here today will serve this lad well.

Vigilante is pleased with the end of this earthly hell for the preacher, teacher and all graveyard ghosts forced to hear them. But it doesn't begin to compare with how grateful he is to Gee for pleading the slain boys' case. For, Hunter lacked the basic sense needed to go beyond the cabin where they met.

Vigilante knows for better or worse for himself, *"The Lord is God, not merely a concept."* The echo regrets he's only a loose collection of mind bursts. An echo has never been alive. Having attempted to make amends for his big mistake, he needs to go somewhere far less challenging.

He retreats back down the river towards his solitary island. This time he doesn't bother to look to up as he passes old house on the hill. Vigilante comes to the Chesapeake and once more heads down the bay hoping for a creative idea. It's something that occurred naturally before his involvement with ghosts and angels. Any good mission he stumbles upon seemed sufficient. He feels like doing something new because of this boost from Clyde,. He drops down into his submerged home to think it over.

A brightly focused beam shatters his meditative state. He looks for its' source. It's coming from the eastern shore. A vaguely familiar woman is probing him. He tries to defend, but his view is obstructed by someone in his direct line of observation. He can't see past her because any living soul, regardless of intent, is impervious to an echoes view.

The obstacle blocking his view is a thief pilfering the crab traps of an honest fisherman. Without hesitation, he inspires the crabs in the boat to scramble in squadron formation forcing the thief overboard. The thief won't drown but unfortunately will return to his ways some other day. The boat was also stolen.

He swims to safety although a considerable distance from shore. The terrified poacher decides to change his wicked ways. But that will happen after tonight when he will tell his wife a big lie; a sudden storm swallowed their boat. In truth: last night, he lost their boat in a poker game. The Coast Guard will return this one he pilfered to its' registered owner. These crabs won't be fooled by traps again. Turning back to the source of the light, Vigilante looks; no one is there.

Although, Oriole became Vigilante's only home; he wonders why he even needs one. Moving from place to place was good enough. This absence of alternatives doesn't make him feel better.

After the adulation of his ghostly groupies something is missing. Back on the river he was a celebrity. He feels a hazy loneliness.

The angels he admires all seem to have some mystical legacy he lacks as an echo. He refuses to accept he's just someone's mind-burst. In a self-pitying depressed mood, he impulsively asks the whole spirit colony of the Chesapeake. *"Am I destined to always be as lonely as Clyde was?"*

To his wonder in eerie response, each sad and lonely ghost, spirit and demon from one end to the other murmurs *"Amen!"* He wonders whether loneliness is as ruthless and abysmal as the loss of ones' soul. Ironically, there would be comradeship among the lonely. If only they could all get together. Perhaps those who are lonely are at very least comrades in their solitude. An even softer *"Amen"* returns in on the waves.

He appreciates how much stronger he feels with the energy boost he received from Clyde. But something from that strange probe bothers him. Why did that woman seem familiar? He doesn't remember meeting anyone from there.

Spontaneously he meditates a prayer of thanks. *"Lord I understand overcoming evil is its' own reward." "Please know that I*

*am grateful to you for my many victories over wickedness... but...
what now?"* He waits; there's only the usual silence.

Silence deeper than he's known recently surrounds him. The
distant chatter has stopped. All in this dimension are struck numb by
the audacity of this mere echoes' pretense to be a creature of the
Lord. For everyone understands an echo is as close to nothing as
anything can be. Because an echo is nothing, then his prayer is
unworthy and is an affront to the Almighty. He decides to fight back
against   this   bias.

Challenging their unspoken disapproval. *"Why doesn't an echo
have the right to pray?"* Digging in, he reaches for inner strength.
Vigilante pushes away his despair. *"I will improve my outlook; I will
be strong!" "Perhaps then the Lord will hear me."*

Soon he is up on the surface above the island. He's frustrated. No
maidens to rescue, no villains to vanquish and not even another
Clyde to challenge. He sighs and subsides into a mellow state
waiting for inspiration. The bay is as smooth as glass.

No great plan comes to him; he's bored. He doesn't become fully
alert again until past noon; nothing has changed. Late afternoon

finds him stalking around the house sweeping out eels and crabs. *"I'm tired of cleaning out this place!"*

He takes leave from deciding his next mission. If only to eradicate the distraction of his insignificance in the universe, he makes an unusual decision for any spirit: *"I'll go on a cruise!"* *"Maybe I need to be more positive."* *"Then, if I am, maybe I can resume my mission and maybe even pray."* Rejecting his insignificance, *"God may prefer to hear from those who are happier."* There is a groan from the heavens. A cherub chirps, *"He doesn't get it."*

But then it occurs to Vigilante, it's just as strange to go on vacation as it was to pursue Lucien, or even try to pray. Shrugging off all negative feelings, Vigilant hopes for something to do and to go somewhere exciting. *"A cruise is certain to make me happy."* Despite its' magnificence, Gee's El Muerte was anything but fun. *"That ship is way too scary."* He turns to the horizon. Looking out over the bay, opportunity is right in front of him.

He is intrigued by a huge cruise ship coming into port. Its' name *Dawns Early Light* is in bold black letters. It will change passengers at the Baltimore marine terminal. Returning, it will pass by venerable Fort McHenry on its' way back down the bay. At least one Brit will point his finger at the fort when no one's looking and say, *"Bang bang - Gotcha!"*

The echo decides to jump aboard near the historic fort. He heads for his chosen rendezvous point just offshore. Arriving there he meditates   patiently.

Dawns Early Light turns into his view, its' brilliantly illuminated decks nearly mesmerize the echo. Enthusiastically, he floats over the rail. He doesn't pause to reconsider. There will be enough time later. Recalling other vessels he saw none except El Muerte made as much of an impression on him. This was designed for fun but only after the passengers settle in.

Waning sunlight drifts gently over the western horizon. Evening paints its' sky in darkening blue shadows. Vigilante gawks at the attractions onboard like any other tourist. He stares up at the Bay Bridge as they pass beneath the lights of cars and trucks overhead. A specter dwelling within a nearby lighthouse waves. Its' ghostly attendant considers the lighthouse it as his heaven. It' unlikely Gee will ever be forced to transport this ghost anywhere against her will. She has a good soul, and the beautiful Chesapeake is her home.

The day is done. Then darkness arrives and the brilliant vessel plows through the night. A bay pilot carefully hugs the center of channel passing clear of the shallows. He'll leave this ship shortly before it flexes its' engines for distant ports.

Grinning to himself, Vigilante justifies being a stowaway. This is the only way any spirit can ride; for who will, or even can, sell him a ticket? *"I'm not stealing my passage." "I need no stateroom." "I have no luggage for the crew to lose or money with which to pay."* He chuckles wickedly, *"Who they can't see they can't catch."*

Still, feeling slightly guilty about taking time off, Vigilante rationalizes, *"Besides, no one has ever told me where I'm to conduct my undertaking."* Reasoning, *"This is going to be a wonderful adventure."*

Near to the railing where the echo came onboard moments ago, an elderly grey-haired gentleman squats on a stool occasionally sipping but mostly watching his beer go flat. Vigilante sniffs his bubbles without having a second thought. The man blinks as the head evaporates from the glass. Still the echo feels no guilt about his petty theft. The gent is inspired to think, *"Flat beer is better for me."*

"No one owns beer bubbles; bubbles are fair game!" *"Sane people don't try to drink the bubbles anyway."* *"After two, they don't even notice they're gone."* He has no shame, reminding himself college students sprinkle salt in beer to make the fizz go away. It takes only this much reasoning for Vigilante to be certain he's doing good... perhaps even carrying out his mission by making the beer go flat. Inanely he wonders whether he's inebriated. *"Good guess!"* The gents' guardian angel replies but does nothing.

An extroverted barmaid refreshes the stool sitters' beer as a singer somewhere on the ship belts out something that he thinks will take him to the top. Vigilante sucks up more ...on the house. But not quite on the house, more on the bubbles-lost gent. Determined to sniff even more, Vigilante ignores both of the barmaid and her elderly patrons' guardian angels.

Two angels are enjoying one another off to one side of the deck. The echo didn't notice them observing him. The somewhat frustrated gent has an untreated high blood pressure condition. While he isn't being directly hurt by Vigilante, they decide not to take a chance. Belatedly, the echo hears one think *"Enough is enough!"*

Quickly Vigilante learns guardian angels can also serve as bouncers. They not quite gently transport him away from the bar. Understanding their concern, he doesn't protest or try to resist. Smiling woozily at these angelic bouncers, the echo allows them to express dutiful concern for their charges.

Even this indignity is way too much fun for him to be upset. Just the same, when they return to their part of the deck he tries to flip them an insolent one fingered salute. They laugh and good naturedly flip the insult back. They aren't angry either. Who could ever be angry for long at a tipsy echo who probably doesn't exist...and whose finger is imaginary?

Gradually he stops moving in the direction in which he was propelled. Vigilante makes his way to a spot even further down the deck. There he pops into a big steaming hot tub. These steamy bubbles are rather sobering. Vigilante playfully swirls around in circles barely skimming the tub surface.

He hopes Gee has made progress with Hunter's case with St. Peter. And he hopes Angela and Hiker are happy. Unknown to Vigilante, in addition to his transportation operation, Gee has been looking into some other amazing monkeyshines as well.

23

Seduction

Feeling relaxed, he stretches out on a deck chair. He isn't just resting; it serves to connect him to the ship. If disconnected in this a bubbly-minded state, he might just float off. Although he wouldn't drown, he might lose this vacation ride. He slips into a happy meditation. His last thought before drifting into meditation is- *"Just like a balloon, over the rail and out to sea."*

Although Vigilante likes the cruise ship he isn't happy about the baggage handling. Some of his fellow passengers new to cruise ships are miserable. As for those who've boarded in Baltimore, many bags haven't arrived at their cabins.

These newbies are still in their cruise tender stage. Their very first mishap began when they boarded. The nervous first timers frantically try to contact the baggage handlers for reassurance. No one at the desk seems to know much. Expensive vacations are starting with a panicky thud.

When her bags finally appear at their cabins, wives will have bought new clothes at one of the onboard shops. Then their bags show up. She keeps her new clothes anyway. Vigilante is ticked off at the stress caused by misplaced passenger luggage. *"How can bags get lost between the dock and ship?"* Of course Vigilante doesn't have baggage, or even a cabin, he feels this is extremely important due to his post-too-many-bubbles hangover.

Crusty old cruise-pros, such as the gent up at the bar, are oblivious to the confusion. Anyone on the swimming pool deck this early in the voyage is a seasoned traveler. These nothing bothers me types won't bother to report missing luggage for another day. For such veterans of many voyages, lost bags nonsense is normal. Although this isn't nearly as depraved as the usual things Vigilante's tackles, helping shape up management on his vacation could be construed as mission.

Vigilante's enjoying his short time onboard just as much as any mortal. Then, for no apparent reason a basic question passes through his mind. It's one that bothered his father- *"What's next?"* While he wants to develop a plan, not having one yet still doesn't spoil his enjoyment. He dreams up a mischievous mini-mission; he'll teach this ships' captain sensitivity.

Vigilante moves quickly throughout the crew areas hiding their luggage, including that of his nibs, the captain. He switches their underwear…even the female crew members'. After sprinkling around a bit of muddle dust, *Aha! The coup de grace…* The ships' captain finds himself sitting at his table wearing only his cruise directors'   bra   and   panties.

Up until this moment, the captain is certain he's in his best uniform, the one with the gold trim. Guests at the captains' table pretend nothing is out of place. He makes jokes throughout the meal. His guests roll on the deck with laughter at everything he says, though it's pure gibberish. At least several in the room post selfies with him to You-Tube. They are immediately deleted by Vigilante who adds "prank" to his list of accomplishments.

He understands considerably more than his father did about his echo mission. But nothing tells him why he's so insignificant in the scheme of the cosmos. *"Why?"* he asks of the Chesapeake and the approaching Atlantic with a streak of self-pity. Neither replies; for them there's only the current and tide. He resolves in the future not to talk to anyone who doesn't answer, except the Man upstairs.

Gradually the fun atmosphere of the cruise takes over and the echo completely relaxes; even his questions pass. He slowly focuses upon the early evening sky. Almost as within a dream he perceives a faint smudge of light. Is it from old Clyde's rainbow trail? Or, where the universe ends, and heaven begins? It's just another question he can't answer.

Forgetting his concerns about answerless questions, he wonders if all great souls ride to heaven on rainbows. He gazes up at the rainbow; it slowly vaporizes and is no more. He muses, *"It must be a long way to heaven…"*

The final threads of day have dissolved. Trees beyond the shores are slowly becoming drowsy. The blue bay fades to black. Well scattered wavelets shine back. This bright ship incessantly plows through them like a beautiful huge white whale. Something flies in the glow above.

The echo is drawn to a winged creature circling over the deck. Whose wings seem to hardly move; it's as if it is held by some unseen hand. It hovers just above. A lone white rosebud descends. It's green stem pierces the ships' glow; it leaves an ever so faint trail. He thinks he might be hallucinating.

Passing down though the glow the bud fully opens, leaves fold away. The rose seems to become an echo and stops beside him. He is astonished. She simply states, *"I am here to meet the fool so insanely romantic as to have loved and been spurned by an angel!"* Shyly he accepts this visitor. Though he cannot clearly see her, she is one whose voice is as clear as fine crystal. In a low voice, *"I am Mercy."*

Defensively he tries to repel her intrusion of his vacation. He isn't ready for a romantic adventure and still misses the angel whose love is lost. The quick fiery courtship of his parents will not be his doom. *"I will resist!"* He tries to see her more clearly but can't in any ordinary way. Mercy is surrounded in haze. No matter how hard he looks, even now he can't see her. Without warning in a magic moment they connect mind to mind. He mutters *"Oh my Lord!"* She warns, raising her eyes to heaven, *"Watch your words; remember you cannot pray!"*

They compare thoughts. Although with very different minds their perspective is quite similar. There are some differences. Vigilantes' way of handling problems is to impulsively rush at what he feels is right at any given moment. It's the opposite of hers. Mercy explains, *"I am patient and compassionate."* Intervention with such juvenile mischief as embarrassing this ships' captain isn't her style. She is far more serious minded.

Her style is to solve problems after giving them very careful thought. His is to come out swinging. By design, they both work in the best interests of mortals whose paths they cross. It's a part of their individual nature. He decides she's perfect, even though somewhat passive. He tries to get her tipsy. Mercy is too smart; she just won't sniff beer bubbles.

He wonders if Mercy really understands their loss of individual identity if they marry as she tries to explain why she would be a good partner. *"We would try to serve others faster and more effective than either of us can as we are."*

Vigilante, worrying about his own loss of identity, flatly states he will always be for swift justice and punishment. The eavesdropping guardian angels who evicted him from their end of the deck yawn rudely. Vigilante directs a surge of hostility in their direction stinging their wingtips. Realizing they are embarrassing him in front of his lady, they smile with sincere apology. His anger dissolves in her presence. The nosy guardians focus on their own duties. The old gentleman, having staggered back to the bar again passes out again. They failed to notice.

Ever the diplomat, his faithful barmaid props his chin atop a glass of beer and positions a newspaper in front of the glass. So, it seems he is reading intently. His chin falls from the beer glass. His angel persuades two barbacks to escort his good client back to the stateroom. It wouldn't be professional to have guests and crew see him floating in air with nothing conveying him. He needs to show someone's feet walking on the deck.

Vigilante and Mercy decide to explore. The new spirit couple glides side-by-side through the ship casino enjoying the colors and sounds. The gamblers returned to play the moment the ship left port. Mercy laments, *"Some play for the game; some play for the pain."* *"Sadly, some who gamble have no money to lose."* Mercy sizes up the situation and inspires those without means to play only the roulette spots she can make win with just a tiny bit of help.

Vigilante rigs the slot machines to pay out much as he did the hospital computer for Angela's medical records. Everyone wins playing slots except the casino. Losing its' margin, the casino suffers a convenient power failure and closes temporarily for repairs. Its' manager baffled; its' bank is busted; the winners are happy.

Mercy didn't just stumble upon the idea of meeting Vigilante. The one who arranged their date truly astounds Vigilante. Because she's concerned by his cautious attitude, Mercy reveals who suggested she come. He admits, *"I'm shocked to learn the dreadful old grim reaper believes in romance."*

She smirks, *"He's an angel; angels are very romantic."* *"It would be a kinder world if everyone could see the beauty and wonder in every other."* She continues, *"Earth will become paradise again if the romance of life returns to humanity.* He agrees, *"Each being potentially has deep-down beauty."*

She establishes her status in their relationship. *"Just because I'm here with you, don't think that I'm your typical echo girl."* Her vulnerability amuses him. *"Mercy, I never thought of getting married; I just wanted to complete my missions and have a little fun!"* He doesn't mention he has no idea what a *typical echo girl* is... He thinks, *"You don't either."* She just smirks again. Both realize they're being silly and laugh together. Gender sparring is their first moment of easy interaction. Round one is a draw.

He hasn't given marrying serious consideration until now. But now, he worries his bachelor days are in serious jeopardy. His earlier laid-back vacation plan has gone out with the tide. Admiration of her stunning presence has gotten to him. Any leverage he has in their relationship is drifting out to sea. His thoughts betray him once more. She teases, *"If I were an old fashioned human echo I'd just go with the first guy with a spark of energy left."* *"But I have my own mind and ideals."* Her mind pierces his and he understands something surprising. *"She is an angels' echo!"* Any rejection is gone.

Now that Mercy has leverage she goes on the offensive. *"Your tête-à-tête with Lucien, a really odd angel over in Elkridge is worldwide gossip."* She giggles. *"You really aren't a great catch."*

"You're tainted by her." If he had physical eyes they would have bugged out of his head with embarrassment. Not only is her awareness of his crush on Lucien out in the open, his last encounter with Mike back in Baltimore leaves him defenseless in this skirmish with Mercy. Ignoring her comment, he goes on the offense.

"If I'm such a sorry piece of ether, why are you bothering with me?" In a softer tone, *"What do you plan to do with your gifts?"* She smiles disarmingly replying, *"I have clients." "Follow me."* With the help of the raven who brought her to him they are guided over the eastern shoreline of the Chesapeake.

A thin winding black road is just beneath them. Following as it narrows and becomes a gravel pathway, soon they pass just over a flat white fishing boat. It's approaching a narrow channel leading into a fishing village. The raven disappears as a large hawk turns to scope her out. But Mercy knows the way.

Two larger scavengers shake out their feathers atop the chimney of a weathered white cottage a short distance beyond the village. A useless rotted crab boat by the waters' edge suggests more prosperous times. Approaching the cottage, clean wash sways in the wind on an old grey clothesline. Vigilante and Mercy descend and peer into the bedroom window. An elderly woman rests beneath the covers of her bed.

A much younger heavyset woman moves a spoon towards her mouth holding warm clam chowder. When little else is available, usually a few clams can be scratched from a nearby sandbar. The thin bedridden figure is very frail and childlike. Mother has become as once was this mothering child. Slowly she savors each gentle spoonful held to her lips. Her strength faded with her youth. Time and toil have taken their toll. Her daughter smiles lovingly to hide her worry and wonders, *"Where is my brother?" "Sam should be back by now with moms' medicine."*

Pity singes Vigilante. His emotion is a last trace of Gin, his own mother. He scans over the waterway until he sees a small island. His mind follows paths of illumination seen only by angels and spirits. One trail is gigantic; another much smaller is a humans. Leaving the women they retrace these paths. They run parallel then meet.

At a point where the two come together, Sam's upper torso is all remaining to be seen. He is quite alive though mercifully unconscious. For his lower half is in the dimension of angels and devils. Clutching his legs is the demon Vigilante, Clyde and Gee thought they chased back to hell. This dragon-like demon kidnaped Sam stopping him from bringing medicine to his mother. Its' slowly dragging him into hell as appeasement to the devil for failing on the Copperhead.

Mercy knows only too well this isolated section of this dimension. However, Vigilante vaguely remembers being here once before. He streamed in by accident during the crazy brawl onboard the Copperhead. From this human side, Sam's lower torso is out of sight; only his upper half is visible. *"Mercy, Sam's halfway to hell."* *"See if you can pull him back from your side."* The demon snorts, *"I'll be damned if you do."* Mercy laughs, *you're damned already!"* But it's obvious the dragon has become weaker.

Vigilante leaps in and begins pushing and shoving the man back out. Mercy seizes the top half of Sam's human worldly end and tugs hard. The demon tries to push Vigilante out of the way, but the echo has nothing for it to grab, push or bite. Overcoming the demons' hold seems to take forever. Finally, Sam is completely in his normal earthly element, but remains unconscious. The cowardly dragon dives for the pits of hell where he hopefully will stay forever.

Sam's facial features are nearly identical to his sister still tending to their mother. Regaining consciousness. although feeling horrible, he starts coming to. Complaining, *"Every inch of my body hurts!"* Getting to his feet he looks around in confusion. *"Where did everyone go?"* *"I know a bunch of people were here just a second ago?"* Vigilante stealthily helps Sam limp to where his small boat sank.

The echoes know he needs to believe there is plausible explanation for what he's been through. It just won't do for him to realize what happened. Learning he was half-sucked into another dimension by a demonic dragon isn't good for Sam's sanity.

Poor Sam had the bad luck of being at the exact spot at the moment when the demonic dragon was leaving the human dimension. Sam has been dragged halfway in and back again. If they restore his memories to reality human society would need to lock him away for the rest of his life. And there's no sign of his guardian angel. Sam will lie to everyone saying he was stuck in quicksand but managed to crawl out…somehow?

Mercy has him awake and alert with a restored sense of equilibrium. Soon he has his boat floating out from under the shallow water. It's sturdy and designed for this marsh. It just wasn't meant to cope with demonic forces.

With Vigilante's help, Sam finds where his medicine and supplies were tossed intact onto a dry spit of land. He rearranges the supplies, launches and heads for home. At each turn he regains his sense of where he is heading. Thinking about his accident, his memories are infused with an alibi. *"A powerful microburst caused me to hit my head and upset the boat!"*

His sister and mother need him badly. His mind returns from where it went before his odyssey. He pushes harder to reach his dear sister and mother. Briskly he unravels the maze of waterways to home. For no apparent reason, at least not one he understands, Sam will always have nightmares about friendly spirits and an evil dragon.

Their work accomplished, Mercy and Vigilante focus upon one another. Her mind probes his thoughts seeking an answer to her ultimate question, *"Can you be with me knowing my ways are so peaceful?"* Vigilante asks her the same question and answers, *"I will embrace your ways if you mine."* He accepts her honest answer. *"I won't have the same spontaneous enthusiasm you have for vengeance."* She accepts his promise to strive for quick justice without undue cruelty. In reality, the discussion doesn't make sense. New echoes have a mind of their own. They know little about their parents.

His aggressive nature and her nurturing one together as a single echo should logically make those whose lives are touched extremely fortunate. Even so, the finality of their merger is more than echoes can comprehend. This is as it has always been for such rare beings.

Vigilante pleads with sincerity and awe … *"Please marry me… for my heart is yours!"* Mercy considers his being and is confident his devotion is sincere. She accepts him, his proposal, love and admiration Then astonishing him, she purrs, *"I want a church wedding!"*

Stunned he nods. In her most mischievous yet angelic tone, Mercy presses her advantage. *"Find the perfect chapel and surprise me."* His mind is rattled and stammers, *"When?"* She replies enthusiastically *"Tomorrow morning!"* With this proclamation all spirits, ghosts and angels of the Chesapeake can barely await the dawn.

Vigilante is pumped! Realizing the possibilities nearby in Maryland and Virginia are enormous he checks in with Mike, at the Anatomy lab. Mike is more than willing. Mike points out the need to exclude all chapels with morning services. Luckily, it won't be a day when most chapels are filled with mortals.

Mike asks, *"How many are coming?"* Vigilante says, *"I give up, just find me a nice chapel."*

Vigilante Spirit

24

Destiny

With every ounce of strength, throughout the night Mike and their angel buddies search for a suitable wedding chapel. Meanwhile, Mercy checks on Sam's family for hopefully the last time. Having accepted the reality they will marry, finding her church is his only foreseeable mission. He doesn't second guess his feelings. Mercy has replaced Lucien who he thought he loved just yesterday.

Vigilante can't get over it; his mind is blown by the realization he's so fickle.

The echo is encouraged by a distant familiar voice; one he can't place saying, *"Don't doubt yourself kid, now's your time..."* It's an angel, but he can't decide whether it's Roman or Michael. He agrees but doesn't realize it's actually Gee.

Mike crew searches small towns along both shores until just before dawn. Finally, they locate a rustic brick church near Cape Charles. Something very unusual about this chapel cinches this location. Its' cemetery is devoid of ghosts. All who were here have moved on to another level. It's the perfect place for beautiful spirits to wed.

Their big day dawns as they enter together carefully. Still not touching, side-by-side they glide down the aisle. Seemingly no one has come; they feel alone. Moving proudly and gracefully, as nearly as echoes can, they emulate the stride of a wedding couple. In moments they approach the empty altar.

Instantly, as though a switch is thrown, both aisles are populated with friends. The bride and the groom are greeted with sounds of joy. Ghosts, angels and even several saints have come to share in their happiness. Vigilante whispers to his bride, *"I hope Lucien and Roman are here and they approve."* He feels some trepidation. Mercy giggles.

Surprisingly, even the rowdy ER angels are also in church. Those who financed Angela's rescue from the hospital by appropriating the money of drug dealers. Mike, the guardian of the twins and everyone involved in the big brawl are seated on the grooms' side. Somewhat out of character this morning, they are respectfully quiet.

Rustic wooden pews glow in lily white strands of sunlight. Mercy is adorned in a heavenly gown, one trimmed in the finest mists. Two cherubs are maintaining her bridal train. Her inner beauty is evident beneath her veil and is visible even to the saints above. Still, her features are shrouded in mystery. That he hasn't ever clearly seen his bride to be doesn't even occur to him.

The repressed excitement and anticipation of those in the pews is beyond earthly comprehension. In awe, from the rear of the chapel, teacher asks of the preacher, *"Who or what clergy can perform such a matrimonial ceremony?"* The preacher shrugs, *"I can't imagine; they didn't ask me."*

A minister dressed in black faces the holy altar. Abruptly with military precision, he turns to the betrothed and congregation. A white roman collar speaks to his authority to officiate. The guests fall silent as his identity is revealed. For this priest is Gee, the Reaper.

Last night his buddy, Mike assured Vigilante someone would come to wed them. Now, the betrothed stand before an altar of the Lord. They promise to devote themselves to one another completely. The minister addresses all in his most solemn tone. *"If there are any who object to this union let them speak now…"*

The words he speaks are surprisingly traditional. But something unforeseen happens … *"I object! I object!"* The cruel specter of Stranglers' echo jams directly in between Gee and the bridal couple. Sneering he lurches at the bride attempting to merge with her by force. No creature at the altar or in the pews of the chapel can react in time. Suddenly a piercing trumpet-like *"screech!"* Its' source spirals down from a rafter directly above.

Quicker than thought, its' wings furiously thrusting, the Raven swallows this final shred of the demonic intruder. Both vanish into the walls' hard brick. The Raven has consumed and made off with this evil for good. Only a lone floating purplish black feather finds its' way into the bridal bouquet. The assembled guests gleefully scream with all their might *"Nevermore!"*

Refusing to allow his ceremony to be ruined by the intrusion, and unwilling to be outdone by this crowd, Gee humbles the disruption with a line from Poe's- *The Raven*, *"...Tis the wind and nothing more!"* And all taunt the devil with *"...the wind and nothing more!"*

The guests are thrilled over evils' failure to destroy this wedding of good spirits. With one voice, they chant *"Nevermore Nevermore!"* Thus, this splinter of Strangler is erased completely. Before anything else interrupts him, Gee is about to pronounce, *"Mercy and Vigilante, you are now one!"* When suddenly another objection arises. This time it's Roman the spurned guardian angel...sober for once.

"Friends, angels and spirits" ... he theatrically croons. He pauses for a moment waiting for the *"boos"* to subside. *"I have not come to protest the marriage, but to be certain all including the groom, recognize the identity of the bride...and to provide all of you with an announcement of great generosity."*

Smiling mysteriously for dramatic affect, Roman produces a parchment engraved with a seal of the highest order. Inscribed is an official directive ennobling one echo spirit to become a special angel. The spirit is Vigilante.

Proclaiming in the holy languages of Latin and old English, Roman reads the promotion of Vigilante to angel and the acceptance of some poor soul named Will Gold into heaven. With these decrees, the new angel's bride lets loose her veil of mist to disclose the angelic face of Lucien. His one true love.

Instantly Vigilante understands his own and their destiny. He is destined to be the bridegroom of an angel. With this he's an immortal as well. He looks in awe to Lucien, then to Gee and grasps Lucien to him with all his newly found might. Neither dissolves!

This moment is their beginning, the end of their past. Vigilante makes a final attempt to pray. He knows that people pray; perhaps now his angelic prayers will be heard. It may have been only a telepathic instant. Yet, it was and was accepted for prayer is inherently mystical. This ceremony is just a prelude.

The bride and groom openly embrace. Roman sobs, Gee dances on the altar; the guests in the isles. The couple is consumed into a new relationship greater than were Spirit and Gin in giving birth to Vigilante. But, in this union no frail echo child is born. Vigilante and Lucien are to create their own legacy.

There is more:

After the ceremony, the preacher and teacher return to the cemetery holding their mortal remains. Once again, they are met by the old-school angel. In his whole fearsome specter, he's like no other still around. This fearful creature is described in ancient texts as *"winged bulls and lions and strange winged men with hawks' heads...."*

Today he's charged to complete a practical necessity of Hunter's salvation. The old angel is entrusted with a rare deed. He must perform the hunters' post-mortem baptism. The teacher must witness this belated sacrament and serve as godfather. He's been relieved from his joint venture in Baltimore with the preacher. Their strained discourse was creating too much strain on the city.... streets were buckling.

When this old angel establishes a path to salvation for the poor lifeless lad from Vigilantes' Buzzardville mishap, his past is now insignificant. A snag in Vigilantes' fabric is repaired. Good, but failed intentions of a spirit should not have led to the Hunter's downfall. However, the boy may still fail by his future deeds.

As his belated absolution occurs, tears fall from the eyes of the angels of the world. And on this fine day even the grim reaper feels joy. Not for this fine deed, but for his friend. Even our Lord has listened to the prayers of a being whose sole self-imposed mission was only to do good. Today, and perhaps always, the prayers of honest and simple beings are heard.

∞

Author- Jack Robertson

www.ingramcontent.com/pod-product-compliance
Lightning Source LLC
Chambersburg PA
CBHW072110250626
47159CB00007B/2388